Would nothing deter her?

He smiled on a sudden thought. 'You have not yet seen the accommodation, Miss Vincent,' he reminded her.

'Nor have I inspected your gambling hell,' she returned with patently false affability. 'At what hour do you close?'

'At three in the morning, Miss Vincent.' His lips twitched with quite irrepressible amusement. 'You are determined to stay? It would be highly improper in you to do so.'

Sarah Westleigh has enjoyed a varied life. Working as a local government officer in London, she qualified as a chartered quantity surveyor. She assisted her husband in his chartered accountancy practice, at the same time managing an employment agency. Moving to Devon, she finally found time to write, publishing short stories and articles, before discovering historical novels.

Recent titles by the same author:

JOUSTING WITH SHADOWS
A HIGHLY IRREGULAR FOOTMAN
SEAFIRE
THE OUTRAGEOUS DOWAGER
FELON'S FANCY

THE IMPOSSIBLE EARL

Sarah Westleigh

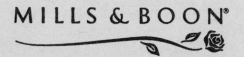

MILLS & BOON®

First published in Great Britain 1997
Harlequin Mills & Boon Limited,
Eton House, 18-24 Paradise Road, Richmond, Surrey TW9 1SR

© Sarah Westleigh 1997

ISBN 0 263 80505 0

Set in Times 10 on 12 pt. by
Rowland Phototypesetting Limited
Bury St Edmunds, Suffolk

04-9802-71853

Printed and bound in Great Britain
by Caledonian International Book Manufacturing Limited, Glasgow

Chapter One

1816

'**A** legacy?'

The faint frown which appeared between Leonora's well-defined brows served only to emphasise her excellent complexion and its general freedom from lines. Her eyes, grey liberally flecked with blue and green within a dark outer rim, widened on the elderly solicitor, who had written for an appointment and undertaken the long and tiring journey from London to Buckinghamshire especially to see her.

Mr Warwick wiped the lenses of his spectacles and put them back on his bulbous, large-pored nose, winding the wires of the frame about his ears.

'Did you not expect it, Miss Vincent?' he asked, his watery blue eyes, set beneath white brows, surprised. 'Mr Charles Vincent did not inform you of his intention to name you as his heir?'

'No,' said Leonora. She made a quick gesture with her hands. 'He was kind to me as a child, but I have not seen or heard from my great-uncle for many years. I had supposed that my uncle the Earl would have benefited upon Uncle Vincent's death.'

She sat on a sofa in the morning room of Thornestone Park, her feet together, her hands folded neatly on the dove-grey muslin of her gown. On no account must she show the excitement, the elation growing inside her. Her Uncle Vincent, the Honourable Charles Vincent, younger brother to her grandfather, who had been the Earl of Chelstoke, had not been rich, but as far as she knew he had not been stricken by poverty either.

There should be something to come—unless, of course, he had died heavily in debt, like his nephew her father. That disaster had left the Honourable Peregrine Vincent's wife and daughter homeless and penniless. His wife had not possessed the strength of character to survive and had speedily followed her husband to the grave.

Leonora, on the threshold of life, made of sterner stuff and valuing above everything her independence, had come here, to Thornestone Park, as governess to Mr and Mrs Hubert Farling's two daughters. She had not thought to be trapped for seven long years but now, suddenly, when she was almost at her last prayers and faced with the problem of finding another, most probably uncongenial, position, the prospect of freedom seemed something too precious to be hoped for.

'As I understood my client's mind, Miss Vincent,' went on the lawyer in his dry voice, 'he remembered you with great affection. Knowing that you had not been offered a home with your uncle the Earl and had not yet found a husband to provide for you, he sought to ease your situation with this legacy.'

'My uncle did offer me a home,' said Leonora honestly.

'But you did not accept?'

'No. I would rather earn my living as a governess than live as a poor relation at the beck and call of Lady Chelstoke and her brood.'

A faint smile touched the whiskery lips of the lawyer. 'I see. I believe my client understood something of the kind. He...er...he held Lady Chelstoke in some dislike.'

'So.' Leonora drew a breath and grinned wryly. 'I have become an heiress, but rather too late in life to hope my good fortune will lure a gentleman of consequence to offer for me.' Her neatly folded hands gripped each other as she sought to hide her overwhelming anxiety to know. 'How much am I to inherit?'

'My client left everything to you, Miss Vincent, apart from a small sum which is to go to his valet, a man who had been with him for many years.'

Mr Warwick made a show of consulting a sheaf of papers on his knee. He was sitting on an upright chair opposite Leonora, with a table by his side. He cleared his throat and reached out for the glass of Madeira he had been offered on his arrival. Leonora quelled her growing impatience, making herself take inaudible but deep, calming breaths as she waited for him to continue.

He took a sip of the wine and then, at last, went on. 'There is a house in Bath, a substantial residence not far from the Abbey. You know Bath?'

Leonora shook her head. He said, 'I am informed that it is an older property, but superior in size to the fashionable terraced buildings designed by John Wood and his son. It is near the Pump Room and Baths and the shops in Milsom Street are within easy walking distance. A conveyance would be required to reach the Upper Rooms, where the Balls and Assemblies are held. The property would be worth a fair sum if you cared to sell it.'

Leonora stirred and he went on quickly, as though he wished to continue without interruption. 'At the moment the ground and first floors are let to a friend of the late Mr Vincent, who himself occupied the rooms on the floor above. The gentlemen shared the kitchen and servants' facilities in the basements and attics.'

The frown, which had disappeared from Leonora's brow, reappeared. 'Would this tenant expect to remain?'

Mr Warwick looked uneasy and coughed slightly. 'That I cannot say, but he holds a sound lease which does not expire for another five years.'

'I see. But unless he goes, I cannot hope to sell the property immediately at its full value?'

Mr Warwick took another sip of wine to cover his hesitation. 'Possibly not, Miss Vincent,' he allowed. 'But in addition to the property, my client had investments, mostly in the five percents, and some cash in the bank. There were, of course, a few debts to be settled and the valet's legacy to find, but the residue of the investments and cash together will total around three thousand pounds.

'Not a great fortune,' he added hurriedly, anticipating Leonora's disappointment, 'but, together with the interest on the investments, the rent Lord Kelsey pays would provide you with a comfortable income should you decide to move into your great-uncle's apartment. Or you could increase your competence by letting that as well.'

Leonora was not disappointed. How could someone who had nothing be disappointed to inherit somewhere to live and enough rent and interest on capital to enable her to set herself up in modest style? In grand style for a period, were she prepared to hazard the capital in an attempt to secure a suitable gentleman's hand in marriage.

An idea was forming in her mind. At five-and-twenty she might be almost at her last prayers, but women older than herself did wed. And, to be quite honest, she longed for an establishment of her own. An establishment with a nursery and an agreeable husband who might, were she lucky, love her and, in turn, win her love.

She said, 'I should like to see the place before I make up my mind.'

Mr Warwick nodded. 'Very wise.'

Rosy pictures of her future flew into Leonora's mind and drifted out again as she forced herself to listen to Mr Warwick's further information; but he had little more of moment to impart. It was arranged that, when she was ready to visit Bath, he would ask a colleague with chambers in the city to represent her interests.

She signed some papers, which were witnessed by himself and the footman stationed by the door. He rose, preparing to take his leave, only to be intercepted by Mrs Farling, who, full of curiosity, must have been hovering nearby. She was not prepared to allow her governess's visitor to depart without being quizzed.

Her round cheeks flushed, her bosom heaving, 'Surely you are not returning to London today, Mr Warwick?' she exclaimed, fluttering her hands and with them the gauze scarf draped about her dimpled elbows.

Mr Warwick bowed. 'No, madam. I shall find accommodation at the nearest hostelry and make the return journey tomorrow.'

'You would think us poor creatures to allow you to

lie overnight at an inn, sir! You must, of course, accept our hospitality!'

'Indeed, madam, you are most kind. I gladly accept but I must dismiss the post chaise and order it to return in the morning. . .'

'Bennett will do that,' said Mrs Farling imperiously. She turned to call out the order to the butler, who appeared in the doorway, bowed and departed on his mission.

Mr Warwick would be happy to enjoy the comforts of the quite extensive country residence of Thornestone Park instead of lying in a possibly louse-infested inn, Leonora knew. But it meant that she would be called upon once again to add the cachet of her presence at the dinner table. On this occasion, though, she resented less than usual the way her employers used her breeding to add to their own consequence. Mr Warwick was here because of her.

But the exclamations, the questions, when Mrs Farling discovered the reason for his visit, were almost beyond bearing. Leonora wanted privacy in which to come to terms with her good fortune but was not allowed the privilege.

Mr Warwick, it transpired, had never had occasion to visit his client in Bath and so had no idea of the exact nature of the residence Leonora had inherited, or of the circumstances and person of the lord who was now her tenant. No amount of questioning or speculation could tell Mrs Farling more than Leonora already knew.

'I must tender you my notice,' Leonora said. 'Perhaps I could plan to move to Bath in two weeks' time? Would that be convenient to you, Mr Warwick?'

'Indeed, Miss Vincent, that will give me ample time to

arrange for Mr Coggan to place himself at your disposal.'

'You wish to leave us so soon!' cried Mrs Farling. 'How my girls will miss you! Husband, persuade dear Miss Vincent to remain with us until everything is quite settled!'

Her stout husband, a gentleman who had as little to do with the womenfolk in his household as possible, wiped his greasy lips with his napkin and grunted. 'I suggest you allow Miss Vincent to do as she pleases,' he declared.

The Earl of Kelsey, who seldom made use of the quizzing glass suspended from his elegant buff waistcoat, raised it to study the broad, open face of the young lawyer, not much older than himself, facing him over the office desk.

'This female now owns the premises?' he enquired, a forbidding frown drawing deep grooves between the straight lines of his dark brows.

'Indeed, my lord. The late Mr Vincent left her everything, apart from a bequest to his valet. Mr Warwick informs me that Mr Vincent's fortune was not great, but the lady will be able to live in some comfort on the income from it and the yield from this property.'

'Hmm.' His lordship's slate grey eyes became thoughtful. He'd known Vincent was only modestly wealthy, but had never discovered exactly what the fellow had been worth. This lawyer would never tell him. He asked, 'How much would this place sell for?'

'On the open market, my lord? With yourself as a sitting tenant?' On Kelsey's nod the lawyer, whose name was Coggan, named a figure.

'And without myself here as tenant?'

Coggan thought for a moment and suggested a larger sum.

'As I thought,' mused the Earl. 'She should be glad to be offered a figure somewhere between the two. I cannot have her living in the rooms above. Such a circumstance would be quite beyond the tenets of decency.'

'Indeed, my lord. To have a lady walking through your part of the property would be most—' Coggan sought just the right word '—unseemly.'

'It cannot be allowed. You must inform her so.'

'I would, my lord,' said the lawyer deferentially, 'but there is little time. Mr Warwick only instructed me yesterday. I am retained to represent her interests on his behalf, my lord, until she arrives in Bath and claims her inheritance. She is due on Wednesday, and proposes to occupy the late owner's rooms. Since Mr Warwick was not aware of your lordship's activities in the part of the house you occupy, neither is Miss Vincent.'

'Is she not?' Kelsey placed a long finger against his pursed lips as he thought. 'The day after tomorrow, you say?'

He abandoned his stance by the window and began to pace the floor. He possessed a finely proportioned figure set off to perfection by the cut of his buff trousers and the fit of his green cut-away coat. He wore immaculate linen and his neckcloth had been tied with subtle flair.

He stopped and stood tapping the long fingers of one hand with the quizzing glass he held in the other. The frown left his face as he turned to the lawyer. The skin about his dark eyes crinkled and his firm, shapely mouth curled upwards at the corners. But it was not a friendly smile.

'Then I shall have to receive her and tell her myself.

The sooner she is appraised of the situation the better. I shall persuade her of the impropriety of her proposal to occupy the rooms so recently vacated, and offer to purchase the building.'

Her worldly possessions packed neatly into two trunks, Leonora arrived in Bath. She had persuaded her friend the local Rector's daughter, Clarissa Worth, to accompany her as companion and seduced Dolly, one of the maids at Thornestone Park, to transfer to her employ. To her surprise and relief Mr Farling had insisted that she make use of the family chariot, drawn by post horses, and had sent a footman with them to make all the arrangements for the necessary overnight stay at an inn along the way.

Winter's early dusk was beginning to fall as the chariot entered Bath. The tower of the Abbey caught Clarissa's attention while Leonora was entranced by the warm, creamy-yellow colour of the stone used for the buildings. Dolly, perched between them on the pull-out seat, simply gazed with her mouth open.

The chariot threaded its way through streets thronged with rigs of every description—barouches, curricles, chaises, phaetons, gigs, wagons and handcarts—while uniformed men carried the gentry about in sedan chairs. Pedestrians—the expensively and modishly dressed along with liveried attendants, a few officers in red coats or blue pea jackets, merchants in more sober cloth and workmen in threadbare coats and breeches and holed hose—sauntered or hurried along according to their need. The infirm, she noted, were pushed in wheeled chairs and wrapped in rugs against the February cold.

It was a different world, an exciting world. Bath in

1816, after this first winter of true peace, was full of people. The *ton*, as usual, was there in force to take the waters before embarking on the exertions and excesses of the London Season.

The post boy seemed to know the town. He turned the carriage into a short street forming one side of a leafy green square surrounded by buildings and drew up before a large, double-fronted house standing on its own between two narrow alleys.

Fancy ironwork fenced off basement areas on each side of a causeway that led to the front door. Three pairs of windows rose on either side of the front entrance, with single windows set between above it. Leonora, scarcely aware of her silent companions, drew a steadying breath as the footman jumped down from the box to lower the step and open the carriage door.

She descended to the pavement and waited, studying the building, while Clarissa and Dolly followed her down. A carved lintel and pediment, with 'Morris House' inscribed on it, topped the single front door, which opened expectantly to reveal a footman, garbed in good but unostentatious livery in two shades of grey.

Leonora crossed the causeway and halted before the step. 'Miss Vincent,' she announced herself. 'Lord Kelsey is expecting me.'

A second person had come forward, dressed in excellently tailored black worn with some elegance. In contrast, his immaculate neckcloth, the high points of his collar, the frills of his shirt, all gleamed starkly white.

'Indeed he is, madam,' said this individual, taking the place of the footman, who retreated into the hall where his powdered wig gleamed in the semi-darkness. 'Allow me to introduce myself. Digby Sinclair, at your service.'

He bowed. Leonora, not certain of the person's standing, acknowledged his words with a nod. Clarissa had come to join her while Dolly and Mr Farling's footman, who wore a tall hat rather than a wig, waited patiently beside the chariot.

'His lordship understands that you wish to occupy the late Mr Vincent's apartments,' went on the individual smoothly.

Impatient at being kept standing on the doorstep, Leonora retorted with some asperity. 'For the time being, at least. Please allow me to enter.'

'Of course, madam.' He made no attempt to let her past. 'But his lordship requests that your boxes be taken round to the back entrance and carried up the stairs there. It will be more convenient.' He looked beyond her. 'Perhaps your maid would accompany them? You will then find her installed in the apartments when you have spoken to his lordship and follow her up.'

Leonora frowned. Enter by the back stairs? Not if she had anything to do with it. 'His lordship is at home, I collect?'

'Oh, yes, madam. He is awaiting your arrival.'

'Excellent. I look forward to meeting him. And you are?'

'His manager, madam.'

Manager? Leonora kept her curiosity to herself. Perhaps the Earl was too old to manage his own affairs. It had crossed her mind that, were the Earl available, he might be pleased to acquire a wife and with her the ownership of this property. She was open to offers from any reasonable quarter. None of those she had received over the years had been appealing enough to tempt her into giving up her freedom, limited as it had been.

Governesses, however well connected, seldom received offers from gentlemen.

She turned to speak to Dolly. 'Wait there with the chariot,' she instructed briskly, 'until it is decided what is to be done about our luggage.' She turned back to Sinclair. Now, perhaps you will announce me to his lordship.

Who might be an earl, but she was an earl's grand-daughter.

'But, madam—'

Leonora lifted an imperious eyebrow. Sinclair bowed. 'If you will follow me, madam?'

'Do you want me to come with you?' asked Clarissa.

Leonora eyed her friend and decided that her presence would serve to hinder rather than help her in the coming interview. Some five years her senior, Clarissa Worth had never been further than Buckingham in her life and although perfectly capable of dealing with her father's parishioners, Leonora doubted whether she had ever learned how to confront a member of the nobility.

'No,' she said. By this time they were in a large vesti-bule with doors on either side and the main staircase, wide and curving, facing them. It was furnished with a small table holding a silver salver, a bench and a number of rout chairs. The muffled sound of male voices came from somewhere above. She speculated momentarily as to who the gentlemen might be and then ignored the sound. She indicated the chairs and said, 'Sit down while you wait for me.'

Sinclair, knocking on a door on the left near the foot of the stairs as he opened it, announced, 'Miss Vincent, my lord.'

His tone was deferential yet there was an undercurrent

of amusement in it that told Leonora that this man, a personable creature approaching the age of forty, she imagined, was on intimate terms with the Earl. He turned to usher her in and she could see something else in his blue eyes, something she had come to recognise over the years. He found her pleasing.

She did not care whether the man Sinclair found her pleasing or not. Her business was with his employer. She lifted her pretty, firm jaw and sailed past him into the lion's den.

The manager withdrew, closing the door behind her. A tall youngish gentleman rose languidly from behind the desk, where he had been sitting perusing some papers, and stepped out to make his bow.

'Miss Vincent.'

He made no attempt to be more than civil. Leonora dipped a polite curtsy and acknowledged the greeting. 'My lord.'

They studied each other. Leonora saw a tall, lean, but well-built gentleman of some thirty years—certainly he was a deal younger than his manager—with short brown hair arranged in the latest careless style, who wore his well-tailored garments with easy elegance. The hair framed a face whose individual features would have been difficult to criticise—a broad forehead; slate-grey eyes set beneath brows of a lighter hue than his hair and fringed by enviable lashes; a straight nose and shapely mouth.

Only his chin gave her cause for concern. It looked formidably firm and determined.

To Blaise Dancer, Earl of Kelsey, heir to the Marquess of Whittonby, Miss Leonora Vincent looked the epitome of a strait-laced governess well beyond her youthful prime. The way she dressed, the way she held herself, the severe expression with which she was attempting to intimidate him, told the tale. But, despite her years, he could not fault the perfection of her complexion, the accumulation of fine features that gave her an appearance of classical beauty which, given the matching stoniness of her expression, he did not find attractive.

Light brown hair tending towards fair strayed from beneath the brim of an elderly velvet bonnet trimmed with wilting silk flowers. It matched the colour of the brown pelisse he could glimpse beneath the enfolding cloth of a grey travelling cloak. Her skirts, by what he could see of them, were of a lighter colour, a dull buff muslin sprigged with brown and green. Her eyes, an interesting mixture of grey, green and blue, were narrowed between gold-tipped lashes with something suspiciously like vexation. He allowed himself a secret smile of satisfaction.

'You,' said Leonora at length, quelling the dismay she felt at having so young a gentleman occupying the rooms beneath hers, 'are Lord Kelsey, my tenant?'

'I am, madam.' They were still standing. He waved her to a seat facing his desk and, once she had settled herself, sank back into his own chair. 'Naturally,' he went on easily, 'I am devastated by the death of Mr Charles Vincent. We dealt well together. That he had left his property to a great-niece came as a surprise to me. Not to say a shock.'

'And to me, my lord. I had not seen my Uncle Vincent for many a year. Not since my mother's death.'

'So you were not expecting to inherit anything,' remarked his lordship with evident satisfaction. 'In that case, madam, you must be grateful for your good fortune.

I am prepared to make you an offer for this building. The money, well invested, will enable you to live quite comfortably wherever you may choose.'

Leonora stared at him. To think that she had once contemplated taking lodgings elsewhere! That had been before she saw the wonderful house Uncle Vincent had left her and met this infuriating, domineering creature. Now, she was determined to make this her home.

She said, 'On the contrary, my lord, I am prepared to buy out your lease. It must be quite immaterial to you where you reside. There must be many more convenient places in Bath.'

'But I have established a business in these rooms, madam.'

Leonora's eyebrows rose. 'Business, my lord? I had not imagined that a gentleman of your rank would indulge in trade!'

'Trade, Miss Vincent?' His haughty tone could not have been more chilling. 'You mistake. I have established an exclusive Gentleman's Club on these premises. Even now, if you will listen, you will hear a party of members being admitted. You must see how inconvenient it would be for you to have such an activity taking place on the floors beneath you.'

Her hands had begun to tremble. She clasped them tightly in her lap, on top of her reticule. 'What activity?' she demanded. 'Drinking? Gambling?'

He smiled. The devil had the most fascinating smile she had seen in a man. Creases radiated from his eyes, which sparked with wicked amusement, and bracketed his mouth, which had assumed the most alluring of curves.

She fought down a desire to smile back. Her hands

gripped each other harder. She would not be seduced by his charm.

'Both of those things, Miss Vincent. But I also provide a Reading Room and serve food as well as drink in the Dining Room. Only two of the rooms are given over to cards and gaming.'

Leonora's lips compressed. 'You are operating a gambling hell in my house,' she accused.

The chilly hauteur returned. Eyes which normally looked upon the world with audacious challenge became cold and repressive. 'If you say so, madam.' He would not deign to argue with the prudish creature. 'I collect that, since you so obviously disapprove of my activities, you will have changed your mind about taking up residence here yourself?'

To his surprise she smiled. Pleats curled round her perfect mouth. Unexpectedly, his body reacted in an all-too-familiar way.

Her eyes challenged his. 'On the contrary, my lord. If it would not inconvenience you too much—' the irony did not escape him '—I will have our boxes carried up the main stairs to my rooms. It will be easier for the servants to carry them up that way, rather than being compelled to negotiate what I imagine are the much narrower service stairs.'

He stirred. He had not expected her to outface him and his annoyance grew. Would nothing deter her? He smiled on a sudden thought. 'You have not yet seen the accommodation, Miss Vincent,' he reminded her.

'Nor have I inspected your gambling hell,' she returned with patently false affability. 'At what hour do you close?'

'At three in the morning, Miss Vincent. And I open

again to serve breakfasts at ten. If you are interested, I shall be pleased to show you round one day before we open.' He raised his quizzing glass and inspected her through it with undisguised challenge, though his lips twitched with quite irrepressible amusement. 'You are determined to stay? It would be highly improper in you to do so.'

She chose to ignore his last inconvenient remark. 'It is my right to live in and to inspect my property, Lord Kelsey. I shall move in immediately and you may expect me down here at nine tomorrow morning to look over your rooms.'

'Very well.' Devil take it, he could scarcely have the aggravating female thrown out. 'Meanwhile, pray consider my offer to purchase the property, Miss Vincent. Or alternatively, I would be prepared to take over the lease of the entire house. The rent I would pay you would enable you to command more suitable premises for your own use.'

Leonora rose. 'Your proposition, my lord, would no doubt sound tempting had I no desire to live in the property left me by my uncle. However it is, in my opinion, ideally suited to my needs. I warn you that, having taken up immediate residence in the rooms my uncle used, I fully intend to consult my lawyer over the possibility of terminating your lease. And now, if you will be so kind as to allow my luggage to be carried upstairs?'

He rose when she did, as was polite. They were on their way to the door when Leonora stopped. She was not short herself, but she had a long way to look up to meet Lord Kelsey's dark, inscrutable eyes. 'About the kitchen facilities. I understand that my uncle shared them with you. I shall need to do the same. And my maid will need accommodation in the attics.'

'Madam,' said his lordship with the utmost civility, 'you may, of course, share the kitchen, provided only that you can come to terms with my cook, Monsieur André. I should point out that Charles—Mr Vincent— was used to order meals to be sent up from the kitchen. I rendered him an account at the end of each month.'

'Astronomical, no doubt,' said Leonora acidly.

'But, no, madam. He paid only the cost of the food. The services of Monsieur André were taken account of in the rent I agreed to pay.'

Leonora eyed him, not certain whether to do the same or not. In the end, 'I will try it for a month,' she decided.

In a month, with luck, he would be gone.

'I will inform Monsieur André of your decision, Miss Vincent. Your maid will, of course, collect the food when it is ready. There are just the two of you?'

'No, my lord. I have with me a companion, a friend and chaperon. Otherwise I could not have taken up residence here without causing a scandal.' She gave him a smile to match his own. 'The presence of Miss Worth, a clergyman's daughter, will quieten the gossips. You do have gossips in Bath?'

He was impelled to laugh. 'The *ton* is here, Miss Vincent, the scandalmongers included. The situation will no doubt give rise to speculation, but if you are discreet you should avoid the loss of your reputation.'

Fire sparkled in her eyes. 'I shall inform everyone I meet of my abhorrence of your activities, my lord, and of my intention to see you off the premises as soon as may be.'

'I think you will find, madam, that your intention will fail. If you wish to avoid the stigma of living above a gambling hell, you will find it necessary to move out yourself.'

Leonora lifted that delightful, stubborn chin. 'Never!' she declared as she walked into the hall.

Clarissa stirred at sight of her, an enquiring look on her rather plain face. Leonora glanced back to the man following her.

'My lord, I name to you Miss Worth, my companion. Clarissa, this is my tenant, Lord Kelsey.'

Clarissa rose, her colour high, and the two made slight acknowledgement of the introduction.

Leonora said, 'Excuse me,' and walked back to the front door to tell Matthew and Dolly that the luggage was to be taken upstairs through the front door.

'When it is all unloaded, Matthew, you may see to the carriage. You know what to do, and have funds to meet any expenses?'

'Aye, miss. Mr Farling were generous, miss.'

'Capital! Thank you for your services on the way here.'

A coin changed hands. Leonora turned back to the Earl.

'Someone, no doubt, will show us the way up?'

'I will escort you myself, Miss Vincent. This once. After this, you must, I fear, use the service stairs and enter and leave by the back basement entrance at all times when the Club is open.'

They had begun to mount the curving staircase, arranged round a small, circular, open well. Leonora snorted.

'You mean that I shall not be allowed to use my own front door? I do not see that you can prevent me, my lord!'

'The lease expressly forbids it,' said Kelsey complacently. 'Naturally, as a member of the Club, your uncle was able to come and go by these stairs whenever he wished.'

He cut off to greet two gentlemen passing them on the landing. Leonora realised that they were more than a little foxed and their bold scrutiny offended her. She tossed her head and trod silently up the next, much narrower flight until she came to the landing and found a screen and a door barring her path.

'You will appreciate the danger of meeting strange gentlemen on the stairs should you insist upon using them,' murmured Kelsey as he leaned past her, uncomfortably near, to unfasten the door. 'Though you need not fear intrusion provided you keep this door locked,' he went on smoothly, handing her the key.

Leonora walked through into a small lobby with some half dozen doors leading off it. The apartment was larger than she had anticipated and her spirits rose. Secure behind her locked door she could ignore what went on downstairs while she made her plans.

'Charles—Mr Vincent,' went on the Earl, 'had old-fashioned tastes. No doubt you will require to redecorate and refurnish in your own fashion.' He flung open the door to a room at the front of the house. 'This was his parlour.'

Leonora entered, curious to see how her uncle had lived. She took in the double window with its brown drapes, the comfortable leather armchair, the writing desk and the shelves of books.

'It looks extremely comfortable to me,' she said, shuddering inwardly at the dinginess of the place. But the furniture was good and the books looked interesting. She could soon change the soft furnishings. 'I shall be quite content living here,' she informed his lordship with conviction.

He could see that she meant it. Of course, she would. The decorations would suit a drab, narrow-minded governess to perfection.

Damnation. He had absolutely no desire to conduct his business with a highly critical female, who was, intolerably, his new landlord, installed above him.

Chapter Two

The Earl departed as the luggage came up, causing confusion on the spiralling stairs.

Anything large, Leonora could see, would have to be hoisted in through the windows. She looked forward to causing a different kind of confusion when she changed some of the furniture. For although she had said, and believed, that she could be comfortable surrounded by her late uncle's things, her ideas on furnishing were rather different to his. Were she to be here long, changes would have to be made.

'The apartments are quite spacious,' remarked Clarissa as they went from room to room together.

Once the Earl had left, they had taken a good look round the front parlour and the rear dining room before inspecting the front bedroom, which Leonora would use despite its masculine decorations, because it was big and had a door through to a dressing room.

'Morris House is nothing like Thornestone Park, of course,' went on Clarissa as they moved on, 'or as grand as what you were used to as a child, I collect.'

'No.' Leonora opened the last door and looked around

approvingly at the smaller bedroom at the back of the house, which must have been used by Mr Vincent's valet. 'This should suit you, Clarissa, if we brighten it up a bit. The bed and rest of the furniture look adequate. It seems my uncle did not scruple to make his man comfortable.'

'Indeed, yes! It is larger than my room at home in the Rectory and look, there is a splendid washstand, and a writing table—even a mirror!' Clarissa's normally rather sallow complexion had taken on a faint glow of excitement. 'But what of Dolly?'

'She will sleep upstairs in one of the rooms in the attic. I'd better go down and arrange it with this Monsieur André. Meanwhile, you could begin to unpack your things.'

'Would you like me to see to yours first?'

'No. Dolly can do it after she has been downstairs with me. You make yourself comfortable.'

The back stairs were discovered behind the main staircase, at the end of a short passage accessed through a narrow door opening from the lobby. Dolly, her boots clattering on the bare boards, followed her mistress down to the basement. A comfortingly warm, aromatic and steamy atmosphere drew them to the kitchen.

Dinner was over, though sounds of washing up came from the adjoining scullery, through which Leonora dimly glimpsed the back area and steps.

In the kitchen itself, pots and pans, mostly iron but some copper, hung from hooks and sat on shelves, shadowy in the light cast by oil lamps and candles. A huge dresser held an assortment of crockery and jars. Beyond the long scrubbed table that occupied the centre of the room, a large range stretched along the opposite wall. A clockwork spit turned a couple of chickens over the glowing fire, which largely accounted for the mouth-watering aromas filling the kitchen, and a couple of pots simmered gently on the hob.

Mixed in with the smell of roasting meat were echoes of coffee, of baking bread, of spices and herbs. Leonora's stomach rumbled. They had not stopped to take more than a light nuncheon on the way.

A small man in a tall, crumpled white hat aimed an excited stream of fractured English at those working about the table chopping, beating and blending. As the door opened he paused in mid-flow to exclaim in scandal-ised tones, 'What ees eet? What you do 'ere, *madame*? What you want?'

Everyone in the room stopped work.

Leonora swept forward with a gracious smile. 'Monsieur André?'

'Zat ees me, *oui*.'

'And you are the cook.' It was a statement. He could be no one else.

'Le chef de cuisine, madame,' he corrected her stiffly, with a small bow.

'I am delighted to make your acquaintance, monsieur,' said Leonora. 'Allow me to introduce myself, since there is no one here to do it for me. I am Miss Vincent, now the owner of these premises. I have spoken with my tenant, Lord Kelsey, who informs me that, through him, you are contracted to supply any meals I might order.'

The cook's stiff manner changed into one of open curiosity as he made a deep, deferential bow. *'Madame! Enchanté, madame!* Hees lordship, 'ee 'as tolded me you come. And you 'ave chose to stay?'

'I have, *monsieur*. I find the house quite charming. This,' she said, pulling her reluctant servant forward, 'is my maid, Dolly. She will bring down my orders and collect the dishes when they are ready.' Dolly dipped a clumsy curtsy and Monsieur André acknowledged her presence with a nod. 'And perhaps she may be allowed to use your kitchen to make me a pot of tea or some other drink or snack occasionally?'

He eyed the girl, who stood awkwardly beside Leonora, her face as red as her work-worn hands. 'Zere will be nossing of any difficulty, *madame*.'

'Thank you. Dolly will need to occupy a servant's room in the attic. Perhaps someone could show her up?'

'Zee 'ousekeeper will arrange zat, *madame*. She is in 'er chamber.'

'Housekeeper?' murmured Leonora, momentarily brought up short. Lord Kelsey had not mentioned a housekeeper, though of course he would need one.

'Mrs Parkes, *madame, une veuve*—'ow you say? A vidow? She 'as zee room in front next zee servants' room. I 'ave zee one next *ma cuisine*.'

'Then perhaps you will introduce us?'

The housekeeper's room had a large chunk cut out of it for a store-room, but otherwise it was the same size as her own drawing room upstairs, plenty big enough to accommodate table, chairs and bed. The fast-fading daylight barely allowed her to see the basement wall, some three yards from the window. As she looked up she glimpsed the railings etched against the flickering light cast on the feet of a man by the torch he carried. The grass and trees beyond were quite out of sight.

The housekeeper herself was of ample proportions and looked middle-aged. Her gown was of dark stuff and a frilly black cap touched by white hid her hair. She rose from a chair drawn up before a bright fire, while candles flickered above on its mantel. Her curtsy was made without fuss and a neutral smile appeared on her smooth-cheeked face.

'Of course there's room for the lass,' she said comfortably and the smile she turned on Dolly was motherly. 'You'll find company up there, my girl.' To Leonora she said, 'I'll be up in a minute to show her where to go. Have you ordered your supper, madam?'

Leonora, surprised by the way the woman spoke, shook her head. 'Not yet. I have a companion to live with me. There are therefore three of us, with Dolly.'

'Dolly can eat in the Servants' Hall, with the others, if that suits. I shall order a meal for you and your companion, madam. Leave it to me. Monsieur André is an exceptional cook, which makes the Club's dining room popular, and I shall see that you are provided with the best.'

'Thank you, Mrs Parkes. When will supper be served?'

'Dinner is between two and five o'clock and supper between eight and midnight.' The excellent Mrs Parkes, plainly a superior woman of some education, glanced at the clock on the mantel. 'It is only a half after five. Would you like a snack while you wait?'

'Thank you, I would appreciate that. And supper early, at eight, tonight. We have had a tiring day. I am obliged to you, Mrs Parkes.'

The spiral stairs seemed to rise up forever. Following Dolly now, Leonora wondered if she would ever be able to mount them from bottom to top without losing her breath. But of course she would! She was comparatively young, and fit, and she would not allow the inconvenience of having to climb innumerable narrow, winding stairs to reach her rooms daunt her. It would please his lordship too much if she did.

She was out of breath by the time she reached her floor, but managed to recover it quickly by inhaling deeply a couple of times.

'Come, Dolly,' she ordered the youngster. 'While you are waiting for Mrs Parkes, you may as well begin to unpack my things.'

Her bedroom was large enough to double as her boudoir, she thought, looking around with more attention than she had given it before. With pretty striped drapes at the windows and new bed curtains and cover, it would be both comfortable and pleasant on the eye.

A mahogany chest of drawers and a cupboard with shelves stood in the dressing room, with a wash stand and close stool. Her clothes would all be kept in there. She would buy a cheval mirror or two and replace the gentleman's chest in the bedroom with a dressing table and perhaps buy a *chaise-longue*.

She would show the intolerable Earl downstairs that she was no wilting lily to be frightened off by his desecration of her premises. What had her uncle been thinking of, to allow him to set up a gambling hell below?

The answer came to her without her even having to think. He had been a man, probably a gambler and had belonged to the Club. Of course he had seen no reason to object!

Apart from the interminable stairs she must climb to reach it, she would have been well satisfied with her accommodation. That she must use the servants' entrance and back stairs was an insult entirely caused by the disobliging presence of Lord Kelsey pursuing his dubious activities beneath her.

Tomorrow, she decided as she consumed the cold ham,

fresh bread and butter and pot of tea Mrs Parkes had sent
up after showing Dolly her quarters, she would confront
Mr Coggan in his chambers and demand that the lease
be terminated. After she had inspected the premises
downstairs.

Tomorrow promised to be an interesting day.

Sharp on nine the following morning, refreshed by a
night of deep and untroubled slumber, Leonora trod down
the main staircase to beard Lord Kelsey in his den. She
took the precaution of taking Clarissa with her. After all,
she was flouting convention by visiting a gentleman in
his rooms, even although it was on business. Besides,
there was something about the Earl she did not—
quite—trust.

The doors on the middle landing were ajar and sounds
of cleaning could be heard. They passed straight down
to the ground floor and Leonora, seeing no functionary
to stop her, led the way to the office she had been in
yesterday.

Most of the doors down here, to private rooms occupied by the Earl and his manager, were firmly closed
against intrusion. The office door, however, was ajar.
She rapped on the panel and entered on a brisk invitation
so to do.

She had not noticed, yesterday, that the room was more
than an office. It was, in most respects, equipped as a
study, with armchairs by the fire and a reading desk near
the single window. The other window, this one's twin,
had been cut off to create an inner room, the use of which
was not immediately obvious.

The Earl, however, had risen from the same large desk
he had been using yesterday. Its surface was strewn

mostly with bills and ledgers. He was not making the entries but checking someone else's work, the scanty daylight augmented by the light from a branch of candles.

'You are punctual, Miss Vincent,' he greeted her, having bowed and received their curtsies in return.

'In business, my lord, it pays to abide by one's promises,' Leonora said. 'I am ready to make my inspection, and have brought Miss Worth with me to take down any necessary notes.'

Clarissa held a pad of paper and a pencil clutched to her breast. She was gazing at his lordship with bright, interested eyes and faintly flushed cheeks. Yesterday, realised Leonora, Clarissa had not had much chance to take in Kelsey's splendid physique and the excellent tailoring which displayed it to full advantage. Neither had she been treated to a smile which conveyed both welcome and a degree of conspiratorial sympathy. As though she, Leonora, was some harridan to be placated!

She looked about her with an austerely critical gaze.

'This room appears to be in satisfactory order—except for that patch of damp by the window.' She walked over and looked up, peering as closely as possible at the stained wallpaper. 'Why have you not had it repaired?'

Kelsey spoke in the resigned tone of one dealing with a fractious infant. 'Because, Miss Vincent, the trouble is outside, in the stonework, for which the owner is responsible. Mr Vincent was intending to have a repair effected before he so unfortunately died. He also expected to bear the cost of having the wall redecorated internally.'

'I shall consult a stonemason,' declared Leonora briskly, hiding her discomfort under a businesslike manner. Dear Lord, how much would that cost her? She had not even considered that repairs might be necessary to the fabric, for which she would be responsible. 'Clarissa, make a note.' She indicated the closed door to the inner room. 'What is in there?'

'I had that room formed, with Mr Vincent's permission, to accommodate my valet. It seemed the most convenient place since my dressing room is little more than a cupboard and has no window.'

He opened the door and Leonora took a brief glance around the small but tidy bedroom.

'Very well. Shall we move on?'

Kelsey closed the door again as they withdrew and strolled across to the office door to hold that open for them, looking indolently tolerant. Leonora seethed. He had certainly had the best of that exchange.

As they passed through she glanced about the hall but could not fault the polished floorboards, the strip of patterned carpet leading to the stairs, the cream walls and brown paintwork or the blue and gold tasselled decorations. Tasteful, mildly opulent yet dignified, it was tilted towards the masculine, of course, but she could scarcely complain about that.

A wreath-like decoration affixed to the wall near the front door caught her attention. She had not noticed it before, or the words it contained.

'"Welcome to the Vitus Club,"' she read aloud. 'Is that what you call your gambling den?'

'The Vitus Club is known throughout Bath, Miss Vincent.'

'I'm certain it is. Do your members all suffer from nervous twitches?'

He laughed, but his tone patronised when he spoke. 'Fortunately, no, Miss Vincent. My family name is

Dancer. St Vitus is the patron saint of dancers. I thought the name appropriate.'

'Prodigiously so. If your clients are not twitching from some nervous disease, they will be from gambling fever or despair,' Leonora scoffed.

The dark brows lifted. Now his tone held an undercurrent of scornful disbelief. 'Do I infer that you disapprove of gambling, Miss Vincent? That you never wager on a hand of cards?'

Leonora flushed. She had allowed herself to fall into the trap of appearing a prude. 'Not at all, sir,' she contradicted him. 'Like everyone else, I gamble in moderation when in card-playing company. I do not disagree with gambling in principle but fear the hold it gains on some people—' like her father, though she would not mention him. Her hand tightened on the handle of her reticule '—and despise those who trade on their weakness,' she concluded quickly.

He waved a hand, indicating that she should enter the door he was opening. She did, and Clarissa meekly followed behind. Leonora wondered what her friend thought of the verbal battle raging between herself and the Earl.

In truth, she scarcely knew why she was being so difficult, except that the entire situation had taken her completely by surprise. White's, Boodle's and Brooks's in London could be regarded as respectable, she supposed, but even so a man could lose a fortune in an evening. The less respectable clubs often set out to fleece their clients.

Unable to meet the high membership fees demanded by White's and the like, her father had fallen victim to such a one on his last visit to Town, a circumstance which had undoubtedly given her a jaundiced view of small clubs like the Vitus. His losses had, in effect, caused his death. He had sold his carriages and horses and his hunters, and been thrown by a devilish animal with an evil eye, the best mount he could afford.

'So no one should deal in the selling of wine or spirits and thus incite drunkenness and delirium tremens?' remarked Kelsey smoothly as he walked to the centre of what must be his parlour-cum-dining room.

Leonora, unwilling to confide her true reasons for her antagonism, chose to ignore this irrelevance while busily occupying herself with looking about. The room was tastefully decorated and comfortably furnished with armchairs. The dining table was small, large enough only for intimate dinners. He would not eat here often, she supposed, he would take his meals in the Club. A side board held an array of decanters and glasses. Leonora could not fault the condition of the the place.

'The bedroom is through here,' said Kelsey smoothly, opening a communicating door leading to the back room.

Not to be hurried or intimidated, Leonora finished her survey of the room she was in before walking through with her chin in the air. Clarissa, reared in the genteel confines of a rectory, held back. Kelsey, a hand in the small of her back, guided her through. Clarissa's colour flared. Her colourless lashes fluttered, revealing and then hiding the pale blue eyes raised to meet the Earl's.

Turning, Leonora felt a small shock run through her. Clarissa was flirting with his lordship! Her voice, therefore, was sharp as she called for her attention.

'Miss Worth! I hope you have continued to make notes?'

'I did not realise that there was anything to write,'

said Clarissa placidly. 'You have found no other fault, I believe?'

'No. But that fact must be recorded, too. Hall, parlour and bedroom are all in excellent order.'

'I am glad you find them so, madam,' came Kelsey's rather amused voice. She had scarcely glanced at the bedroom and in her hurry had ignored the middle-aged gentleman's gentleman occupied in tidying his master's clothes beside a cubicle containing a cupboard and washstand, and he knew it. He might not intimidate her, but his huge canopied bed did.

'There are other rooms on this floor, I believe,' Leonora said, making speedily for the door to the hall.

Kelsey followed her out of his bedroom, a small smile denting one corner of his mobile mouth. He crossed to the door next that of his office. 'Only one. This is Sinclair's room. I have arranged with him that you should be admitted.'

Leonora merely raised her brows at this piece of nonsense. She had every right to be admitted!

Kelsey knocked. A voice bade them enter.

Sinclair had risen and met them near the door, his manner almost effusive.

'Good morning, Miss Vincent. I believe you wish to inspect my room?'

Leonora gave him her sweetest smile. 'I merely wish to discover the general condition of the part of the building Lord Kelsey rents,' she explained.

'Then you must be quite reassured,' observed Sinclair, returning her smile and transferring it to Kelsey as a grin. 'He is most particular and Mrs Parkes is an able housekeeper.'

'Your apartment looks comfortable, clean and

well-decorated,' observed Leonora. 'You are well suited here?'

'Indeed, madam, I am happy in my accommodation and my association with his lordship. As you can see, he has provided me with every comfort. Is there anything else you wish to know?'

'I think not,' said Leonora, noting that he had a small desk in his room, at which he had been working, as well as a dining table and chairs, a well-stocked side board, several armchairs and a narrow bed behind a screen in one corner. 'Thank you, Mr Sinclair. Miss Worth, note only that there is a little paint peeling from the window frame.'

'There is? murmured Kelsey, his brows rising. 'You did not tell me, Sinclair.'

'I thought the matter too trifling,' said the manager.

They all dutifully inspected a small area near the sill where the paint had flaked.

'Strictly, it is,' said the Earl. 'But I will undertake to have it touched up. And now, madam, if you are satisfied with this floor, we can mount the stairs to see those rooms I use for the Club. I fear we must not linger, for the doors will open in half an hour. I will lead the way.'

'Very well.'

This flight of stairs was wider than the next one leading up to her rooms, as she had already noted. It was usual, of course, for stairs to become narrower the higher they climbed. She became even more determined to gain possession of the lower rooms, particularly the main rooms served by the wider staircase, as soon as possible. Otherwise, how was she ever to receive?

'This is the Dining Room,' he said, ushering them into one of the back rooms through an already half-open door.

'But you may even think that selling food holds out the danger of encouraging gluttony?'

He wanted to throw ridicule on her views. The question in his voice held the ring of irony. Leonora shook an angry head.

'Pray do not be absurd,' she snapped. 'If a man chooses to drink or eat himself to death, he does not necessarily leave his family bereft of anything but his presence. A man who is stripped, of intent, of all he owns and dies deeply in debt, leaves a destitute family. There is a difference.'

There was a considering look in the slate-grey eyes. Leonora flushed again, conscious that she may have given away more of her past than she had intended.

He bowed. 'I give you best, madam. A prudent, honest gentleman will have a care for others. It is the imprudent who find themselves with pockets to let, be it through over-indulgence in the good things of life or in gambling.'

'Imprudent? Maybe.'

Leonora stood by one of the circular tables, her fingers smoothing the polished mahogany surface. Her father, for one, had not in general behaved rashly. She collected her scattered thoughts and looked about her.

Like others of its size the table was set about with four padded chairs. Some were meant only for two, one for a larger party. White damask cloths were already in course of being spread and cutlery placed in position. The clatter of continuing activity distracted her for a moment.

She realised that it would be pleasant to eat in this room, with its buff walls divided into panels outlined in blue, while above gold leaf and blue paint decorated

the wide cornice. A gilt—it could scarcely be gold—
chandelier holding dozens of candles and dripping with
crystal hung from the centre. Rich damask curtains
matched the blue and gold chair seats.

She stirred, only now ready to finish what she had
begun to say. 'But gambling is like a fever. The compulsion can be caught; once in its grip, an individual is
helpless until the bout is over.'

'The addictive compulsion to alcohol is equally
deadly, Miss Vincent, particularly for the poor, where
families starve because the father spends what little he
earns on drink. Yet alehouses remain open and merchants
continue to peddle spirits without rousing condemnation.
I see no reason why I should be damned for providing
the facilities for gentlemen to eat, drink and amuse themselves in congenial company.'

He shrugged his immaculately clad shoulders. 'I no
more encourage anyone to indulge to excess than does
your wine merchant or the hostess who sets up card tables
in her home. The stakes at the tables here may be a little
higher than at a rout or at the Assembly Rooms, but that
is the gambler's choice, not mine.'

He was, she realised, attempting to justify himself and
using all his charm to win her over. He did have a point,
if what he said was true. But how could she know that
it was? He must take a percentage of the stakes. She
shook her head, the slightest of involuntary movements.
The very fact that he had chosen to profit from the frail-
ties of others must condemn him.

She met his dark, quizzical eyes without flinching,
going straight to what she conceived to be the weakest
part of his argument. 'You set no limit on the stakes, I
collect.'

He shrugged shoulders encased in immaculate blue broadcloth. The shadows on his neckcloth shifted and changed but his expression did not. Not a trace of guilt showed in his manner. 'No, madam. A man must have somewhere to go where he is allowed to do as he determines.'

'To go to hell if that is his choice?'

'Exactly, madam.'

Leonora's soft lips compressed into a tight line before she said, 'I should prefer such an activity to take place somewhere other than beneath my roof.'

'I regret, Miss Vincent, that I cannot oblige you in that respect. Have you seen all that you require in here?'

So he wanted to abandon the argument for the moment. Leonora's frustration grew. Nothing she could say or do could shift him.

She could feel nothing but righteous pleasure that she had made her position so abundantly clear. She had no desire to prolong the argument. What she did most urgently want was to find some flaw in his lordship's tenancy agreement or in his adherence to it, which would allow her to evict him.

'Yes,' she answered him. 'This room is in excellent repair.' The double doors leading to the front room stood open. She moved to pass through. 'This is the Reading Room?'

'As you can see, Miss Vincent.'

If anything, it was decorated, furnished and equipped in better style than the Dining Room. High-backed arm-chairs, each with a small table beside it, predominated. Where the walls were not lined with shelves bearing books, they were painted cream with white, blue and gold decorated panels. Rich brown velvet curtains hung at the windows.

Besides the central chandelier and a number of wall brackets, a branch of candles stood on the table by each chair, ready to be lit with a taper from the jar standing near the grate where a fire was already burning. The supply of candles must form one of his greatest expenses, she thought, he was so lavish with his lighting. One side-table had newspapers spread upon it while another held an array of glasses. The drink itself must be out of sight in the locked cupboard behind the main door.

Leonora found herself fingering the leather spines of some of the books. Perhaps she allowed her longing to show. His lordship lifted a brow and smiled. Sweat pricked uncomfortably under her arms and a pulse throbbed in her throat. She would so much rather he had not smiled in the way he had, in warm enquiry rather than in censure or irony.

'You would be most welcome to borrow a volume at any time, Miss Vincent,' he invited. 'Although,' he added, 'you would require to come down at about this hour to make your choice, while the room is unoccupied.'

'Thank you.' Despite the unwelcome response his smile had provoked and the caveat about the time, she wanted to explore the books so much she found she could not hide her pleasure. 'I had feared I would miss the library at Thornestone Park, but I expected that there would be a subscription library in the town?'

'There is, in Milsom Street.'

'Then between the two I shall not lack for something to read.'

'Reading can give great joy, can it not?' he remarked, apparently with all sincerity. 'No doubt, as a governess, you have felt the need to extend your knowledge.'

'I have enjoyed reading since I was a child,' responded Leonora, inordinately annoyed that he should think her interest in reading due entirely to the profession forced upon her.

He bowed slightly in acknowledgment of her protestation. He said, 'If you would care to come through, I will show you the other rooms,' and opened the door to the landing.

Card rooms, of course, were a feature of every large house, of every Assembly Room, and card tables graced every private gathering. She could never have entered any level of society had she not been willing to play cards and lay down her stake, however small! Kelsey had known this and deliberately misunderstood her. The more generous perception she had begun to have of him suffered on this reflection.

So she entered the other front room with a frown between her brows, her eyes narrowed, looking for evidence of foul play or sharp practice.

'The Card Room is reserved for those desirous of playing whist,' said Kelsey. He regarded her frown, the intent expression in her grey-blue-green eyes, with relaxed amusement.

As well he might. It was impossible to tell, of course. The room was equipped with perfectly ordinary green baize-covered tables large enough for four people to sit around, with a candle and an unbroken pack of cards on each. And the decorations, as elsewhere, proved to be both tasteful and faultless.

'Nothing to be done,' she said abruptly to Clarissa, who faithfully recorded the verdict.

Here again, double doors led through to the back room.

This was fitted out rather differently. A large padded, baize-covered table predominated, with small tables and their attendant chairs scattered about in random fashion.

'This is the Gaming Room,' Kelsey informed her. 'Members are free to play whatever they like in here. Vingt-et-un and other games involving many participants are played at the large table, piquet, cribbage, dominoes and dice at the smaller ones.

'That book there,' he went on, pointing to a leather-bound ledger-like article, 'records all the non-gaming bets and the stakes laid between members. Gentlemen will wager on anything under the sun, as you must know. But once a bet is recorded in there, no gentleman can deny its existence or refuse to honour the debt. I do not make the book,' he observed mildly. 'I merely keep the record.'

'Has anyone,' asked Leonora fiercely, 'ever lost their inheritance in here? Gambled away the deeds of their property?'

Kelsey's face remained inscrutable. 'Would you like to be the first to do so, Miss Vincent?' he asked amiably.

'You are unbelievable, my lord!' cried Leonora. 'You are suggesting that I should bet my ownership of this property on the winning of a game of cards? What, may I ask, would be my reward should I win?'

'I should set my lease against your deeds,' responded his lordship imperturbably.

'Ha!' exclaimed Leonora. 'And both of us are very sure that you would win! No, my lord, you cannot bamboozle me in that fashion! I was not born yesterday!'

'No,' he agreed, his gaze considering. 'You are certainly not in the first flush of youth, Miss Vincent.'

Her choke of shocked outrage and Clarissa's surprised

gasp almost overset him. Lights danced in the dark eyes and his mouth gave an involuntary twitch. Leonora was too angry to notice.

'You are no gentleman, sir!' she managed to gasp.

'But then, madam, you do not behave like a lady,' came the instant riposte. He bowed languidly and gave her a lazy smile. 'May we not call a truce while you inspect the last room over which I have temporary dominion? May I show you the office?'

'You may show me the office, my lord, but I do not accept your truce. I shall proceed to my lawyer's rooms immediately after breakfast.'

'That will be your privilege, madam.' He sounded not in the least perturbed.

She scarcely looked at the small room above the entrance hall, where an elderly clerk sat on a tall stool working at a sloping desk surrounded by shelves and strong-boxes. She could not escape Kelsey's presence soon enough. She flounced off up the narrowed stairs, her front-door key conspicuous in her hand, with Clarissa following meekly behind.

And did not see the amused, reluctant admiration with which Blaise Dancer, Earl of Kelsey, watched her undoubtedly attractive posterior disappear from his view.

Chapter Three

Despite her fury, Leonora managed to consume two soft-boiled eggs and several crusty white rolls spread with butter, and to drink two cups of coffee. Anger made her hungry and the food was delicious.

'An excellent repast,' offered Clarissa as she, too, pushed her plate aside. She had broken her fast with kidneys and bacon.

'Yes.' Leonora was in no mood to be fulsome over anything which had its origins in Kelsey's management. 'Can you be ready to go out in half an hour?'

'I am ready now, except for my bonnet and cloak. Shall you take a sedan chair? I believe there is a rank nearby. Dolly should be able to find it.'

'Not this morning,' Leonora decided. 'Mr Coggan's chambers in High Street cannot be far away and I should like to see something of the town.'

'Oh, so should I,' cried Clarissa, her pale eyes shining. 'I am so grateful to you for bringing me here, Leonora! The very atmosphere makes me feel quite young and giddy!'

'Does it?' So far, Leonora had not felt either young

or giddy but that was because of the infamous use to which the Earl of Kelsey was putting her property. The only feelings she had known were those of uncomfortable awareness of his lordship's personal charm and frustration and anger at his attitude. And utter mortification that he should think her old.

Mortification brought a lowering sense of unease to her entire being and she could feel a flush rising up her neck when she remembered his look and words. She would hazard a guess that she was several years younger than he was. But then, he was a man. He did not have to fear that his child-bearing years were dwindling with depressing rapidity.

She must make her utmost endeavours to have his lordship evicted. She jumped to her feet. 'If you are ready, then we may leave immediately,' she declared. 'Dolly, my bonnet, my cloak, gloves and muff if you please.'

She, like Clarissa, already wore her pelisse, for the morning was chilly and the fires had not yet had time to make the rooms warm.

Dolly dropped the dishes she was clearing with a clatter and rushed out, hurrying along the landing to the dressing room. Leonora followed her, shivering slightly at leaving even the comparative warmth of the dining room. She glanced quickly into the rather mottled mirror above her uncle's dressing chest—she must do something about mirrors as soon as possible—as Dolly handed her her bonnet, and examined her features as best she could.

She undoubtedly lacked the fresh bloom of real youth, the bloom she had possessed at eighteen when her parents had died. But she did not look old.

He had not said that she did. He had only spoken the truth in such a way as to imply it. Devil take the man! Her soft mouth tightened as she determinedly thrust all thought of Lord Kelsey behind her. She did not have to think about *him* to arrange the termination of a lease.

With her outer garments on, she bobbed about and stood on tiptoe to see as much of herself as she could.

Depression settled in. No wonder the man was so scathing about her appearance. She looked every inch what she had been—a governess. She would never engage the attentions of a suitable gentleman of means dressed as she was. The second thing she must do was to buy some new clothes. Mr Coggan would know about her money, though she would doubtless be able to purchase what she needed on credit.

She passed through the comparative warmth of her bedroom to pick up her reticule and emerged on the chilly landing to find Clarissa waiting.

'You know what to do, Dolly,' said Leonora to her hovering maid. 'Take the dirty breakfast things downstairs to the scullery and then come back and clean the rooms. Remember, we found the brooms and dusters in there.' She indicated the dark oak cupboard standing on the landing. 'Have your dinner with the rest of the staff. I shall not trouble Monsieur André on the way out.'

She did not wish to make a production of her use of the back entrance but to slip out, as far as possible, unseen. 'Tell him that I shall dine at four o'clock,' she went on. 'If there is mutton I should like that, but otherwise whatever is available. I cannot fuss over what we shall eat today. Do you understand?'

'Oh, yes, miss,' said Dolly fervently.

She was devoted and willing and not the most able

girl she had ever dealt with, but Leonora liked her and appreciated the effort the child made to please.

'By the way,' she said as an afterthought, turning back with her hand already on the knob of the door to the back stairs, 'is your bed comfortable? You slept well?'

'The room's lovely, miss, such a nice view as I've got, over the trees. I slept like a log.'

'Capital,' said Leonora with a smile. 'I'll leave you, then. Don't forget to keep the fires stoked.'

'No, miss,' said Dolly with another bob.

Having descended the stairs, the two ladies passed through the scullery without speaking to the cook, who was busy at the far end of the kitchen.

Leonora's only real disappointment in the actual property she had inherited was its lack of a garden, but the leafy green fronting it largely made up for this deficiency. It was, after all, a town house built before John Wood and his son had begun to build the Palladian-style terraces, with long gardens at the rear, which now prevailed in Bath. She was, indeed, rather glad that Morris House stood in isolation.

Mounting the back-area steps, they found themselves in a street they soon discovered was called Abbeygate.

'Which way?' wondered Leonora.

'The Abbey will be in the town,' suggested Clarissa.

Its tower beckoned. 'Very well,' decided Leonora, 'we will go to the Abbey and ask our way from there.'

'It truly is a huge building,' murmured Clarissa as they walked its length to arrive at the West Front. 'Dare we go in?'

'It is so,' agreed Leonora 'But we must not linger. I have no appointment and we may have to wait to see the lawyer.'

'We could attend a service here on Sunday,' suggested Clarissa.

'Perhaps,' said Leonora. She did not intend to be seen in public before she had acquired a more becoming wardrobe.

High Street was nearby and they had no difficulty in finding Mr Coggan's offices. He, it seemed, was free to see Miss Vincent immediately.

'Good luck,' murmured Clarissa as she took the seat offered by a clerk and prepared to wait.

Leonora was ushered into a dimly lit room where she discovered a youngish man in legal garb, who rose from a chair behind a desk strewn with parchments and papers intertwined with red tape, to greet her.

'Miss Vincent! A privilege to meet you,' he cried, bowing deeply before asking her to be seated and sitting down again himself. 'Sadly,' he went on, 'I never knew Mr Charles Vincent, but Mr Warwick asked me to represent him here in Bath, and to act in your interests as beneficiary under Mr Vincent's Will. You have appointed him to act for you in other matters?'

'No,' said Leonora, frowning. 'He is, I suppose, not acting for me but for my uncle still, as his executor. It did not occur to me that I myself had need for a lawyer.'

'I should be delighted. . .should you think it in your interests. . .should it please you. . .to act for you in whatever way you might need, Miss Vincent,' he said, eagerly yet with a diffidence which appealed to Leonora.

He was really quite a personable creature, even distinguished, in his wig. He was young, keen and surely ambitious. He might be just the one to take on the Earl.

'You have met Lord Kelsey?' she asked, without committing herself.

'Once, Miss Vincent. To inform him of your being named as beneficiary under Mr Charles Vincent's Will.'

'And what was his reaction, pray?'

Coggan looked embarrassed. He flushed. 'He was dismayed,' he admitted. 'He proposed to offer you a sum of money to purchase the house. Has he done so?'

'He has. And I have refused. Morris House is mine, is it not? There can be no question under the Will?'

'Indeed, no, madam. You have taken possession of the property, its deeds and all the investments have been transferred to your name and the cash rests in an account at the bank in Milsom Street, which needs only your signature to make it operable. No doubt you will present yourself there as soon as possible.'

Leonora nodded.

Coggan resumed speaking. 'I have presumed to write a note of introduction to the manager. Thus the Will has been fully executed. Mr Warwick's duty, and therefore mine, is at an end.'

'Thank you,' murmured Leonora, accepting the sealed paper handed to her. 'Mr Coggan,' she went on, tucking it into her reticule, 'I shall be glad if you will advise me on the matter of the lease.'

'Ah,' said the lawyer thoughtfully. 'You are dissatisfied with the terms? They could, by agreement, be amended.'

'I want it terminated,' said Leonora baldly.

'Terminated,' repeated Coggan. His voice had gone flat. 'I do not believe that to be possible, except, of course, by agreement. I take it Lord Kelsey is not willing?'

'No. But I want him out. I cannot endure to have a gambling hell on my property.'

'A hell?' Coggan sounded surprised. 'Do you have proof of your contention, Miss Vincent? As far as I am aware, the Vitus Club is a legitimate business and the use of the rooms for the purposes of cards and gaming is not forbidden in the lease.'

'Then find proof that Lord Kelsey is in some other way breaking the terms of his lease or even of breaking the law! I cannot believe that he does not use the Club as a cover for relieving gullible gentlemen of their fortunes. Small establishments are notorious for this.'

'Gentlemen lose fortunes at White's, Brooks's and Boodle's, madam. No one condemns those clubs as gambling hells.'

Leonora rose. 'I see you are on Lord Kelsey's side,' she said stiffly. 'Thank you for your time. I must seek another lawyer to represent me.'

Coggan jumped to his feet. His wig slipped and he clapped it hastily back into place. 'No, Miss Vincent. You mistake me. I am not on his lordship's side. I merely point out to you the difficulty you face in attempting to overthrow the lease if his lordship is determined to remain in possession of his rooms. Do please sit down again and let us discuss the matter further.'

Leonora sat. She liked Coggan and thought him honest. But as the discussion continued, she came to see that there was little either she or her lawyer could do to evict Lord Kelsey unless he was proved to be violating the terms of the lease.

'He must be,' said Leonora with growing lack of conviction. 'Find someone who will investigate the way he runs the business. Find someone he has fleeced.'

'I will do my utmost,' promised Coggan.

And with that Leonora had to be content. For the moment.

'I have to go to the bank,' she told Clarissa as they left Coggan's offices. 'This way, I believe.'

The streets were narrow and busy. Leonora and her companion picked their way through to Milsom Street, eyeing the shops and the dressmakers' and milliners' establishments on their way.

'There is the circulating library!' exclaimed Clarissa suddenly.

Leonora was engaged in looking for the bank, but was sufficiently interested to stop and take a good look at the quite impressive façade of the library. 'We must take out subscriptions,' she declared. 'But look, there is the bank. Why do you not go into the library and make enquiries? I will join you there when I have finished my business.'

She had almost reached her destination when she recognised the gentleman walking towards her. He wore a many-caped top coat, a tall hat set at a rakish angle on his brown head, carried a silver-knobbed cane and had a ravishing female dressed in blue velvet and sable fur on his arm.

Kelsey. She could not ignore him. She acknowledged his pleasant but formal greeting with the courtesy demanded.

He turned, smiling, to his companion. 'Alicia, may I name to you Miss Vincent, the new owner of the property in which the Vitus Club has its rooms?'

The woman's scrutiny held slightly amused interest. 'Of course,' she murmured. Leonora suspected that she had been the subject of some earlier discussion between them.

'Miss Vincent,' he drawled, 'I have pleasure in presenting you to Lady O'Brien.'

'My dear!' exclaimed her ladyship once the formal curtsies and avowals of pleasure had been made. 'How intrigued I was to learn of your good fortune! My husband is one of the Vitus Club's most devoted members!'

Leonora did not know of the O'Briens or what rank the woman's husband held. She forced an amiable smile, inclined her head in acknowledgment of the pleasantry but said nothing.

'You are alone?' asked Kelsey. He sounded disapproving.

'My companion is in the circulating library,' said Leonora shortly. 'I shall join her there after I have seen my bank manager.'

'Ah! Money!' sighed Lady O'Brien. 'How it rules our lives!' She did not appear to study Leonora's dress but was moved to say, 'You must allow me to recommend my excellent modiste, Madame Fleur—so clever, so reasonable! Her establishment is in New Bond Street—you may have passed it?'

'I believe we did, my lady. I thank you for your interest. I shall, of course, be renewing my wardrobe now I have the means at my disposal.'

'There is a fine emporium for gloves and other accessories further down. Shopping in Milsom Street is vastly rewarding.'

'So I suppose. I look forward to investigating at my leisure.'

'I will leave my card,' promised her ladyship, preparing to move on. 'You must call on me, I am at home on Tuesdays and Thursdays. I look forward to meeting you again. And now, Blaise, we must take our leave of your friend, for I have an appointment at my milliner's—another excellent creature, Miss Vincent, her place is next door to the dressmaker—and I must not be late.'

Blaise. Blaise Dancer. So that was his name. And the woman who had erroneously called her his friend was looking up at him in a way that suggested to Leonora that they were rather more intimate than that, more intimate than the lady's husband might wish.

He was returning the look. Leonora became hot under her collar despite the chilly wind. She bent her knee in farewell and hurried on.

The encounter disturbed her. She had imagined Kelsey safely caged in his Club but, of course, he had a manager. He could come and go as he wished. She could never count on not meeting him when out and about in Bath. She would feel better able to cope with chance meetings after she had been to the modiste.

She was in two minds as to whether to patronise Lady O'Brien's dressmaker but had to admit that her ladyship had been tastefully gowned in the height of fashion. Whatever her morals, she possessed stunning good looks, knew what suited her—the sable furs had emphasised the spun-gold of her hair and the fairness of her skin—and looked every inch a lady. No wonder Kelsey had fallen victim to her lures.

But in all probability she had purchased her clothes in London. Her recommendation may not have been kindly meant.

She forgot Kelsey and his mistress while with the bank manager, emerging from his presence with a cheque book, a pouch of golden guineas and a wad of Bank of England notes complete with the recently introduced serial numbers. She had never felt so rich.

She sailed out of the bank, walked to the library with a spring in her step, discovered Clarissa engrossed in a book by Mrs Radcliffe, paid her own subscription out of the haul from the bank and took out a novel by a writer more to her own taste, *Mansfield Park* by Miss Austen.

'Come with me to the dressmaker,' she invited Clarissa as they left the library. 'I met Lord Kelsey on my way to the bank, and he had a lady with him—a Lady O'Brien. She has recommended me to visit Madame Fleur. I shall go, but am not perfectly persuaded that she will suit.'

'I shall be most interested. Papa gave me some money before I left,' Clarissa told her. 'I must have a new gown if we are to visit the Assembly Rooms.'

'Then perhaps we may both be suited.'

Leonora did not mind Clarissa patronising the same modiste if she could afford it. A well-dressed companion would add to her own consequence, which she had already decided to enhance in every way within her power. No one knew the exact extent of her inheritance. There could be no harm in her aim to persuade Bath society that it must be much larger than it was. To instil such a belief remained an essential element in her campaign.

As they arrived at Madame Fleur's, Lord Kelsey was leaving the milliner' next door.

'Ladies,' he murmured, raising his hat.

'Lord Kelsey. We meet again,' said Leonora, stifling a desire to scream. 'You have abandoned Lady O'Brien?'

'She understands that I have urgent business to attend to, Miss Vincent. During your inspection yesterday I noticed that the carpet in the Dining Room is showing signs of wear. I must arrange for it to be replaced. I am about to drive to Bristol to visit an excellent warehouse

I know of there. Should you desire to renew any of your own carpets, I can strongly recommend it.'

'Thank you,' said Leonora icily.

He went on, quite unperturbed by her tone. 'My oddjob man is already attending to the faulty paintwork. Do you have a mason in mind who will attend to the rear wall?'

The desire to scream increased. 'Whom did my uncle intend to consult?' asked Leonora grimly, torn between independence and ignorance. The last thing she wanted to do was receive help from the Earl.

'A man called Black, I believe. He has a yard on the outskirts of the town.' He smiled engagingly but the dark eyes taunted. 'Shall I send a boy with a message asking him to call?'

'Thank you, but no. If you will supply the direction, I shall send a note myself.'

'With pleasure, Miss Vincent. I shall see that the information is provided without delay.' He bowed. 'Miss Vincent. Miss Worth. I bid you good day.'

Clarissa, blushing, returned his smile. Leonora merely inclined her head. Both ladies watched his retreating figure. He strode along, his stick swinging, as though he had not a care in the world.

Leonora indulged her desire. 'Ar-r-gh!' she uttered.

Clarissa eyed her warily. 'You dislike the Earl?' she asked diffidently.

'He sets my teeth on edge,' said Leonora grimly. Her teeth were not the only parts of her anatomy he put on edge. 'There can be no place for his business on my property.'

'I cannot see that his Club is so very objectionable,' said Clarissa. 'And I find him pleasant enough.'

She was blushing again. Leonora glared. 'Of course

he has a pleasant manner! That is all part of his despicable character!'

'You cannot know that his character is despicable!' protested Clarissa with unusual heat.

Everyone thought her unwarrantably prejudiced, irrational, even obsessed by her opposition to gambling for high stakes. But the discovery of a gambling club on her own property had shaken her badly. Even to herself she would not admit that her main battle now was against herself and her reaction to Lord Kelsey.

For however much her body might wish otherwise, her mind insisted that he was a rogue, a rake, and not a suitable gentleman of means to be lured into the bonds of matrimony.

Madame Fleur, petite and voluble, had an impressive variety of made-up gowns on display.

Her assistants fluttered in the background as she explained, that *madame* could have any of the finished garments altered to fit. Her English was almost faultless.

'Or I can make up any of the designs in another material and to your exact measurements. Or, if *madame* prefers, I could suggest some slight alterations to any pattern, or create something exclusively for you.'

Her practised eye ran down Leonora's person and back up again. The cloak had already been discarded. Now Madame Fleur suggested that she take off her bonnet and pelisse. After another close scrutiny, she announced her verdict.

'*Madame* has a figure that will display my creations to admiration. So shapely, so graceful! I shall be delighted to dress you if you will honour me with your order.'

Prices were discussed. Leonora realised that to have a dress designed exclusively for herself did not come cheap. She could allow herself one, perhaps, for special evening occasions. For the rest, she could select from those delectable muslins, silks and velvets already made up and on display. Her eyes glowed. Choosing from those, she could instantly be gowned as she would wish.

Clarissa was much taken by a white muslin, but the style was more suitable for a young girl and the colour would most certainly emphasise her sallow complexion, Leonora knew. She was reassured to hear the modiste skilfully turn her companion's attention to a rose-tinted gown patterned in mulberry, a shade which reflected a faint glow to her skin.

Leonora herself could wear white. She was entranced by an exquisite evening gown in white silk with an over-skirt of the flimsiest oyster-coloured chiffon, which shimmered in the light. It had satin ribbon trimmings. The neckline was modest and the fashionable sleeves long, which, being winter, would be an advantage.

The price was high but it needed the minimum of alteration and Leonora, turning about before the mirror, decided that she would enjoy presenting herself at a concert at the Assembly Rooms wearing it. It would do excellently well were she to be invited somewhere to dine. Regardless of the cost, she bought it.

Her other purchases were more modest: a couple of pale-coloured muslins for the morning in simple styles— though one needed some of what Leonora considered to be excessive frills removed—a walking or driving dress made from a wool and cotton mixture in an attractive shade of green trimmed with dark green velvet, a matching pelisse and a less costly evening dress in pale primrose muslin with a low neckline and short puffed sleeves for dancing.

She had no idea whether she would ever be invited to a private ball of any consequence but could not resist the temptation to order a gown in case. Surely, one day, particularly should she attach the interest of an acceptable suitor, the occasion to wear it would present itself. *Madame* was delighted to bring all her artistic talents to bear and promised Leonora a stunning creation.

'Your eyes,' she murmured. 'Let me see.' She rummaged amongst her samples and returned with a length of shimmering aquamarine silk, which she draped over Leonora's shoulder. 'Yes. This will enhance your beautiful eyes. Trimmed with ivory and gold. . . Yes. A low neckline—'

'Not too low,' interrupted Leonora quickly.

Madame Fleur smiled. 'Trust me, *madame*. Modest yet revealing. The skirt gathered at the back to give you room. . . Elegant and stylish—fit for a duchess!'

Leonora hoped so, considering the huge sum it was to cost her.

Being minor, the necessary alterations to those gowns which were already made up could be accomplished overnight. They would be delivered next day. Those made from the same patterns but in a different colour or material, within the week. The special ball gown would take a little longer. *Madame* would have to return for a second fitting in a few days.

'I shall bring the altered gowns to you myself,' announced Madame Fleur. 'I must be satisfied that there are no further adjustments needed.'

'That is most kind of you, *madame*,' said Leonora.

'Mine will be delivered too?' asked Clarissa anxiously.

As well as the ball gown, she had ordered a modest walking dress in heavy russet twill trimmed with coney.

'Indeed, Miss Worth.'

For the first time, Leonora was faced with the difficulty of explaining her predicament.

'Once I have terminated the lease and the Vitus Club has moved out there will be no problem,' she explained. 'But meanwhile, if you cannot deliver before ten o'clock then you must use the back stairs. I am sorry. The situation is not of my choosing.'

'How unfortunate for you!' exclaimed Madame Fleur. 'I know Lord Kelsey, a quite superior gentleman,' she added with distinct admiration. 'He has been in here with. . .er. . .'

She trailed off in confusion.

'Lady O'Brien,' supplied Leonora drily. 'She recommended me to visit you.'

'I must thank her! She is an excellent customer. Her husband the Baron, you understand, is elderly and rather infirm. They are in Bath to enable him to take the waters.'

And if he was like to die, then to obtain the hand of an earl in marriage would be a step up the social ladder for his widow, thought Leonora rather sourly.

'Is he very ill?' asked Clarissa.

Leonora, grateful for the question she had not liked to ask, concentrated on smoothing her gloves.

'Gout,' said Madame Fleur succinctly.

Looking up, Leonora saw her own relief, which she declined to acknowledge, mirrored on Clarissa's face. Surely Clarissa had not decided to set her cap at Kelsey? The idea was ludicrous.

The modiste was still talking. 'But the Club is popular and Lord Kelsey will not easily agree to change its location, I am certain. He has spent lavishly on refurbishing the place to make it more acceptable to his members. He must regret Mr Vincent's death for many reasons. They were, I believe, on the best of terms.'

But he had not been in her uncle's confidence regarding his Will. No one had been, it seemed. 'I am sure he does,' concurred Leonora drily, donning her bonnet and cloak. 'I will expect you tomorrow morning, then.'

'I shall come at nine, if that would suit you?'

'Capital,' agreed Leonora. The gowns could not arrive soon enough for her.

All they had to do now was to visit the milliner next door and then walk home without being noticed. Since Kelsey was going to Bristol she did not expect to encounter him again. But she particularly wished to avoid Lady O'Brien, too.

When she thought of Lady O'Brien, all sorts of complicated emotions coursed through her. The one she recognised was jealousy, and it irked her. But soon she would have no material cause to envy the delectable Alicia. With decent gowns and becoming hats to wear she would have no reason to feel loweringly dowdy and old-maidish in her presence.

Except that Lady O'Brien possessed an assured manner and an easy elegance Leonora knew that she herself lacked. Never having experienced a London Season and subsequently having been exiled from Society for seven long years, she had had no chance to acquire it.

Unaware that her own innate dignity, elegance and charm were far more engaging than the affected deportment of many a Society beauty, or that her sharp intelligence set her apart from the vapid nonentities trained by governesses at the prompting of proud mamas, and could captivate far more effectively than demure acquiescence, she decided that she must learn fast.

With her new wardrobe to keep in trim she needed a lady's maid, someone who could also do clever things with her hair, perhaps provide her with the perfect grooming needed for her to take her place in Society with a similar degree of confidence.

Then she would be able to meet her ladyship without suffering those uncomfortable pangs of jealousy the woman's manner and appearance inspired. The fact that Alicia was also blessed with looks any man must admire caused Leonora little concern. Any gentleman she might consider suitable as a husband would not be misled by a pretty face alone. He would admire character above beauty.

No, it was the creature's dress and grooming that had given Leonora that lowering feeling of inferiority. That sudden burst of jealousy.

Lady O'Brien had long ago left the milliner's when Leonora, having first satisfied herself on the point, entered the workroom. By the time she left, with Clarissa carrying a bandbox, Leonora had discovered where to go to engage a lady's maid. Clarissa dutifully accompanied her to the Agency where the woman promised to send along several highly qualified applicants that very afternoon.

'She will have to sleep in my dressing room,' Leonora told Clarissa as they at last made their way back to Morris House. 'I shall lose my privacy, but there is a bed in there.'

'She would not like to sleep in the attics,' observed Clarissa.

She had bought a bonnet in brown velvet to match her new walking gown. Leonora had purchased and was wearing a hat with a small brim and a dashing bunch of feathers in a neutral yet pretty shade of grey and had ordered a similar hat to be fashioned from the same velvet used to trim her new walking gown. She had been promised that tomorrow morning as well. The milliner would obtain the material from Madame Fleur and work all night if necessary to finish it.

They climbed the stairs and were met by a hugely beaming Dolly.

As she took their outer garments, she explained with gleeful satisfaction that they could have a pot of tea and toasted muffins straight away, if they liked. Since they were back earlier than expected, four o'clock and the dinner she had ordered—mutton was available as miss had requested—was still more than an hour off. But she had borrowed a kettle and teapot from the kitchen, and the cook had given her tea, milk, sugar, muffins and butter.

'You sees, miss, there are trivets as can be turned over the coals and I found a toasting fork among the fire irons. So I asked downstairs and he were only too happy to oblige.'

'Well done, Dolly,' Leonora praised the girl, who had shown surprising initiative. 'I should be most grateful for tea and muffins.'

'The kettle's singing on the hob,' said Dolly smugly, dumping their garments on one of the chairs furnishing the hallway. 'The tea can brew while I toasts the muffins.'

By the time Leonora had washed her hands and tidied her hair the tea was ready. The muffins, running with melted butter, proved delicious. Seeing Dolly's longing gaze, Leonora offered her one. Not until that moment did she realise that Dolly had nowhere nearby that she could go to eat it except up to her room in the roof.

'Is there a bell in your room, Dolly?' she asked.

'Yes, miss, but it don't ring. Not like them in the servants' hall. If I was down there I'd soon know if you wanted me.'

'I dare say the one upstairs is not connected. Mention it to Mrs Parkes, tell her I would like it to work. Then you would be able to go to your room whenever you are not needed and do not wish to go down to the basement. Go up there now, Dolly. I shall call if I need you.'

Tomorrow she must remember to see about the mason.

'Shall you go to the Pump Room and sign the book tomorrow?' asked Clarissa.

That, too. Once she was decently gowned.

The third lady's maid Leonora interviewed proved to be youthful but experienced. Her mistress had come to Bath for her health and had died a week since, she explained. She had references. . .

Leonora read them, smiled at the woman, calm, capable, neatly dressed and probably about Clarissa's age, and offered Juliette Tranton the position.

Juliette smiled, accepted without hesitation, and took up her post immediately. She only had to collect her trunk.

Leonora felt that by tomorrow she would almost be set up in the style she wished. A carriage of her own would not be practicable in Bath. If she wished to drive out into the country she could always hire an outfit. There were still one or two ends to be neatened off, but by and large she was settled.

Apart from the nagging irritation of having Lord Kelsey's Vitus Club operating below. The rumble of men's voices, the occasional burst of laughter, could not fail to remind her. The sounds were not overly intrusive, but they were there in the background. And during the day she could not use her own front door to receive callers.

Which was intolerable.

Chapter Four

The following morning Leonora drew the bolts on the door closing off the main staircase and put the key in the lock.

Dolly answered the anticipated knock to admit Madame Fleur and her assistant, loaded down with boxes. Leonora received them in her bedroom.

Juliette was on hand to assist as the boxes were sorted and opened. Clarissa took possession of hers and carried them to her own room.

Leonara's gowns, removed from the layers of tissue paper and spread over the bed, created a breathtaking confusion of colour and texture.

In a mood of sheer delight, Leonora tried them all on. Only the smallest additional alteration was necessary to the morning gown, a mere stitch, which the modiste undertook personally while her assistant went to wait upon Clarissa.

Another knock announced the arrival of the milliner's assistant with her hat. Leonora happened, by lucky chance, to have tried her walking dress on last and was still wearing it. She watched eagerly as Juliette took the hat from its bandbox, and sat obediently while her new lady's maid set it upon her head.

Juliette had made a remarkable difference to her appearance already, Leonora knew, dressing her hair in a softer style, arranging her chignon in a most clever fashion, even using hot tongs to coax some curls to hang by her ears.

When she stood again to peer into the mirror over the dressing chest she was amazed and pleased by the transformation. And by what little she could see, the soft leaf-green of the costume and the darker velvet trim, together with the matching pelisse and hat, constituted an outfit of which she could be proud.

'I am going out after breakfast. I shall keep the gown on,' she decided as Juliette removed the hat. 'I need new gloves and a muff.'

The modiste, busy packing up her tape measure, scissors, needles and thread, straightened up. 'I am gratified that you are pleased, Miss Vincent. The other morning dress and the undergarments you ordered will be delivered in a few days, as I promised.'

'Thank you, *madame*. Clarissa!' Leonora exclaimed as her companion walked into the room behind Madame Fleur's assistant. 'How very à la mode you look!'

She was glad to be able to utter such a genuine compliment. She had thought the russet walking gown a good choice and her opinion was confirmed. Clarissa's new brown bonnet went with it well.

She wore a cap, had done so for several years as the Rector's daughter and, unlike Leonora, who had discarded her badge of servitude upon leaving Thornestone Park, continued to assume one as Leonora's companion. It was fashioned in ecru lace, much the same straw colour as her hair, and its pretty frill beneath the dark velvet was most becoming. She looked almost attractive.

Clarissa was making the most of her change of circumstances and Leonora could scarcely blame her. She had asked her to accompany her to Bath because she needed a respectable companion and felt sorry for the quiet, repressed young woman, already dwindling into an old maid, with whom she had come to be on terms of friendship.

The modiste had scarcely left when an imperious rap on the landing door sent Dolly scuttling to open it. Leonora was still in her bedroom with Clarissa. The two ladies were discussing the things they intended buying and doing once they had partaken of the breakfast Dolly had just brought up.

Leonora recognised the voice at once. She stiffened. Lord Kelsey, and not in the best of tempers by his tone.

'I will be with him immediately,' she told Dolly when the girl came to inform her rather nervously that she had shown him into the parlour.

She drew a deep breath.

Clarissa's eyes widened. 'I wonder what he can want?'

Her colour had heightened again. To her chagrin, so had Leonora's own.

'Nothing pleasant, I'll warrant,' Leonora snapped. 'Wait here.'

She patted her hair, for the hat had squashed her chignon somewhat, and straightened her gown. Would he notice it? It did not signify whether he did or did not. With set mouth and determined tread, she marched across the lobby—which she had decided to call the hall—and swept into the room which did duty for morning room, drawing room, sitting room and parlour. It was convenient to call it the parlour.

'Miss Vincent.'

His greeting was curt and accompanied by a stiff bow. His cold gaze did not alter at sight of her improved appearance. Her mouth set in an even firmer line as she returned his bow with a slight dip of her knee.

'My lord. You wished to speak with me?'

'Indeed, madam.' He clasped his hands beneath the tails of his cutaway coat and rocked back and forth on firmly planted feet. 'I reluctantly gave you permission to use the front door of this establishment before I open at ten o'clock in the morning. I can tolerate you and your companion passing through my private living quarters, though it is dev—most inconvenient. But I cannot allow your tradespeople to make use of my hall and stairs as though they had the right.'

'No?' murmured Leonora, deceptively quiet.

'No. In future, madam, whatever the time of day they may choose to call, they will mount by the service stairs. My footman has been instructed to refuse them admittance. The back entrance is designed for the use of such persons.'

Leonora went cold. He had the right of it in a way, although even if she was admitted by the service door, a modiste of Madame Fleur's standing would be invited to mount the main stairs to see her client.

She lifted her chin. 'Your tailor enters through the basement?' she enquired tartly.

He smiled. Wolfishly, she considered.

'My tailor is in Savile Row, in London, Miss Vincent. I normally find it preferable to visit him. And were your sempstress a man I might not be so averse to his traipsing through my private apartments. As it is, I forbid it. I made an exception in the case of yourself and your companion. Do not force me to regret my generosity.'

Leonora drew a fulminating breath. '*You* forbid it, my lord? Have you forgot that I am the owner of this property?'

'Have you forgot that I hold a lease which is not due to expire for another five years, Miss Vincent? At that time I shall be quite ready to vacate the premises. I shall have no further use for them.'

'Why not?' The words were out before she could stop them.

He regarded her down his fine, shapely nose. 'I am not persuaded that my reason is any business of yours, madam. I merely inform you that you will regain possession of the floors below at that time. Not a moment before.'

Leonora suddenly lost the use of her legs and sank into a chair. Lord Kelsey had the most devastating effect upon her. His broad shoulder looked to be such a comfortable place to bury her face while she wept with frustration.

She recalled her wandering wits and straightened her back. That she could entertain such a notion positively appalled her. Besides, she refused to turn into a watering pot.

'We shall see,' she ground out.

His attitude changed. Dear Lord! Had he noticed her weakness?

'You still have the ability to take more suitable accommodation,' he reminded her, his look and voice kindly. No! Condescending! The insufferable creature! 'The choice is yours. I believe you could lease an entire house

in the Circus for the amount I pay in rent at the moment.
I am willing to extend my lease to include these rooms,
and to raise the rent I pay accordingly. I could use
the space.'

He looked round, his gaze considering. 'This floor
would make adequate overnight accommodation for
members who wished to stay, something which I cannot,
at the moment, offer.'

'No, I thank you,' said Leonora stiffly. 'You have just
voiced an excellent reason for you to seek alternative
accommodation yourself. Were I you, I should do so.'

'But you are not me, Miss Vincent, and I have no
intention of abandoning all the hard work and money I
have invested in making the Vitus Club the select and
comfortable club that it is, patronised by all the prominent
members of Society when they are in Bath, whether they
gamble or not. Overnight accommodation to offer my
members would be an asset, but I have managed thus far
without it and can continue successfully as I am.'

She was not getting the best of her contests with Lord
Kelsey, for he appeared to hold all the aces. But if he
could make her life difficult, she could disturb his.

Strengthened by this thought, she stood up again. His
eyes flickered over her as she moved and she thought
she detected surprise in his expression. He had cooled
down enough to notice her improved appearance at last.
She smiled. An insincere, provocative smile. At least,
she hoped it was provocative, but she lacked practice in
the art of flirtation.

'I shall remember what you say, Lord Kelsey. But at
the moment I consider this apartment adequate to my
needs. And now, if you will excuse me, I believe my
breakfast is served.'

'Of course, Miss Vincent. I have said what I came to say. But may I first congratulate you on taking Lady O'Brien's advice? Madame Fleur in an outstanding modiste.'

How expertly he managed to turn compliment into condescension! Leonora drew breath.

'You approve of my choice of gown, sir? I cannot tell you how happy it makes me to know it.' Her tone, she hoped, implied the opposite. 'Now I have the means and the leisure, I can dress as I have always wished. Good day to you, sir.'

He left. But as he ran down the stairs a broad smile lit his features. What a spirited, captivating creature she could be! Scarcely a trace of the governess remained, except, of course, in her narrow-minded attitude to his Club. The smile left his face. How devilish unfortunate that she should be so obdurate, so determined to remain resident on the premises. But he would not allow her presence to inhibit his own activities, either in business or in private.

Leonora was still fulminating when she and Clarissa mounted the back area steps to the street an hour later.

But she would not allow his lordship to alter her intentions. She had considered herself settled, but she was not. There were numerous matters which still had to be dealt with.

The mason must be contacted. Kelsey had handed her a note of the man's name and direction as he left. The purchase of mirrors, a dressing table, a *chaise-longue*. The choosing of material for new curtains. New gloves and muff. The signing of the visitor's book in the Pump Room, although she did not regard herself as a visitor.

The *Bath Chronicle* listed new arrivals and local society would read her name and know she was in Bath.

Meanwhile, a sight of both would tell her who else was here at the moment. There might be someone with whom she could claim acquaintance. She must order some cards. And then there was the matter of tickets for balls, concerts and assemblies at the Upper Rooms to be settled. It should still prove worthwhile to take out subscriptions, the Bath Season not being over for a few months yet.

'Come, Clarissa,' she said, striding out towards Milsom Street. 'We have a busy few hours before us. Our first call will be at the draper's emporium, to purchase curtain materials. You may choose what you wish for your bedroom.'

'Thank you, Leonora.' Clarissa glanced sideways at her with a genuine smile of friendly admiration. 'And I must tell you that you look delightful and quite as you should in that outfit.'

Leonora smiled an acknowledgment of the compliment. And a small thrill of some indefinable emotion ran through her when she remembered that Lord Kelsey had thought the same, although he had refused to say so in plain language, bestowing his praise on his mistress and Madame Fleur instead. 'I feel distinctly more presentable than I did yesterday! You look charmingly, too. What a pity we have not yet met anyone we know!'

Her companion blushed consciously. 'Not in the street, at least. You saw Lord Kelsey.'

Leonora noted the blush, felt unreasonably annoyed with Clarissa, and snorted. 'He had no mind to compliment me! Condescending creature!'

'Oh, dear. What a pity it is that you two are so at odds.'

'It doesn't signify,' said Leonora tartly. 'Here we are.'

Clarissa's choice of curtains for windows and bed surprised Leonora almost as much as her idiotish crush on Lord Kelsey. Her companion revealed a liking for frilly pink and white, which Leonora thought fussy. The rather dowdy, strait-laced Rector's daughter showed signs of metamorphosing into a feather-brained, vain creature without much discernment. Her own tastes ran to less frill and more stylish colours. And did not include admiration for Lord Kelsey.

With the materials chosen—a lime green and cream stripe for her bedroom and mulberry, silver-grey and pale blue for the parlour, enough to be going on with; the dining-room could be dealt with later—they visited a furniture warehouse.

There, Leonora purchased a cheval mirror framed in gilt and white for the dressing room. Then, for her bedroom, a long pier-glass to hang between the two windows and a dressing table complete with a mirror to stand on it.

The matter of mirrors and adequate dressing facilities for a lady dealt with, she looked about her more generally. A comfortable *chaise-longue* covered in blue-and-grey striped material with a touch of gold caught her eye. It would match the curtains chosen for the parlour to perfection. She could visualise it stood in front of the windows, where she could relax in comfort and watch the world go by. So she ordered that, too.

As an afterthought she bought an oval mirror, delicately but ornately framed by swags and bows painted white with a touch of gold leaf, for over the mantel and a suitably patterned rug to lay before the fire. As she left the warehouse she felt that she had at least made a start on brightening up the apartment.

A secret smile pleated the corners of her mouth. The *chaise-longue* and dressing table would have to be lifted in through the windows by ropes. They were due to be delivered at two o'clock the following day and their arrival was bound to cause confusion in the road outside.

She suppressed a broader smile. Members inside the Vitus Club would see furniture flying past the windows. The big dressing mirror, too. She would oblige his lordship by having the smaller pieces carried up the service stairs, but the large stand of the cheval would make it difficult, if not impossible, to bring that up the narrow stairs.

She would not even ask if it could be carried up the main staircase. He could not prevent her from having her new pieces brought in through the windows of the rooms they were intended to furnish.

Her spirits had recovered much of their normal buoyancy by the time they arrived at the Pump Room, having purchased her gloves and muff and called in at the printer's to order her visiting cards on their way.

Leonora looked eagerly around as the soothing strains of a small orchestra met her ears. The players sat behind a metal balustrade in a gallery at one end of the large room. A number of ladies and gentlemen paraded up and down to its strains.

Opposite the entrance several other people clustered around what she supposed to be the famous King's Spring, an urn-like contraption with a tap, waiting to purchase a curative glass of water.

'Will you take a glass?' asked Clarissa.

'I cannot see what good it could do me since nothing

ails me,' replied Leonora. 'I have heard that it tastes dreadful.'

'I shall try some,' decided Clarissa. 'Simply from curiosity,' she added, seeing Leonora's sceptical look.

'Well, you can tell me what it is like,' Leonora said. Spotting a statue set in a niche in the curved wall at the opposite end to the orchestra, she pointed it out. 'That, I believe, is of Beau Nash. I once had it described to me. I wonder whether the Master of Ceremonies, Mr Le Bas, is in attendance.'

He was. A moment after Clarissa had left her to obtain her mineral water, two gentlemen appeared from an inner door which led to the Roman Baths behind. Leonora had never met Mr Le Bas and therefore did not know that the first to enter the Pump Room was he, but she did recognise the elegant figure following close behind.

'Oh, no!' she groaned, feeling inclined to indulge in strong hysterics. 'Not Lord Kelsey again!'

So it was that she was introduced to the Master of Ceremonies by the one man in the whole of Bath she wished to avoid. Yet he made the introduction in the most pleasant manner possible and Mr Le Bas, an ageing but spry gentleman possessed of exquisite manners, must have thought them to be on the best of terms.

His lordship, in the guise of an elegant man about town, wielded such an aura of masculine charm that Leonora, despite all her resolution, found her heart beating faster.

But very soon, with civil apologies, he took his leave. Leonora's eyes followed the lithe form until it disappeared through the door. Only then did she realise that Mr Le Bas was urging her to come with him and sign the visitor's book.

'Your name will appear in the *Bath Chronicle*,' he confirmed. 'If it would please you to attend the Dress Ball at the Upper Rooms on Monday I will introduce you into Bath society, Miss Vincent.'

Clarissa joined them, nursing her glass of mineral water, and Leonora introduced her.

With a flourish, Le Bas produced cards from his pocket and offered them to Leonora. He bowed again and said, 'Please accept these tickets for the Ball for yourself and Miss Worth, with my compliments.'

Leonora thanked him prettily and promised that they would attend.

'Your uncle was a much-valued resident of Bath and many persons of consequence will wish to make the acquaintance of his niece. Although—' he hesitated deprecatingly '—I have no wish to usurp your family's attentions in this matter. You are aware that Lord and Lady Chelstoke are in residence here?'

Leonora could not hide her surprise nor, perhaps, her dismay. 'No,' she admitted. 'We do not keep in touch. Have my uncle and aunt been here long?'

'A week or so.'

'I see.' Expecting to benefit from his Will, no doubt they wished to discover what it had denied them. A more generous assessment must acknowledge that he was the Earl's uncle, a close relative, and the Will's contents must have come as a shock. Yet they had not troubled to contact her, either to inform her of her great-uncle's death or, later, to congratulate or berate.

'I was not advised of my great-uncle's demise until after the Will was read,' she explained, 'and so I did not see them at the funeral.'

'You were not invited to attend the obsequies?'

'No. No one expected me to be interested, I dare say. Even his lawyer did not know the terms of the Will until it was read, and then had to discover my whereabouts. Mr Vincent, who had some training in the law in his youth, had entrusted the sealed document to the lawyer with instructions that it should remain unopened until after his funeral.'

'A most unusual course to take. No doubt he had his reasons.'

Why was she confiding all this to a total stranger? Because she knew Mr Le Bas would circulate the information and she wished wild speculation to be minimised.

'Yes,' she acknowledged.

Knowing his nephew—or rather, his nephew's wife—he had not wanted the Earl to know that she was an heiress. She was grateful for his foresight. Her life would have been made a misery.

Nevertheless, she would say nothing against her relations. She merely said, 'I must call on my aunt. Where do they stay?'

'In Queen's Square. They have taken a house there.' He told her the number.

'I shall at least leave my card,' said Leonora later as she and Clarissa made their way home, tired and longing to sit down with a cup of tea. 'They have made no move to call on me; if my uncle and aunt do not wish to receive me, then I shall not trouble them further.'

'Why should they not?' wondered Clarissa.

'They may resent my good fortune. You do not know my aunt,' said Leonora grimly. She knew she could depend upon Clarissa not to tattle.

'Will you call on them when you deliver your card?'

'Yes, or at least I shall try. And you shall come with me, Clarissa! If she receives us, you will see why I did not wish to be dependent upon them for my welfare.'

She sighed, reluctant to remember those unhappy days. 'My elder cousins were still at home at the time of my mother's death,' she explained, 'and I had always found them and their mother intolerably condescending. The younger girls were turning into spiteful, unattractive young women although they were still in the schoolroom, and the boys loutish individuals with no respect for their tutor. I had no wish to become their unpaid servant.'

'Would not the Earl have forbidden them to treat you so?'

'He is wrapped up in his estates and his horses; he would scarcely have noticed my arrival. He allows his wife a free hand in the household arrangements and as long as he is fed on time he asks no questions.'

'Dear me,' said Clarissa sympathetically. 'You were certainly better off at Thornestone Park.'

'I thought so. The Farlings were kind, the girls amenable and reasonably bright.' Leonora sighed. 'But I must confess I had not intended to remain with them for so long. I had thought—' she laughed suddenly. 'But you know how difficult it was to meet eligible gentleman in that district!'

'Indeed I do! I almost settled for Mr Endersby, you know.'

'Your father's curate?' Leonora pictured the tall, severe, humourless clergyman and shook her head. 'You would not have found happiness with him, Clarissa.'

'That is why I resisted the temptation, Leonora. It was a difficult decision to make, for he had been offered a living and I would have had my own establishment. But in the end I decided that I could not endure to live with him for the rest of my life. Even the prospect of children could not reconcile me to the idea.'

'Nor me to any of the offers I received,' admitted Leonora. 'I would rather end up an ape-leader than be wed to an uncongenial man.'

On this they were fully agreed.

Leonora approached the lodgings her relations had taken with some trepidation.

Not that she was fearful of her aunt, her uncle or any of her cousins who might be present, but she did not relish unpleasantness, and since neither the Earl nor his wife had seen fit to communicate with her she could anticipate nothing but a chilly welcome.

She therefore presented one of her newly acquired cards and waited patiently with Clarissa in the small front parlour while the footman went to see whether her ladyship was at home.

She was. Leonora and Clarissa were led back into the entrance lobby and up a circular staircase almost as narrow as the back stairs at her own house, to the morning room, on the floor above.

There, Lady Chelstoke waited to receive her, accompanied by her youngest daughter, Adelina, a young lady of some nineteen summers looking decidedly cold in a white muslin gown, who had not yet netted a husband despite her London Season last year.

Neither lady rose as they entered, but inclined their heads in greeting. Leonora and Clarissa made the required curtsies in return.

'Thank you for receiving me, Aunt,' said Leonora,

punctiliously polite. 'This is my companion, Miss Worth. Miss Clarissa Worth.'

Both her aunt and her cousin eyed with disapproval the despised relative they had last seen at her mother's funeral and whom they remembered only as an unnaturally colourless, penniless orphan, dressed in a cheap black gown.

A chit who had steadfastly refused the offer of a home at Chelstoke Park where she could have made herself useful, and who had now become transformed into a self-possessed lady dressed in the first stare of fashion in a green walking dress with a velvet pelisse, and rendered unexpectedly attractive by a most becoming hat which must have cost a small fortune.

'Well, miss,' said Lady Chelstoke at length, unable to quite hide her annoyance at her niece's change of circumstances, 'so you are arrived in Bath to claim your inheritance.' She waved a be-ringed hand at a sofa. 'Sit down, do. I declare, I cannot imagine what Mr Vincent was about to leave his fortune as he did.'

'I had not expected it, madam,' returned Leonora gravely. 'But I shall be eternally grateful to him for remembering the necessity I was under either to find a position and earn my own living or to exist as a poor relation dependent upon the generosity of my relations, and for deciding to relieve my circumstances. The possession of a property, particularly one of such distinction as his residence has proved to be, is an asset above all price.'

'I'm sure you must be most gratified,' declared Lady Chelstoke pettishly.

Leonora inclined her head in acknowledgement of the remark but otherwise ignored it. She went on, 'My only

regret is that it is at present partly occupied by Lord
Kelsey. But I hope soon to have the entire building to
myself and to set up my establishment in a proper
manner, for Uncle Vincent's estate allows me the means
to do so.'

'Oh?' muttered her aunt glaring through
narrowed eyes.

'Until then,' Leonora continued undisturbed, 'I fear
that any acquaintance must climb the back stairs to call
on me. However, I shall be glad to receive you at Morris
House on any day you care to call, provided I am at
home, although unfortunately you will not be able to
ascertain that until you have climbed to my apartments—
unless my maid, Dolly, happens to be in the basement
for some reason.'

'You have a servant, then,' remarked Lady Chelstoke
peevishly.

'Two at the moment, madam, Dolly and Juliette, my
lady's maid. Miss Worth, as you know, is my companion.
But as I was about to say, the stairs are no more difficult
to negotiate than those in this house.'

'Narrow, twisty things,' muttered her ladyship. 'Not
at all the kind I'm used to.'

'No,' agreed Leonora. 'I remember the fine oak staircase at Chelstoke Hall. My uncle's was an admirable
inheritance. I trust he is proving a worthy steward of the
Chelstoke estates. Shall I see him this morning?'

'I doubt you will. He is probably in the place you call
yours at this very moment. He is become a temporary
member of the Vitus Club.'

'Really?' Leonora was quite taken aback. She
remembered her uncle as a kindly intentioned man,

though careless of others' finer feelings. It was his wife and family she had so disliked.

Would it be possible to recruit him to her cause? 'Then he will have access to my apartments by the main door and staircase,' she said thoughtfully. 'In any case, cards may be left at the front door and will be delivered to me, but Lord Kelsey has the exclusive right to its use for himself and therefore his members under the terms of his lease.'

Lady Chelstoke settled more comfortably into her arm-chair, arranging the frilled skirt of her elaborate morning gown about her plump knees. For the first time, she smiled. 'How unfortunate for you, Leonora. And to have such a rake inhabiting the floors below!'

'Lord Kelsey is not a rake!' protested Adelina in a fierce whisper.

This defence of his lordship surprised Leonora until she remembered Clarissa's reaction to his practised charm. Clarissa had coloured up again and was sitting with lips compressed, forcing herself to remain silent because that was a companion's duty, unless directly addressed. Otherwise, Leonora felt certain, she would have ardently agreed with Addie, who must have met the Earl and, like Clarissa, developed a most unsuitable tendre for him.

And was not above arguing with her mother. But the look of smouldering resentment she directed at herself made Leonora glad she was not throwing out lures to gain his lordship's attention. Not that she would have minded pitting her more mature charms against those of her cousin, had any other gentleman been involved.

Leonora returned the look with one of mild distaste. 'I should have judged him to be so,' she said coldly.

'Forget Blaise Dancer!' Lady Chelstoke ordered her daughter. 'His father's estates are mortgaged to the hilt; the Marquess has not the slightest interest in running them economically and his heir spends his time gaming and running after married women. Your father may consort with him in his Club but you will not speak to him, Addie, do you hear me?'

'I hear,' muttered Addie rebelliously. 'You wish me to wed Lord Ransom, who is old, dreary and probably incapable.'

'Addie!' cried her mother, outraged. 'Mind your tongue, my girl! To utter such a sentiment at all, let alone in public! Pass me the hartshorn! I declare, you have given me a fit of the vapours!'

Addie, not much concerned by this attempt to manipulate her emotions, got up to fetch the vinaigrette and handed it to her mother in sullen silence.

Lady Chelstoke inhaled, coughed and wiped her streaming eyes. When she was capable of speech again, 'Such lack of conduct will condemn you in the eyes of respectable society if you do not have a care!' she declared. 'Then not even Lord Ransom will wed you!'

Addie, her lips compressed into an angry line, bowed her head as she sat down again. Leonora felt a stirring of pity for the girl. She had shown a spark of spirit and had it crushed.

If only Addie would look upon her as a friend! She had been a lively youngster of twelve when Leonora had last seen her, though already showing signs of acquiring the imperious condescension of her elder siblings. In fact the gawky, boisterous child had behaved in the rudest fashion then and did not seem inclined to be more than distantly civil now that she had grown into a passably agreeable-looking young lady. It seemed to Leonora a great pity.

But in all conscience, however much she felt for her, she could not encourage the girl to set her cap at Lord Kelsey, even though he was the heir to a marquess. The prospect of acquiring such a distinguished title could never compensate for his lordship's conduct. He would make the worst kind of husband.

But curiosity drove her to ask, 'Kelsey's father is a marquess?'

Lady Chelstoke, fully recovered from her imaginary vapours, arched her brows until they almost disappeared beneath the lace frill of her cap. 'You did not know? He is Whittonby's heir. *His* fortunes have been in a sad state these many years. He made some poor investments, I collect.'

'I see.' Kelsey, heir to a gravely encumbered honour, had decided to abandon his inheritance. Her opinion of him dropped even lower. He should be working to improve the estates, not wasting his time with the Vitus Club here in Bath. But he would be a marquess one day and that would be enough for most designing mamas. Since he was not yet married he was probably holding out for a fortune to recover the family finances, and taking the chance to enjoy his freedom while it lasted.

Which put both Clarissa and Addie out of the running. Addie would have a dowry of some sort but it would not be large. Clarissa could command practically nothing at all, not even so much as five hundred pounds, as hers.

'So even were he not a rake he would not do for you, my girl,' Lady Chelstoke told her daughter. 'Your papa would never allow you to wed a pauper, however grand his title.'

'Does Lord Chelstoke spend a great deal of time at the Club?' asked Leonora.

'Too much. Says there is nothing else to do. He did not wish to visit Bath but I persuaded him that it would be good for Addie to spend at least some part of the winter here. So many of our friends are presently residing in the town.'

'Do you intend to remain long?'

'Until the end of next week. We have not taken the house for longer. And since there do not appear to be many eligible gentlemen here, apart from Lord Ransom, there is little point in remaining longer. He has already asked for Addie's hand,' her mother informed Leonora smugly. 'She will be engaged before we leave. He is both rich and titled, which cannot be said of a great many of the nobility these days.'

'And old and infirm,' muttered Addie savagely.

'All the better, my girl. In a year or two you will be a very rich widow. You could do far worse.'

Addie's features assumed a calculating expression. Leonora could almost see her mind working. Her parents must have been trying to persuade her of this before but something about the argument had struck her anew.

'Very well, Mama,' she said eventually. 'I will do as you wish and marry Lord Ransom.'

What she did not add, but which Leonora suspected she thought, was that once wed she could take Lord Kelsey as her lover. After all, her mother had said that he took married women as his mistresses.

Addie, however, must be cherishing false hopes, as was Clarissa. With Lady O'Brien available, he would scarcely be inclined to look at either of the other women, who could not match his current mistress in either looks or address.

Within half an hour she rose to take her leave of her relatives. She badly needed refreshment to wash the sour taste from her mouth.

Chapter Five

Leonora, to her relief, did not run into Lord Kelsey on the way back to Morris House, but he dominated her thoughts and the relief was tinged with some other emotion, which she refused to acknowledge as disappointment. She responded to Clarissa's remarks with only part of her mind.

She had a puzzle to solve. The Earl of Chelstoke had joined the Vitus Club as a temporary member. Kelsey must know him, and equally must know the relationship she bore to him. Why had he not mentioned that Lord and Lady Chelstoke were in Bath?

Did he think the presence of her relations unimportant? Did he have a reason for not wanting them to meet? Did he wish to stand apart from a family unpleasantness? For he must know that her relatives would resent the terms of the Will even more than he did. Or had it simply slipped his mind?

Not the last, she felt certain. Nothing would slip the analytical, enquiring mind he must possess to run a successful gambling club. But probably he cared little how her relations felt towards her. It was, after all, none of his business. She doubted he engaged in gossip so why should he bother to inform her? She would find out from others soon enough.

As she had. And much good it had done her.

Kelsey's manager, eager in his attentions, had knocked early that morning to tell her that any correspondence or visiting cards for her which were delivered to the front door would be placed on a salver and brought up and left on a small table on the sliver of landing outside her door. Back in her parlour awaiting the delivery of her furniture, she sent Dolly to see if there was anything waiting there.

To her surprise, her uncle's crested card rested in lonely state upon the gleaming silver. She studied it as Dolly departed to return the salver to its place. A scrawled note on the back told her that he would call again later, before he left the Club.

So he could not know that she had visited his wife. Leonora smiled to herself. Her aunt, no doubt, would be most put out to discover that her husband intended to visit his niece without telling her! The timepiece on the mantel told her it was just midday. She prayed he would not decide to come upstairs while her furniture was being delivered. In all probability, though, he would now dine at the Club before coming upstairs again.

Two of the clock could not come fast enough for her. Meanwhile, a dish of tea, a small minced mutton patty and an orange fortified her for the coming excitement.

The delivery cart arrived at the house at the appointed time. Men came up the back stairs carrying the small pieces, together with the ropes and blocks to clip to the hoisting rings fixed inconspicuously under the eaves of the building. With speedy expertise they removed the sashes from a window in both bedroom and parlour, thus leaving large openings for the furniture to pass through.

First came the cheval mirror, bound round with cloths, handled with great care and accompanied by a deal of shouting. Leonora noticed that a crowd had gathered in the road outside to stand gawping as the anonymous bundle, guided by the ropes, slowly rose up the face of the building and disappeared into her bedroom.

They were still securing the ropes around the classically designed, satinwood kneehole dressing table with its exciting array of drawers and compartments, when a furious tattoo beat upon her door.

The workmen who had remained upstairs continued operations at one bedroom window while, her stomach muscles knotting with tension, Leonora prepared to withdraw from the other, open at the bottom so that she could satisfy her curiosity. Clarissa, who was leaning out of the parlour window, called across to wonder who it could be.

Leonora returned no answer, merely making a rueful face before taking her head in. If Clarissa could not guess, she could. The interruption was not unexpected, she had been ready for it, but all the same she found her composure sadly shaken as Lord Kelsey, his air of amused tolerance having quite deserted him, ignored all the tenets of polite behaviour to push past Dolly and stride into her bedroom.

'What the devil are you up to now?' he fumed.

Leonora, keeping a tight hold on her jumping nerves, arched her brows in assumed shocked astonishment. 'Mind your language, if you please, my lord!'

He sucked in a fierce breath. His eyes sparked chips of pitch at her but he moderated his tone and cloaked his anger by resuming his usual urbane manner. 'What game, madam, are you playing at now, may I ask?' he enquired in a more moderate tone.

'Game?' Leonora's astonishment would have provoked a saint. 'No game, sir. I am merely taking delivery of the new furniture I ordered yesterday.'

'You did not inform me that you were expecting it!'

Leonora's eyes widened. Suddenly she was enjoying herself. 'Should I have done? I could not conceive the necessity, sir. The operation will cause you no inconvenience. I was most particular to instruct the men not to use the main stairs, and the larger pieces would not pass up the back ones.'

She turned down the corners of her lips and spread her hands in a helpless gesture. Kelsey opened his mouth as though to speak and she hurried on quickly, before he could utter a word. 'I doubt whether they could have negotiated the *chaise-longue* up the main staircase beyond the first floor, even had it been available for use.' He closed his mouth again and stared at her in what appeared to be incredulous disbelief. 'I imagined that the rings at the eaves were put there for this very purpose,' she offered deprecatingly.

He continued to stare at her for what seemed a long moment. Then, suddenly, all the controlled tension left his body and he threw back his head and laughed.

It was the most delightful sound Leonora had ever heard, not at all harsh, full of genuine amusement, a sound, she suddenly knew, the thought entering her mind from nowhere, that she would enjoy hearing every day of her life. His eyes, brimming over with mischief now, sought and held hers.

Her lips curved without her even knowing it, the

corners compressing to produce the pleats he found so
fascinating. Still less did she realise that her luminous
eyes had become the colour of the sea on a sunny day
and that his lordship found himself drowning in their
depths.

'You are a devious woman, Miss Vincent,' he told
her, the edge of laughter in his voice taking any sting
from his words and disguising the very different kind of
tension now gripping his body. 'I know when I am beat,
ma'am, but such tricks will not induce me to leave the
building. Is there much else to be brought up?'

Leonora indicated the workmen, who were leaning out
of the window to guide the dressing table on its upward
journey. Kelsey followed her gaze and, reminded of their
presence, produced a rueful grin. But what inferiors
thought of his behaviour did not concern him.

'A dressing table is being brought in here and then they
will lift a *chaise-longue* in through the parlour window,'
Leonora told him. 'That is all. For the moment,' she
added recklessly.

'You have taken your revenge, Miss Vincent. I cannot
pretend to relish having you take up residence so unsuit-
ably above the Vitus Club, but I accept that I cannot
prevent it.'

His smile blazed down on her. 'Can we not call a
truce?' he suggested. 'Given warning, I am willing to
allow anything that will pass up the main staircase to be
delivered that way, provided it arrives before ten o'clock
and there are no women involved in the operation. Is
that fair?'

'A truce, my lord, certainly.' She felt less inclined to
resist his offer of peace now. 'But,' she continued, her
tone determined, 'I shall not cancel my instruction to my

lawyer, who is looking into the terms of your lease in order, if possible, to terminate it.' Only then did she return his quite unnerving smile. 'But until you are forced to leave, I agree that we should attempt to occupy Morris House together on civil terms.'

'I can assure you that he will find no loophole to terminate the lease. And so, madam, it seems we are destined to irritate each other for the next five years.'

'Perhaps not, my lord,' said Leonora, watching her dressing table enter through the window to be placed on the floor with infinite care and attention. 'Much may happen in five years.'

'True,' agreed his lordship. 'I will leave you to arrange your furniture. I imagine the members of my Club are being much entertained by the activity outside. You seem to have gathered quite a crowd in the street. The chairs are finding difficulty in getting through.'

His ill-temper had quite gone. Her poor opinion of him wavered somewhat. But no amount of good-tempered charm could overcome her aversion to a gentleman who set out to fleece any unwary flat that came his way. Since his family fortunes were in such poor case, she supposed he was trying to finance an expensive lifestyle.

She still considered that he would do better to wed an heiress. At least then only one poor creature would suffer as a consequence of his poverty. And whoever she was she would acquire a title to compensate and a tall, broad-shouldered, handsome and devastatingly attractive husband to warm her bed.

The sour taste had returned to her mouth. Once Kelsey had done the pretty and excused himself, she left the workmen to their task and ordered Dolly to make a fresh pot of tea.

The Earl of Chelstoke called, as Leonora had expected, after his repast. She had just finished her own ample and delicious meal and was enjoying a cup of tea in Clarissa's company when the knock came.

He entered the parlour, a stocky man with a weather-beaten face, a man who spent his time riding about his estates when not following the hounds in the hunting season. He looked more at home in her drawing room, furnished almost exclusively by his recently deceased uncle, than he did in his own at Chelstoke Park.

There his wife had installed modern flimsy furniture and frilly hangings. Leonora's new *chaise-longue* by the windows and the mirror over the mantel, with its delicate tracery of a frame, were the only modern or remotely feminine articles in the room, yet she prided herself that they blended well with her uncle's things and would do so even better when the new curtains were hung.

Once introductions and courtesies were over, 'Hrmph,' grunted her uncle as he lowered himself into his uncle's large padded armchair, 'comfortable place you've got here.'

'Yes,' agreed Leonora, 'I am fortunate. I was surprised to discover, yesterday, that you and Lady Chelstoke were in Bath.'

'Addie, too. We came for her sake. I didn't want to leave the huntin', but Lady Chelstoke thought the girl might pick up a husband. Seems to lack the power to fix the interest of any man she fancies and is proving deuced difficult to persuade to wed some fellow she don't like. Not accommodatin' like her sisters,' he muttered.

'So I was given to understand. I called at Queen's Square this morning. They knew I had taken up residence here. Lord Kelsey must have told you?'

'Did ye now!' He glanced at her sharply. 'Yes, Kelsey mentioned it in passing. Thought I'd let you get settled before I called. My wife don't like your inheritin' above half, I can tell you.'

'So I gathered,' said Leonora calmly. 'Neither do you, I collect.'

'Can't say I do,' Lord Chelstoke admitted. 'A town house in Bath would suit Lady Chelstoke to admiration and I could have used the funds.' He emitted a heavy sigh. 'My sons have become expensive young gentlemen. Can't think what Uncle Charles was thinkin' of, leaving it all to you. Thought you was destitute, I collect, didn't know ye was invited to live with us.'

'He knew,' said Leonora. 'He also knew my reasons for not wishing to become a dependent relative. I preferred to earn my own living.'

'Foolish notions you young chits do have these days. Could've been comfortable enough at Chelstoke Hall.'

'But you had three daughters to see wed. You did not need an independent-minded niece to add to your tally of available females.'

This time Lord Chelstoke gave his niece a long hard stare. 'No,' he admitted at last. 'Damn difficult enough as it was. . .and is. And none of 'em could hold a candle to you for looks, Leonora. You'd've queered their pitches, I dare say.'

'Not intentionally, Uncle, and I had no dowry to tempt a gentleman to make an offer. But you were all far better off without having my welfare to concern you, and it has turned out well as it happens. Confess it now, you do not need another residence, especially one which you could not occupy, and forgive me for saying so, but it will not harm my cousins to curb their extravagance.'

A vision of her spoilt male cousins' heavy visages, as she had known them, briefly crossed her mind. She wondered what they were like now. Dissipated, no doubt. She could truly dredge up no warmth for any one of her Chelstoke relatives, even her uncle, although he was conducting himself with more nicety of feeling than she had expected.

'In fact, it may positively do them good!' she went on in a spirited tone. 'Meanwhile, I am free and able to command the means to live in respectable comfort.'

'Aye. Uncle Vincent weren't exactly a warm man,' said Chelstoke, 'but he weren't extravagant, neither. Always managed on what he had. Lived cramped up here and took rent from downstairs and saved his blunt instead of making a show and running into debt. Sensible fellow, but dull. Still,' he added grudgingly, 'you've benefited.'

'Except that I must confine myself to this floor, as he did. I should be vastly pleased if I could terminate Lord Kelsey's lease. I do not enjoy having a gambling hell beneath me.'

Lord Chelstoke's heavy brows drew together in what could only be described as a scowl. 'Don't talk foolish, Leonora. The Vitus is a respectable gentleman's club. D'ye think I'd belong to it otherwise?'

Maybe he would, maybe he wouldn't. How was she to know? However, she could scarcely voice her doubts. So she made do with saying, 'But you are new in town, Uncle. You cannot know how many youthful gentlemen—and older ones, come to that—have been ruined playing at its tables. I know whist and Vingt-et-un are played, and no doubt hazard and faro are, too, although they were not mentioned when I inspected the place.'

Her uncle snorted. 'What if they are? The members indulge in whatever game they choose and if they can break the bank at faro or hazard, so much the better. Kelsey seems to hold his own.'

'But—' began Leonora only to find that he gave her no chance to argue.

'Brooks's Club in London is famous for its faro table,' he declared forcefully. 'Many of both White's and Brooks's members belong to the Vitus Club. Have ye studied the list of those who do? No? Then allow me to inform you, miss!'

He reeled off the names of a number of distinguished gentlemen, making Leonora's head whirl and her heart sink. She had a suspicion that faro and hazard were still nominally illegal, but with noble lords, Members of Parliament, mayors and judges as members, no one was going to listen to any complaint she might make. She was wasting her money employing Coggan to snoop.

'I ain't suggestin' that it's suitable for you to be up here, mind,' went on Lord Chelstoke. 'Last place a young woman like you should live. Take my advice, miss, move out to a place where decent ladies like Lady Chelstoke could call on ye. You won't find many who will climb the back stairs of a gentleman's club. Enter Society. You're not ill-looking. Ye might find yourself a suitable husband yet.'

Leonora smoothed the skirt of her new gown, controlling an urge to jump to her feet and dismiss her uncle with a sharp word, but she positively would *not* take offence.

'I have every intention of entering Society, Uncle,'

she responded mildly, earning herself a sideways glance from Clarissa, though whether it expressed approval of her forbearance or surprise at it she could not tell. 'Will I see you at the Dress Ball at the Upper Assembly Rooms on Monday?' she went on in her most dulcet tones. 'Mr Le Bas has presented me with tickets. Clarissa and I intend to go.'

'That coxcomb?' snorted Chelstoke. 'No time for the likes of him, nor for fancy balls and suchlike. Your aunt will be there, I make no doubt, with Addie. Girl don't know what she wants, don't know what's best for her. Should wed Lord Ransom and to the devil with it! She'd be a rich widow in no time at all.'

'That is what her mother persuaded her of this morning. I believe she may be willing to listen to your advice now.'

'Really?' Lord Chelstoke lumbered to his feet. 'Then I'd better be off back to our lodgings and make certain she don't change her mind again.'

Leonora rose too. Clarissa, who had remained silent throughout the exchange, set aside the piece of embroidery on which she had been working, intended as decoration for an old gown, and made her farewell curtsy.

Once Lord Chelstoke had retreated to the more congenial all-male atmosphere of the Vitus Club—for Leonora placed no reliance upon his declared intention to return to his wife and daughter immediately—Clarissa sat down again and resumed her seat and her sewing.

Leonora paced the room.

'You will wear out the carpet, Leonora,' Clarissa chided at last, breaking a rather lengthy silence. 'Do calm yourself, pray. No purpose can be achieved by losing your temper.'

'I have not lost my temper!' declared Leonora, her inward fuming made worse by what she conceived to be Clarissa's sermonising tone. 'But really, I could never have lived with Lord and Lady Chelstoke! You must see how impossible such a life would have been!'

'For you, perhaps. But in your position I should have accepted a place in their household with gratitude. It would not have been ideal, I grant you, especially if your cousins are as hateful as you say—and I must admit I did not take to Lady Adelina above half.'

'She,' said Leonora sourly, 'was the best of the bunch. I should have become nothing but a put-upon, unpaid servant.'

'So you chose to be a paid one, instead! Don't you see, Leonora, at Chelstoke Hall you would have mixed with the nobility, moved in true first circles, not with those who constituted the first circle around Thornestone Park! Mr Farling is a jumped-up nobody who happened to make a fortune in India in his youth. No one of real consequence recognises him.'

'That is why they were so pleased to acquire my services,' admitted Leonora. 'I had no experience and yet they paid me well. They were kind, Clarissa, whereas my aunt and cousins were not.'

'But at Chelstoke Hall you might have fixed the interest of a gentleman of consequence. Of a peer of the realm, indeed! We are already agreed that no one even remotely suitable crossed your path at Thornestone Park.'

'You would have submitted to petty tyranny, Clarissa?' asked Leonora curiously. Perhaps she had not known the real Clarissa Worth before bringing her to Bath.

'For a year or two, yes, if it had served to allow

me to meet a suitable future husband.'

Such a thought had never entered Leonora's head. She had simply refused to contemplate living in abject misery, preferring to find her escape quickly and by her own efforts. That she had remained at Thornestone Park for far longer than she had intended did not change the fact that she had been free to give in her notice at any time and, after the first year, to leave with enough of her salary saved to sustain her until she found another situation.

'Well,' she said at last, 'I cannot regret my decision, especially now. How I shall enjoy making my entrance at the Assembly Rooms on Monday!'

Clarissa smiled. 'So shall I. Let us hope there are plenty of unattached gentlemen present, who will ask us to stand up with them!'

'There are plenty of half-pay army and naval officers parading the streets. You may be sure that some of them will attend.'

'Yes. They must be the only persons not glad to find the country at peace.'

'They may well attend church on Sunday.'

Still restless, Leonora walked over to pick up and study one of the elaborate yet tasteful cards she had had printed.

'Tomorrow,' she declared, 'I shall return to the Pump Room to study the visitor's book, and also seek to obtain a copy of the *Bath Chronicle* and read the announcements there. If there is anyone in town with whom I can claim the slightest acquaintance I shall call and leave my card. Now I possess some new clothes I shall not mind my presence being widely known. Why, I may receive some agreeable invitations! And you, in course, will accompany me wherever I go, unless you do not wish it.'

'I should like nothing better! I do thank you most

fervently for this opportunity to mix in better society than was available at home.'

Leonora merely smiled. Clarissa had declared herself willing to endure servitude at Chelstoke Hall in order to meet eligible young gentlemen, so she was unlikely to refuse any opportunity to mix with members of the polite world now.

Of all those currently in Bath Leonora recognised only two names from the past, apart from that of her uncle and aunt. Both had been acquaintances of her parents.

She delivered cards to their doors but did not expect a return of the civility. By now they would scarcely remember that Mr and Mrs Vincent had left a daughter called Leonora.

Sunday dawned bright though cold. Leonora dressed for the Abbey in expectant spirits. For the first time for many years she would appear in public dressed and groomed, with Juliette's help, as befitted her true station as the granddaughter of an earl. Her cousins, of course, looked down upon her but she sprang from the same stock and, in her opinion, her father had been superior in intelligence and in character and had possessed a more kindly and affectionate disposition than his elder brother, who had inherited the title.

'Will that suit you, madam?' enquired Juliette, the curling tongs still hot in her hand.

Leonora pulled experimentally at one of the attractive curls framing her face. It sprang back into position immediately, and she smiled her approval. 'Just pray that it does not rain!'

'If it should, madam, simply tuck the hair out of sight

beneath your hat. That will save you from looking bedraggled.'

'Thank you, Juliette, I will remember your advice. Am I ready?'

Juliette put down the tongs and nodded. 'I believe you will do, madam.' And she added, sincerely Leonora thought, 'You are the most rewarding lady I have yet had the pleasure of serving, madam. I can take real pride in your appearance.'

Clarissa, even without the attentions of a lady's maid, appeared to her best advantage that morning. Her usually sallow skin held a faint flush of excitement. She was making her first appearance in the superior sort of polite society that frequented Bath and was, perhaps, more expectant even than Leonora, who had moved in it in her youth.

The singing in the Abbey filled Leonora's soul with peace. The sound seemed to rise to the vaulted roof and descend again infused with the spirit of God. She would, she felt, be happy to live within the Abbey's ambience for a while, although after even such a short time in a town she yearned for the open country, to live surrounded by fields rather than streets crowded with houses, carriages and people. When. . .if. . .she married she must chose a husband who also pined to live in the country. If she did not find such a gentleman then she would, eventually, sell Morris House and find herself a country cottage—in a village, perhaps. . .where she could live in quiet seclusion.

Living in the country appealed, but not the cottage or the seclusion, she realised. What would she do all day? She must be in reach of stimulating company, of a decent library, or she would sink into melancholy.

But she had no wish to live in a town for the remainder of her life. Until her father's death she had been used to living in a large house, set in several acres of grounds and within easy reach of other such establishments which afforded agreeable company and a lively social life. It had not been as splendid or expansive as Chelstoke Hall, of course, but adequate to the needs of a growing, active girl with a lively mind and a gregarious nature.

Thornestone Park, for all its faults, had not been a bad place to live. She had walked and driven about the grounds with her charges, had had free access to the library and, perforce, attended many of the dinners and social gatherings sponsored by her employers. She would have enjoyed those occasions more had her presence not been demanded for reasons other than the simple pleasure of her company.

The congregation stood, Leonora with it. She had not heard a word of the sermon, she realised as the final hymn was launched. But one thing had become clear to her. All her future happiness depended upon her being able to engage the affections of a gentleman of means with a country residence in need of a mistress. This was the destiny she had been born to and no alternative would adequately suffice.

It was as she came to this conclusion that a movement in the congregation as they knelt for the final blessing gave Leonora a glimpse of a head she recognised. Her heart thumped in her chest as she realised that Kelsey was kneeling a few rows forward.

His presence was a surprise. She had expected him to be otherwise engaged at the Vitus Club, glad of the excuse not to attend church despite the Club's ban on gambling on the Lord's day.

As they emerged from the great doors of the West Front she found him at her elbow.

'God give you joy, Miss Vincent, Miss Worth.'

He included Clarissa in his greeting and both ladies responded suitably. Small groups of worshippers gathered in the churchyard to speak together and Lady O'Brien passed by on the arm of an elderly gentleman whom Leonora took to be her husband. She raised a hand and inclined her head in greeting, including Kelsey in her acknowledgment, while Lord O'Brien lifted his tall hat to Lord Kelsey and ignored the ladies.

Lady O'Brien laid a hand on her husband's arm to halt him.

'My dear,' she said, 'I do not believe you have met Miss Vincent. May I name her to you?'

Clarissa was included in the ensuing exchange of introductions and civilities and before long Leonora found herself walking beside the portly Lord O'Brien while Kelsey strolled ahead with Alicia and Clarissa. Their object was to cross the Abbey precincts to the North Parade—in company with most of the other polite residents of Bath, it seemed.

Never mind, Leonora had wanted to be seen and had no objection to joining the promenade. But O'Brien had no conversation and she, after a brief comment on the weather, relapsed into silence, more intent on admiring her new half-boots and wishing they would not pinch than enjoying the walk itself.

O'Brien's eyes were fixed on his wife as he stumped along with the aid of a stick and Leonora could not but feel sorry for him and reflect upon the likely consequences of a man's marrying a woman so much younger than himself.

She watched with caustic amusement as Alicia and Clarissa vied for their escort's attention. His lordship, it seemed, had the ability to make amusing conversation, for Alicia's musical trill rang out from time to time, accompanied by Clarissa's subdued, conscious titter. She could hear his pleasant baritone but could not make out what he was saying so she attempted to quicken her pace, and that of her escort, in order to draw nearer.

Eventually, 'We are dropping behind,' she urged O'Brien. 'Can you not walk a little faster, my lord?'

He grunted and speeded his pace slightly but they were not making up much ground. Then, it seemed, Kelsey realised that his party was outstripping the other and paused, turning to see what had become of them.

Alicia exclaimed and walked back towards them. 'Why, Lord O'Brien,' she exclaimed. 'Were we walking too fast for you? Fie on us! Come, my dear, allow me to take your arm.'

O'Brien visibly relaxed as his wife threaded her gloved fingers about his elbow. Kelsey smiled and turned to Leonora, holding out his own arm, crooked to invite her hold.

'Will you not take my arm, Miss Vincent? The ground may be a little slippery after the frost.'

'Thank you, my lord,' said Leonora, who did not like to refuse to take the proffered arm, though she much disliked the prospect of such close contact with this particular gentleman and would be unable to use her muff properly.

With her gloved and reluctant hand resting on the thick wool of his greatcoat Kelsey turned to Clarissa. 'Allow me to offer you an arm too, Miss Worth.'

Clarissa's eagerness to accept his invitation was evident. Why was it, wondered Leonora to herself, that whenever she was with Kelsey and Clarissa she needed something to take away the sour taste in her mouth?

'Your furniture is all safely installed?' enquired his lordship as the stroll resumed.

'Quite safely, I thank you, my lord. Lord Chelstoke called on me after he had eaten. You did not inform me of my relatives' presence in Bath.'

Now it was Kelsey's turn to assume innocent amazement. 'Should I have, Miss Vincent? We had scarcely exchanged a civil word, as I remember. I thought it a kindness not to burden you with the news,' he added with a grin.

'I had already called upon Lady Chelstoke,' Leonora told him.

'Ah!' He turned to include Clarissa in the conversation. 'You accompanied Miss Vincent, Miss Worth?'

'Yes, my lord. We enjoyed a most civil reception.'

Clarissa had learned diplomacy in a hard school, considered Leonora. Her reply could not be faulted. In fact, she possessed all the attributes necessary to make an excellent wife to some country gentleman. But not to a peer of the realm, surely. Yet Kelsey had taken pains to walk with her, to offer her his arm, to include her in the conversation, and was now smiling down warmly into her shyly radiant face.

'Who would not receive you with civility, Miss Worth? Tell me, has your father held the living at Thornestone for many years?'

From that moment on Leonora walked in silence while Clarissa told Lord Kelsey about her family, her interests and her gratitude to dear Miss Vincent for giving her the opportunity to come to Bath.

'It was indeed most kind,' agreed Kelsey. 'You see, Miss Vincent, you have secured the devotion of at least one admirer by your goodness. To introduce Miss Worth into Society was an act of great generosity. But here are acquaintances you must meet. Allow me to introduce you.'

His manners were perfect. The introductions were made, civilities exchanged and they passed on. This happened several times and to persons of importance in Society. Lord Kelsey clearly moved easily in first circles where he was accepted as being both agreeable and worthy—by the gentlemen, at least. In one or two of the older matrons she detected just the slightest coolness of manner, echoing, she thought, her aunt's reservations.

All the same, when she entered the ballroom the next evening she would be able to claim acquaintance with a number of influential members of the *ton*, several of them eminently eligible gentlemen, whether wearing a red coat, a pea jacket, or merely the latest offering of a London tailor.

Kelsey was doing her a service. That he had some ulterior motive Leonora did not doubt.

Were she to wed, she would be obliged to abandon Morris House, leaving him in possession.

But that would mean that she had achieved her purpose in coming to Bath. So why did she feel so outraged at the idea of being manipulated? Did it truly matter by what means she accomplished her aim?

It should not. But it did.

Chapter Six

The novel experience of riding in a sedan chair gave Leonora a sense of adventure as she stepped into one of the two she had hired to take herself and Clarissa to the Upper Assembly Rooms, which were situated in the newly fashionable north of the town.

Leonora settled into the plush-lined, rather stale-smelling interior. The door closed and the two bearers bent to the poles. She waved a hand at Clarissa, similarly ensconced, as their chairs were lifted and the men began to thread their way through the narrow streets. A broad back topped by a tricorn hat filled most of Leonora's view through the front window, the man's shadow sometimes made grotesque by the fluctuating light afforded by the infrequent flambeaux along their way.

To make a truly impressive splash she should purchase a sedan chair of her own and engage footmen to carry and escort her about the town, she supposed. But. . .no, to hire a sedan chair when needed would serve as an adequate indication of her consequence, especially with Juliette walking alongside, accompanying her to her engagements in order to be on hand to repair her toilette as necessary.

She guessed that Juliette did not object to the outing. She would gossip with other ladies' maids while her mistress was engaged in the ballroom or sitting listening to a concert. Her duties would not be onerous.

Having been deposited at the entrance to the Upper Rooms, Leonora ordered the chairs to return at eleven to carry them home.

They divested themselves of their cloaks, Juliette ensuring that Leonora's toilette had not suffered during the journey, and then made their way to a ballroom brilliantly lit by dozens of candles set in five scintillating cut-glass chandeliers and a multitude of wall sconces.

The entertainment was in full swing. The orchestra played in a semi-circular gallery positioned above the entrance door, its music floating down to the throng below, who were either dancing or taking their ease on the benches banked against the walls.

Mr Le Bas noticed them enter and immediately came to escort them to seats he had reserved for them. Leonora walked proudly, knowing that her toilette was perfect and that Madame Fleur's primrose gown, with its lacy cream overskirt trailing just slightly at the back, suited her to perfection. Juliette had suggested the purchase of ribbons of a deep bronzey-orange together with a matching chiffon scarf. The ribbons were threaded through her hair and the scarf draped about her elbows. Silk gloves, satin slippers and an ivory and silk fan completed her ensemble.

She felt supremely confident. And the approving and enquiring glances she drew as she passed did nothing to disturb her self-assurance.

Her aunt was seated on the other side of the room and acknowledged her by an inclination of her head. Adelina was dancing, partnered by an older gentleman who must be Lord Ransom, Leonora supposed.

He did not look nearly as old or incapable as Addie had made out. The prospect of his dying within the next two years appeared remote, but perhaps he suffered from a bad heart or something. In any case, it was no business of hers. For good or ill, the Chelstokes would dictate their daughter's future.

Mr Le Bas introduced Leonora to several rather intimidating matrons as they made their way to the seats, most of whom produced their cards and invited her to call. She gained some half-dozen acquaintances in this way and decided to begin her round of morning calls the next day, starting with Lady O'Brien, who had acknowledged her during her transit of the room and who had, after all, been the first to offer an invitation.

Leonora had barely taken her place on the end of a front bench, with Clarissa immediately behind her, when a gentleman wearing full hussar regimentals bowed before her, reminded her that he had been introduced by Lord Kelsey the previous day, and asked her to stand up with him.

The hussar was an ordinary young man with no pretension to good looks but his manner, apart from the pride common to all young officers wearing a similar prestigious uniform, was faultless. She accepted gracefully.

He danced well and Leonora enjoyed herself. Not until he returned her to her seat did she see Kelsey. He stood conversing with Clarissa and, she discovered on greeting him, had engaged her companion for the next dance, a stately minuet like the others before supper.

By his lordship's side stood a weatherbeaten naval officer, whom he introduced as Captain Lord Cunningham. Cunningham immediately requested the pleasure of her hand for the next dance.

The captain was not old—in his early forties, Leonora judged. She was, she gathered, expected to be flattered by his notice and to respond eagerly to his attentions.

'I'm no hand with the ladies, ma'am,' he assured her, 'but I've always found females eager to entertain a British sea-officer, in whatever part of the world I've found m'self.'

Because his manner was bluff and ingenuous, and he was probably only stating the truth, Leonora could not take exception to his observations, made at intervals in a booming voice whenever the stately steps of the dance brought them together. But she did not feel inclined to humour him beyond polite civility.

'I was made post in seven,' he informed her, and went on to tell her, at tedious length, that he'd had a good war, fought at Trafalgar whilst still a lieutenant, had earned plenty of prize money and eventually been commissioned as the captain of a ship of the line, a seventy-four.

'What is the name of your present command?' she enquired politely, almost certain of the answer before it was made.

His face took on a gloomy aspect and she knew her guess had been right. 'Ain't got one now,' he admitted sadly, his voice sinking to a modest rumble. 'Me old seventy-four is laid up and I'm beached on half-pay.

'Mind you,' he added with a sudden return of spirits and volume, 'while I remain on the active list of post captains I'll still become an admiral one day. Admirals are appointed on seniority, y'know, and I'm nearing the top of the list. My wife, when I take one—' he gave her a significant look '—will be Lady Cunningham, Admiral Cunningham's lady. I ain't got a better title to inherit, but admirals are often made up into viscounts.'

'Really? Like Admiral Lord Nelson?' Leonora opened her eyes wide and since the dance had just ended, was able to flutter her fan in a gesture of shy interest. 'You are not yet wed, then, Captain?'

His laugh rose above the general noise and several heads turned. Leonora gazed up at him, wishing she could look to see whether Kelsey was watching. The dog, to land her with this nice but impossible man!

'No, ma'am,' he said, eyeing her earnestly, 'but I aim to take a wife as soon as maybe. I have a decent little estate in Sussex and shall settle into the life of a country squire without much trouble, I daresay. And I need an heir for the barony, y'know.'

'Naturally,' murmured Leonora, turning towards her seat and managing not to blush at his forthright statement. Really! Had the man no delicacy of feeling?

Kelsey was escorting Clarissa back but he was looking her way. She placed her hand on Cunningham's arm and Kelsey's gleaming smile reached her across the room. She smiled back, a distant smile that she might have bestowed on a stranger under certain circumstances.

She spotted Addie, too, looking mumchance as her suitor led her back to her mama, and felt glad that she was of an age when she might choose a husband for herself.

Not that it was necessarily going to be easy. A small group of gentlemen had gathered about her seat and Kelsey seemed only too ready to introduce them so that they might ask her to stand up with them.

By the time supper was served, the rivalry to escort her into the Tea Room was intense, and she was engaged in a laughing protest that she could not be expected to choose one gentleman above another, when Kelsey, who had been watching her success with sardonic interest between dancing with Alicia O'Brien and several other ladies of his acquaintance, stepped in to resolve the issue.

'As Miss Vincent's earliest acquaintance in Bath, and since, as her tenant, I must seek her favour, I claim the privilege of escorting her in to supper. Miss Vincent?' he said, bowing and offering his arm.

Leonora wanted to refuse Kelsey, but his dark, brilliant eyes both challenged and laughed and she found it quite impossible. Besides, it was a way out of her dilemma. Clarissa had already attached the interest of a mature gentleman of some girth, and stood with him awaiting her benefactress's pleasure. So she returned Kelsey's bow with a curtsy and took his offered arm.

'I thank you, sir. Gentlemen, please excuse me?'

Murmurs of feigned outrage and a degree of genuine disappointment met her decision, but the protests were good humoured.

'I shall claim the privilege on a future occasion, Miss Vincent,' promised Captain Lord Cunningham in his distinctive boom and several other gentlemen, including the hussar, raised their voices in agreement.

'You are a success, Miss Vincent,' murmured Kelsey in her ear as they progressed to the Tea Room, where supper was being served.

'I believe,' said Leonora, refusing to be overset by his flattery, 'that I have you to thank if it is so, my lord. You have introduced me to every eligible gentleman present, I declare. I wonder at your taking the trouble.'

'But, my dear Miss Vincent, my landlady must be well regarded and in demand socially, or my own consequence must suffer. That I could not allow.'

His eyes laughed at her although his face was grave. He had abandoned his initial antagonism and, as she had suspected, was attempting to seduce her by charm into giving up her determination to live in Morris House and, above all, her aim to have him evicted. And not only by seducing her with his own charm, but by placing as many eligible gentlemen as feasible in her path, possible or impossible.

'Besides,' he was going on smoothly as they crossed the Octagon, resplendent with chandeliers, carved mantels and ornate mirrors over the fireplaces, 'you have astounded me by your transformation into a veritable diamond of the first water. Such a gem must not be allowed to remain in obscurity. You deserve a wealthy and devoted husband and a thriving nursery and school-room of your own, my dear.'

Leonora's heart leapt. So her efforts had not been in vain; her object had been achieved. She was equipped to procure for herself an agreeable and secure future—although his flattery could not be accepted entirely at face value, for those most usually considered to be diamonds of the first water were young girls making their come-out, not ladies approaching their last prayers. A certain amount of scepticism would be advisable.

She suppressed a sigh. If only she could feel the slightest interest in any of the gentlemen to whom Kelsey was so assiduously introducing her. The post captain would, she was certain, make an offer given the slightest encouragement, but the prospect merely depressed her.

It dismayed and angered her to realise that she was content to enter the Tea Room on Kelsey's arm and that it would give her more pleasure to take supper with him than with any of the others. The most ineligible of all the gentlemen in the room!

Nevertheless, she fluttered her fan and lifted her eyes to his. 'You approve of my gown, my lord?'

'I approve of everything about you,' he told her with the merest hint of a wry grin. 'From your hair to your slippers. I would not have believed such a transformation possible, and in so short a time.'

'I am,' said Leonora severely, 'exactly the same person beneath the finery and change of hairstyle. And for those things, you must thank Madame Fleur, various other tradespeople and my new lady's maid.'

'But you provided the raw material on which they have worked. Had I seen you as you are now when we first met, I should never have offended you by implying that you lacked youth. You are positively blooming, my dear Miss Vincent.'

He sounded sincere. Leonora resorted to raillery to ease the tension which suddenly gripped her. 'Flattery, my lord, will get you nowhere without you bring me some food, for I declare myself to be starving!'

His smile bathed her in a warm glow. 'Despite Monsieur André's wonderful cooking? You cannot be such a philistine as not to appreciate that?'

'I do. It is miraculous. But it is hours since I rose from the dinner table.'

'Then I only hope that the cold meats, the jellies and the biscuits and sweetmeats served here will also meet with your approval.'

He led her to a table already occupied by Lady O'Brien

and a gentleman friend, who had absented himself in search of food. Clarissa brought her beau over, who asked if they could join the party, to be assured that they would be welcome.

'Will you take wine?' asked Kelsey, seating her before himself going, accompanied by Clarissa's escort, to forage behind the screen concealing the food.

Leonora, smiling graciously towards Alicia O'Brien and nodding acknowledgment of Clarissa's new friend as she took her seat, said, 'If you please.'

'I declare,' said Alicia archly, following Kelsey's retreating figure with her eyes, 'you have worked a miracle, Miss Vincent. It is an age since Kelsey graced the Assembly Rooms with his presence. I can only conclude that you are the lure.'

'Really?' murmured Leonora, feigning indifference. But a new thread of excitement inexplicably flashed along her nerves. She must, she thought, beware of Lord Kelsey's charm.

While he was away, several of her new admirers sought seats at the same table or nearby. She wondered whether Kelsey would mind suffering the other gentlemen's company and then decided that it would serve him right if he did. He had, after all, prompted their pursuit.

But his lordship, it became clear as the meal progressed, was not so much concerned with keeping her to himself as in acting as referee in the competition for her attention. The mood of excitement settled into one of cynical amusement.

Her admirers all believed her to be a considerable heiress. Kelsey did everything in his power to reinforce the impression.

Leonora's initial amusement turned to annoyance. Not

because her financial status was being assessed and over-valued—that fitted in with her plans—but because Kelsey so clearly wished to marry her off so that he could occupy the whole of Morris House.

She was tempted to drop her intention to wed and remain at Morris House come what may, at least until his lordship's lease expired. If she married and left she would be playing into his hands. . .but five years on she would undoubtedly be firmly stuck on the matrimonial shelf, her own future in ruins.

Drat the man! He had her at a distinct disadvantage.

Upon their return to the ballroom he asked her to stand up with him for the first set of country dances, which followed the interval. She had watched him perform the minuet with elegance and grace, so was not surprised to find herself led with engaging expertise and confidence into the lively steps of the cotillion.

Despite her resentment of his machinations, she enjoyed that dance. She would have enjoyed it still more had she not felt certain that his asking her was all part of his plan to show her off to advantage so that, in the end, he would be rid of her.

The temptation to rebel and behave outrageously was strong. But if she did she would defeat her own plan, which she had not yet quite decided to abandon.

And which was, in effect, the same as his.

That conclusion deserved some thought.

'Thank you, my lord,' she said politely as he returned her to her place. 'That was most enjoyable.'

He bowed. 'It is I who must thank you for doing me the honour of dancing with me. And now I fear I must leave you to the attentions of your other admirers. As you may guess, my presence is required at the Vitus

Club. You have a sedan ordered for your return?'

'Yes, I thank you.' She curtsied. 'Good night, my lord.'

The remainder of the evening passed pleasantly enough. Leonora could not deny that it was flattering to be so sought after. Although all social intercourse had not been denied her—she had attended local assemblies from time to time and met the Farlings' circle of friends—her youthful years had been singularly lacking in romance.

She had never even fancied herself in love, and knew that she had not excited that emotion in any of the three gentlemen who had offered for her. She had been the governess. They had condescended to favour her with their attentions while seeking to add to their own consequence by wedding an earl's granddaughter. One had sought, in addition, to secure an unpaid governess to his several motherless children.

So she welcomed the genuine admiration she roused in her present suitors as a boost to her confidence.

Alicia found it difficult to conceal her growing annoyance. Leonora smiled to herself. The erstwhile dowdy governess that Lady O'Brien had patronised with her advice had taken it, and now threatened to rival her in the elegance of her person and her power to attract the attention of so many of the gentlemen present—for young beaux and old roués alike were competing to dance with her.

She forgot Kelsey in her enjoyment of her triumph.

But not for long. Gaming still being in progress, lights were still blazing outside Morris House when she and Clarissa, who had been quite a success herself with certain of the gentlemen present, arrived home. Perforce, they had to be carried round to the rear entrance.

Leonora had dismissed Juliette soon after the supper interval, but she would be waiting up for her. Dolly, who rose at an early hour to see to the fires and clean the dining room and parlour before her mistress stirred, would be in bed.

'Did you enjoy yourself? she asked Clarissa as they finished climbing the stairs and entered the apartment.

'Yes, indeed! How different it was to the Assemblies I attended in Buckingham!'

'To receive the attentions of so many gentlemen was certainly pleasing,' agreed Leonora. 'Did you like any of them well enough to consider. . .?'

She left the question trailing, finishing it with an enquiring look as Juliette took her cloak.

Clarissa looked conscious but shook her head, 'It is too soon to tell, Leonora. How about you?'

'I agree, it is too soon to say, but I expect that those least acceptable will be the most persistent!'

She was thinking of the post captain as she spoke. He had remained in attendance throughout the evening, although he had abided by the rules and not asked her to stand up with him more than twice.

Kelsey had asked her only once.

She thrust the remembrance aside as she bade Clarissa a restful night and went to her bedroom, a wry expression on her face. Lord Kelsey might have declared a truce in their disagreement, but tonight he had taken his revenge for her previous interruption of his business. She would call on Coggan tomorrow, before she set out on her round of social calls.

*   *   *

Coggan was engaged with another client when she arrived unannounced at his chambers the following morning and she had to wait some thirty minutes to see him. She did not object since it was her own fault—she should have made an appointment.

When she was ushered in, Coggan was already on his feet to greet her.

'Miss Vincent. Good morning. Please sit down. How can I help you?'

Leonora arranged the skirts of her smart walking gown, aware that Coggan was eyeing her with surprise and appreciation. Of course, she had still been wearing her governess's clothes when she last called. She smiled.

'As you may see, I have been spending some of the money you were so obliging as to make available to me.'

'The bank manager raised no problems, I collect?'

'Indeed, no. Your letter of introduction proved entirely adequate.' She paused while he murmured a response, then went on, 'I wished to see you again to ask whether you have obtained any results from your enquiries into the Vitus Club and its owner. If, in fact, you have any information which might enable me to evict Lord Kelsey.'

Coggan shook his head and fiddled uneasily with his quill. 'I fear not, Miss Vincent. All the staff have been approached, discreetly, of course, but all are happy to be in his lordship's employ and singularly reluctant to criticise. My man did not feel it wise to offer a bribe which he knew would be refused. It would only have drawn particular attention to what had seemed until then purely idle questioning. I agree with him. His lordship, should he learn of it, would roundly oppose such a move.'

Leonora shifted slightly. She could imagine Kelsey's cold anger should he discover that, indirectly, she had

been attempting to bribe his servants into disloyal indis-
cretions, even were there no incriminating information
to be disclosed. She did not fear his anger, but did not
wish him to think her a low, skulking creature in her
dealings. She nodded agreement.

Coggan went on. 'As for his members, several are my
clients, including the gentleman who was here when you
arrived. Those I have been able to ask in the course of
conversation deny any irregularity at all in the running
of the Club.' He paused to eye her directly and at the
same time absently scratched his temple beneath his wig.
'Except, of course for the gambling on games which are
strictly illegal.'

'Then——' began Leonora eagerly, but Coggan waved
a dismissive hand.

'They are indulged in so widely as to make the clubs
where they are played immune from prosecution.'

'Like Brooks's,' observed Leonora wearily. 'I have
discussed the matter with the Earl of Chelstoke and am
forced to the same conclusion. Mr Coggan, is there really
nothing we are able to do?'

He scratched his scalp again. Perhaps he had an itch,
but Leonora suspected it to be a nervous habit. 'The
law has been ignored for so long that it has become
unenforceable. There is little point in pursuing that
course. However, I shall read the lease carefully when it
arrives from London and find a loophole if I can, of that
you may be assured, Miss Vincent.'

'You have not seen it yet?' asked Leonora, astonished.

'No. My information as to its contents, which I passed
on to you, came as notes attached to Mr Warwick's letter
of instruction. The lease is on its way to me now, together
with the deeds to the property, the bonds and all the other

papers which are now yours. Mr Warwick retained them on your behalf until everything was settled and you had appointed your own lawyer. I wrote asking for them after receiving your instructions last week and expect his reply at any moment.'

Leonora rose to her feet. 'I trust you will find something, Mr Coggan. I rely upon you to try. Meanwhile, I shall pursue my own enquiries. I thank you for your time. Good day to you, sir.'

She left the premises, escorted by an attentive Coggan, and in the street let out a sigh of frustration.

'He was not able to help?' enquired Clarissa who, as before, had been waiting in the ante-room.

'Not yet,' said Leonora grimly. But she herself now had a whole army of gentlemen to question. All were either members or visited the Vitus Club with someone who was. She looked forward to deepening her acquaintance with each and every one of those to whom Kelsey had introduced her. Even Captain Lord Cunningham.

As they walked towards the house rented by Lord O'Brien to call on his wife, Leonora became prey to a strange feeling. On the surface she felt angry and frustrated, eager to continue her challenge to Kelsey's occupation of her premises. Yet something kept rising in her which brought a touch of pleasurable excitement, of keen anticipation of the future.

In the end she recognised that, much as she wanted Kelsey's gambling hell removed from Morris House, she did not relish the thought of Kelsey's going with it. That almost hidden part of her that kept obtruding itself desired only to prolong her acquaintance with his lordship. She really must cure herself of such foolishness.

*   *   *

Several other ladies, including the Duchess of Broadshire, a personage of great consequence, were already seated with Alicia O'Brien in her morning room when Leonora and her companion were announced.

She was greeted charmingly by her hostess, who effected the introductions to those ladies she had not met the previous evening. Discreet enquiries were made as to her status and intentions. Clarissa, as was expected, was ignored and remained mute.

Leonora, in expressing herself delighted with her inheritance, stressed her relationship with the late Mr Charles Vincent and his brother, her grandfather the Earl, and mentioned that she had already paid her respects to the present Countess of Chelstoke, currently resident in Queen's Square.

'It is a pity,' remarked one of her new acquaintances, shaking her head so that the mass of silk flowers decorating her blue velvet bonnet shook as though in a breeze, 'that Morris House is in such an unfashionable part of Bath.'

Leonora's wide eyes expressed surprise as she examined the florid face, surrounded as it was by slightly grey lace beneath the brim of the large floral bonnet.

'You think a position so near the Abbey and the Baths unfashionable, my lady?' she enquired mildly. 'Perhaps it is, a little, but the house is so much more spacious than most of those in the new terraces. It is only in the Royal Crescent that any new residence can compare with it in size.'

She paused a moment to let her words sink in and then went on disarmingly, 'No doubt that is why, to my distress, Lord Kelsey insists that he will not surrender his lease. I was prodigiously distressed to discover that he was not simply living in the rooms he rents, but had founded the Vitus Club on the premises. I fear that he is making a fortune out of his more gullible members.'

There was a moment's silence. Then Alicia said, 'Of course, we ladies are inclined to be critical of gentlemen's clubs and of the sums our husbands hazard at cards.' She made a graceful, deprecating movement. 'I must confess, however, that I myself enjoy playing deep whenever I have the opportunity.'

'So do I!' put in another matron.

Alicia acknowledged the interruption with a smile. 'Kelsey is merely meeting a need, I protest—you must not condemn him for doing so. The gentlemen would find somewhere else to gamble their fortunes away were the Vitus Club not available.'

'And they do not go there only to gamble,' put in the florid-faced matron severely. 'They find congenial company and good food and wine. At least,' she had the grace to add, 'so my husband informs me.'

'You do not object to his spending much of his time there, my lady?'

'Of course she does not,' snorted her friend, a lady as thin and acid-looking as the other was plump and fussy. 'Gentlemen must have something to do besides hang about the house. In London, my husband spends much of his time at White's. He tells me he finds the Vitus equally congenial when we are in Bath. He meets all his friends and acquaintances there.' She gave Leonora a scornful glance. 'Why, he came home five hundred pounds the richer only the other night!'

'Kelsey has been known,' put in the Duchess of Broadshire gently, 'to help young men who have come to *point non plus*.'

The small Duchess displayed all the dignity of a great lady tempered by a charm and delicacy of manner Leonora could only envy. The Duchess, it appeared, was another of the Earl's conquests, for all her advanced years.

'I can scarcely credit—'

But Alicia sprang to Kelsey's defence again and cut her off. 'My husband insists that Blaise often refuses to issue counters against an IOU if he thinks the gentleman is about to hazard more than he can afford and, on occasions when the play gets too deep, he declares the faro or hazard table closed.'

Leonora realised that she was fighting a losing battle. She was the only one, it seemed, who thought Kelsey irresponsible, if not precisely wicked, to offer his peers the opportunity to gamble their fortunes away whilst at the same time lining his own pockets. No one else seemed concerned that the more counters he issued the richer he became for, naturally, he took a commission on each transaction. She compressed her lips in annoyance, for to argue further would have been pointless.

She did not remain long, and afterwards made more brief courtesy calls on new acquaintances. By the time she returned to Morris House she knew that in most ladies' eyes—her aunt providing a conspicuous exception—Kelsey could do no wrong and that his consequence had suffered not one iota by reason of his enterprising venture into a business which could not be scorned and dismissed as trade.

Who could resent or patronise a peer of the realm who offered hospitality and entertainment of such a high standard, even if it was at a price? The more expensive a club was, the more fashionable it became. A display of wealth was vital to one's standing in the *ton*.

Which was why she had decided to spend liberally now in order to secure for herself an affluent future.

Had it not been for her father's misfortune and the shock of finding her treasured house invaded for such a purpose, she would probably have joined everyone else in lauding his enterprise and character. It had enabled him to retain his position in Society.

But she could not forget the anguish her father's brush with gambling had caused to himself and his family, or reconcile herself to having men tramping about beneath her engaged in what she considered to be little short of criminal activities.

Kelsey, she told herself firmly, should be engaged in an attempt to restore his family fortunes by improving his father's estates, not involving himself in a frivolous enterprise in order to sustain his own expensive lifestyle. She had no room in her life for a gentleman so lacking in principle.

Chapter Seven

The following day an attentive Mr Sinclair came up to inform her that Lord Kelsey had gone to Herefordshire to visit his parental home.

Having bent over her hand and refused the offer of a seat, 'Everything here is in my charge while he is absent,' he explained. 'I merely came up to say that if I may be of any assistance during the next few days, please do not hesitate to ask.'

'Does Lord Kelsey often leave Bath?' asked Leonora. His absence settled one thing for her. She would not encounter him at the Assembly Rooms or anywhere else for a while. It would be a relief if he chose to absent himself a great deal.

'No, nor does he remain away for long. He will briefly visit his own estate, which is in the same neighbourhood, but he don't like to leave the Club for long.'

'He does not trust your management?' enquired Leonora provocatively.

Sinclair did not rise to her bait. He merely smiled. 'Oh, yes. We have known each other for ever since I, too, come from Herefordshire.'

'You are old friends?'

'Yes. When Blaise began this enterprise he sought me out in London, and since I was tied up from too much gaming and my father was threatening to disinherit me, I agreed to be his lieutenant.'

'You did not object to working for him?'

'Lord, no, why should I? Gave me somethin' to do apart from driftin' about Town ruinin' myself.'

'Surely this is the last place you should work, then! Do you not find the temptation to gamble too strong?'

He shook his head. 'No. I am perfectly happy watchin' others make cakes of themselves instead.'

Leonora leapt on the implication. 'So gentlemen are ruined while playing at your tables?'

He pulled a wry face and spread his hands in a gesture of impotence. 'Only if they are determined to be. Blaise discourages excessive betting, y'know.'

She'd heard that story before. She frowned. 'I thought someone who ran a gambling hell. . .club,' she amended in response to Sinclair's offended look, 'must be quite ruthless, quite prepared to see people ruined.'

'Blaise is not and neither am I,' protested Sinclair. 'We both know what it is like to be at *point non plus*— his reaching it wasn't because of excessive gambling, though; in fact, not his fault at all—and neither of us would wish the same fate upon our worst enemies. The betting downstairs is strictly regulated.'

'You surprise me,' she admitted, doubt in her tone.

'I can assure you it is so, Miss Vincent. But as I began to explain, when only one of us is present it means the one remaining ain't able to leave the premises. Otherwise I should be honoured to escort you to the concert tomorrow evening. You do intend to go?'

'Why, yes.' Leonora was intrigued by this glimpse into both Sinclair's and Kelsey's former lives. 'Your father did not disinherit you, I collect?'

He grinned. 'No. He don't like what I'm doing above half, but in truth it keeps me out of mischief, Blaise pays me well and I'm in funds, so he don't forbid it. I shall inherit a barony one day and an estate to go with it, but meanwhile, if it weren't for Blaise, I'd have to manage on the paltry allowance Papa makes me.'

'I wonder you have not sought to wed an heiress, Mr Sinclair. That would surely bring you about.'

'If there were a likely heiress in sight Blaise would be the one to land her,' said Sinclair without rancour. 'But neither of us is keen to enter parson's mousetrap just yet.'

Leonora smiled. What young gentleman was? They imagined they would lose their freedom if they allowed themselves to became what they termed leg-shackled. Unless, of course, they fell in love—then nothing would stop them from rushing to the altar, fortune or no. Both Kelsey and Sinclair must be immune to that sickness.

'When are you expecting him to return?' she asked, a polite enough enquiry but one she was unable to prevent herself from making. In some extraordinary and disturbing way, knowing he was not near, she had already begun to miss him.

'On Friday. It is to be only a short visit. He wouldn't have gone at all just now except that there seems to be some problem only he can solve. But he intends to to be back in time for the Duchess's dinner on Saturday. Have you met the Duchess?'

There was only one duchess in town. Leonora nodded. 'Yesterday.'

'Did she offer you an invitation?'

'No. But I would not expect her to. We were not acquainted before I was presented yesterday.'

'But you are the talk of Bath society, Miss Vincent.' At Leonora's incredulous glance, 'Did you not know? A stranger, a considerable heiress who made such a successful appearance at Monday's Ball—everyone wishes to meet you. I would not be surprised—keep an eye on your post, Miss Vincent!'

Leonora laughed. 'I doubt an invitation will arrive, sir! I disagreed with her views!'

'Oh, the Duchess admires a chit who can stand up for herself!'

She could not resist a mildly flirtatious rejoinder. 'A chit, sir?'

He grinned again. 'To her you must be. To me you are a beautiful, mature young woman. I think you must know how much I admire you.' He seemed to recollect himself. A faint flush stained his high cheekbones. 'But I must go. Good day to you, Miss Vincent.'

Well, thought Leonora, that was what came of entertaining a gentleman alone in her parlour, even if the door was decorously left open. Her unseemly behaviour had invited such a response. It had not amounted to a declaration, but such an admission of admiration must surely be regarded as a sign of interest. She resolved to be more careful in her future dealings with Mr Sinclair; she did not wish to lure him into a proposal she could never accept.

Later, when Dolly answered a knock on what must be considered her front door, she heard an unmistakable man's voice asking for her. The post captain.

But Captain Lord Cunningham was accompanied by

the hussar major and one of the other gallants she had met on Monday evening. Sitting in the parlour with them, Leonora found entertaining them hard work. She made several discreet enquiries as to the Vitus Club's activities and received short, glowing answers that profited her not at all and sent her into a gloom.

Disgusted, she gave up trying to be more than polite. She drew Clarissa into the conversation and her companion responded with some spirit. She was used to making small talk with her father's parishioners and, somewhat to Leonora's surprise, seemed well able to hold her own in the current company. Leonora scarcely had need to open her mouth.

She was, in fact, amused by the promptness with which the gentlemen had chosen to call, and the way they all, perfectly discreetly, eyed the contents of her room. She sat with Clarissa on the new *chaise-longue* and the gentlemen seemed to find her uncle's selection of armchairs comfortable. As indeed they were.

An offer from any one of them would result from a careful calculation of her worth. She found this conclusion entertaining rather than insulting, because it was her own fault—she had set out to impress them with her supposed fortune and was using it to secure a wealthy husband.

Suddenly, though, the idea that she could bamboozle any gentleman of more than slight means and encumbered acres to make her an offer seemed ludicrous. It was the fortune hunters who, so far, had shown most interest. Except, perhaps, Captain Lord Cunningham. She could not be certain of his financial status.

Still, if the lures she had thrown out did not land a large enough fish, she would still have enjoyed a Bath

Season, living in some style and moving in first circles, which in itself would be something to remember when she retired to her cottage. Once it was known that her supposed fortune was an illusion she would be dropped, so such an opportunity to take her rightful place in Society for a while would not recur. She could not regret her decision.

Although, were she absolutely honest, the first enthusiasm with which she had set out from Thornestone Park to capture a prize on the marriage market had already dimmed in the face of reality.

She was, she realised now, largely allowing Clarissa to entertain her suitors. But she had no particular wish to fix the interest of the captain, the major or the pink of the *ton*. They bored her. She was relieved when, after the prescribed twenty minutes, they rose to take their leave.

Not one of her new female acquaintances called. But then, she had scarcely expected to find them eager to climb the service stairs to visit her.

Sinclair's intuition had been sound, however. An invitation to the Duchess of Broadshire's dinner arrived. Clarissa, however, was not included.

'It makes no matter,' declared Clarissa, although Leonora could sense disappointment beneath her companion's show of unconcern. 'I possess no suitable gown. You'll wear the white?'

'Yes. I am glad I was tempted into purchasing it or I would have had nothing suitable myself,' she observed. 'It will do splendidly, and I shall wear the sleeves.'

She sent Dolly off with an acceptance and later interviewed the mason, who called in response to the letter she had sent earlier. The cost of the repair, she was relieved to find, would not be great. As for the redecoration inside, she decided to allow Kelsey to organise that and reimburse him when it was done.

While Kelsey was away, she took the opportunity to venture downstairs to take a closer look at the books on the shelves in the Reading Room. The circulating library was excellent for novels, but sometimes Leonora fancied something more meaty.

She had investigated her uncle's shelves but there was little there to interest her. She wondered whether Kelsey's interests—or rather, perhaps, those of his members—ran to more than the breeding of racehorses and the elements of navigation.

Her uncle had been in the navy in his youth. Perhaps prize money earned in the American War of Independence and the early French Wars had formed the basis of his financial security. But it was so many years since he had resigned his commission—almost before she was born, in fact—that she had forgotten he'd ever held it.

She was gratified to discover not only a copy, in several volumes, of Gibbon's *Decline and Fall of the Roman Empire*, but other works by the same author, together with biographies and travel books which might interest her. Having obtained Sinclair's permission, she took a volume of one of Gibbon's other works upstairs with her.

Both she and Clarissa enjoyed the concert that evening, particularly since their company was so eagerly sought by the gentlemen of their acquaintance. Once that was behind her, however, the coming dinner at the mansion of the Duchess of Broadshire filled her thoughts.

*   *   *

Early on the Saturday morning a knock on her front door heralded a visit from Lord Kelsey, who had returned from his travels looking worn rather than rested.

'Did the journey tire you?' she asked solicitously.

He eyed her with amusement, knowing the enquiry had been made tongue-in-cheek. 'Why? Do I appear exhausted?'

'Not exactly,' she allowed, 'but hardly as rested as I would have expected after a few days in the country.'

'Life in the country,' he observed languidly, 'can be far from restful. But I drove hard yesterday, knowing I must be back in good time to prepare for the Duchess's dinner, which I had engaged to attend. I hear that you are also invited?'

'Yes.'

'Capital. I am come to offer to convey you there in the chariot I have hired for the occasion. Or had you already made other arrangements?'

'I had intended to take a sedan chair. Mr Sinclair has offered to detail one of your footmen to escort me.'

Blaise raised his brows. The devil he had! Lacking notice of Digby's generosity he had hired the chariot entirely to accommodate her. Although the mansion was situated on the outskirts of the town he would normally walk to such an engagement unless it was raining. Not that, he admitted to himself, knowledge of her arrangement with Digby would have dissuaded him from hiring the carriage and attempting to persuade her to accept his escort.

'But,' Leonora was going on, 'if it would not be too inconvenient, I should be most glad to accept your escort, my lord. I find the sedan chairs useful but rather cramped inside.'

He smiled, hiding his triumph. Dressed by an artiste and with the help of a talented lady's maid, she had become the most exquisite creature currently in residence in Bath. Her success at the ball had been unexpected but not, once he had seen her in that delightful evening gown, surprising. The young gallants to whom he had introduced her had fallen at her feet and he had let them have their day.

But he now saw the conquest of Miss Leonora Vincent as a challenge. He could not stand aside and allow one of those coxcombs to fix the interest of the most desirable female available. He had no intention of offering for her, of course. She had been scornful of him on first acquaintance and still thought him an unprincipled swindler, so it would amuse him to see her develop a *tendre* for him.

He could achieve this end, he knew, for she was not unaware of him as a man. Without conceit, he knew women found him attractive—how could he fail to, when they fell so embarrassingly at his feet at every turn? Miss Leonora Vincent would prove no different.

Besides, if Alicia and certain other hopeful females thought his affections engaged elsewhere, he might free himself from their clutches. Alicia was a charming companion and an accommodating mistress but she had become too possessive.

'Then I shall come up for you at five-fifteen since we are summoned to arrive at half past, with dinner to be served at six. You will be in my company so you may descend by the main staircase, Miss Vincent. The chariot will await us at the front door.'

'I cannot allow that, my lord,' protested Leonora, scandalised. 'It cannot be proper for me to pass among your

members, even in your company. I shall be glad indeed
if you will come up to collect me, but we will descend
by the stairs I normally use. I insist.'

She had scored a hit, a palpable hit. He had laid down
the rule forbidding her to use the main staircase and now
she was keeping him to it, forcing him either to withdraw
his offer to escort her to the carriage or to descend by
the back stairs.

He was not a petty man. Or he hoped not. Her lovely
eyes were meeting his with such limpid innocence he
simply had to laugh. All his initial disdain and harsh
antagonism had disappeared, he found, and now he had
become used to her living up here he would not have it
any other way.

But he could not allow her free access through the
Club for cogent reasons that still held good. So he must
abide by his own rules and descend through the kitchen.
André would be astonished. As would the footman who
was to accompany them on the box!

'Then I shall be happy to ask the carriage to wait in
Abbeygate Street,' he said. 'Do you wish to take your
lady's maid with you?'

The delightful pleats formed at the corners of
Leonora's mouth. So much more attractive than dimples.
'No, I thank you. Since I am to travel in a closed carriage
to a dinner engagement and there will be no dancing to
disarrange costume or hair, I shall be able to manage for
myself. I have done so this many a year past.'

'But you no longer need to. The chariot will not seat
more than two in comfort, but Juliette shall travel in
a chair.'

Leonora did not argue. To have her maid accompany
her would certainly not diminish her consequence. His

lordship was being both helpful and charming, although she was excited by the attention, she was also suspicious of his motives.

She inclined her head. 'Then we shall both be ready when you call, my lord.'

Although Leonora had 'come out' at sixteen, attending local balls and functions in the company of her parents, she had never before dined at the table of a duchess. She was, therefore anticipating the event with eagerness blended with trepidation.

She had been well taught in the customs and demands of high society in anticipation of a London Season, during which a lack of conduct would have proved damning, but had never, before her advent in Bath, been accorded the opportunity to practise them on other than minor social occasions.

This evening must set the seal on her entry into the *ton*, for the Duchess of Broadshire was indeed a great lady in every sense of the word. Her ailing husband had remained in the country and so would not be present to act as host, although, as Leonora understood from the gossip of her acquaintance, her grace's grandson, Viscount Grath, had newly arrived in Bath and would stand in his grandsire's stead.

She heard Lord Kelsey arrive to escort her a few moments before time. Dolly, following instructions, showed him into the parlour to wait. Clarissa, freed from her duties as companion for the evening, had retired to her room.

Leonora did not keep him long. Juliette, already wearing bonnet and cloak and with a bag of necessary toiletries to hand, was putting the last touches to

Leonora's headdress as Dolly came to tell her that his lordship had arrived.

She had woven satin ribbon through Leonora's abundant chignon and finished the arrangement with chiffon roses to match the overskirt and trimmings of the gown.

Leonora blessed the day she had engaged Juliette. Tonight she had not used irons to create curls to frame her mistress's face but drawn the hair back in such a way as to reveal its fine bone structure. For years Leonora had arranged her hair in a somewhat similar manner but Juliette's magic touch had produced an altogether different effect. Fine wispy strands had been allowed to escape to soften the hairline without concealing it. Leonora scarcely recognised the regal yet flatteringly feminine head framed in the dressing-table mirror.

She stood, moved to regard herself in the long cheval glass and almost gasped with pleasure. Not only her head had been transformed. No one would recognise in the stylish, graceful creature staring back at her the ill-dressed governess who had arrived in Bath less than two weeks since.

She slipped her feet into the satin slippers standing ready for her, gathered up an ivory-framed, painted silk fan and a small evening bag, and smiled at Juliette. 'Thank you.'

Juliette smiled back as she picked up Leonora's latest indulgence, a white velvet evening cloak lined with shot silver-grey silk. She was a friendly soul, not standoffish and jealous of her own dignity as were some lady's maids Leonora had known.

'It is, as I suspected, a pleasure to dress you, madam,' she said as she hung the cloak over her arm, ready to place it about her mistress's shoulders just before they left the apartment.

Leonora felt almost shy as she entered her parlour where Lord Kelsey waited. She was quite unused to feeling so grand, but the sensation was intoxicating.

He was already on his feet, standing by the fire looking into the flames. He turned as she entered.

She had not seen him so splendidly attired before. A black superfine coat fitted perfectly over a grey brocaded waistcoat, which allowed the frills of his shirt to ruffle down his front. The shirt's collar was high but not ridiculously so and his neckcloth lay in exquisite folds about it. White silk breeches swathed his thighs and were fastened below the knees by gold buckles set with diamonds. Silken stockings led down to shining black pumps decorated by similar buckles. His only other adornment was the gem-set quizzing-glass hanging at his breast.

Her heart gave a strange thump and her knees trembled.

Just for a moment Kelsey stood holding his breath. The sight of her dazzled his eyes as the leaping flames had failed to do. She was exquisite. But he was too practised to allow his normal address to be overset for longer than that imperceptible instant. His legs carried him forward and he bowed over her hand while the shock waves of awareness surged, rippled and died.

Straightening, he resorted to the quizzing-glass he seldom used, lifting it to survey her through its distorting lens.

'Madame Fleur is indeed an artiste,' he murmured. 'You look ravishing, my dear.'

The familiarity did not escape her. Juliette hovered behind in the doorway. 'So is my maid, my lord,' she said as airily as she was able. 'I trust a chair is waiting for her below?'

'It is.' He turned to the maid. 'I must congratulate you, Mistress Juliette.' Juliette bobbed, accepting the compliment with perfect composure. 'Go on ahead,' ordered Kelsey. 'The men know where to take you and it would probably be an advantage for you to arrive before your mistress.'

Juliette inclined her head. 'Very well, my lord. If that is madam's wish?' she asked as she moved to place the cloak about Leonora's shoulders.

Leonora nodded. Kelsey intervened. 'I will take that.'

Juliette handed him the garment, said, 'Very well, my lord,' again and departed for the stairs.

Leonora struggled to retain her composure. He was behaving in a vastly high-handed manner, yet she found it strangely comforting. She had seldom had a gentleman fuss over her before.

'Did Dolly offer you a glass of wine, my lord?' she enquired, remembering her manners. 'If not, perhaps you would like to partake of one before we start out?'

'She did, and I refused.' He held out the cloak. 'Madam, may I place this about your shoulders?'

She accepted his offer and the *frisson* his touch always compelled shivered through her. His strong, shapely hands smoothed the fabric over her shoulders and then tweaked the high collar into position behind her head. He was too close. The instant he had finished she stepped back. 'Thank you,' she murmured.

He held out his arm. 'Allow me to escort you to the carriage.'

She wished convention did not decree that to refuse would show lack of conduct. It was incredible that she should be so aware of him, impossible that she should begin to like him.

Clarissa unexpectedly emerged from her room to bid her goodbye. A conscious blush tinged her sallow skin and her lashes fluttered in Lord Kelsey's direction.

She had no need to come out, especially dressed in her best gown—she was thrusting herself forward. Leonora felt a flash of annoyance.

Her instinct suggested that Clarissa was playing the poor neglected companion for Kelsey's benefit. Why, if she so wanted to meet him, had she not joined him in the parlour to await Leonora's arrival?

The courtesies exchanged were brief, although his lordship did express his regret that Clarissa was not to be one of the party. Clarissa made a deprecating gesture and Kelsey, having bestowed on her companion a regretful smile, followed Leonora through the narrow door to the service stairs.

Had it not been for the way he had greeted her own entrance into her parlour, Leonora would have been seething with anger and jealousy.

As it was, as she fled lightly down the stairs, she acknowledged a feeling of distinct disgust that he had the power to rouse such emotions in her. Why should she care if he chose to flirt with her companion? Not only, she recognised with mortification, because it suggested that he must place her on a par with Clarissa. No, she did not really believe that, and her feelings ran deeper than mere pique.

He was, of course, an exceptionally attractive creature and his attention was flattering, although she guessed it to be superficial. Never in her life had she contemplated being seduced solely by a gentleman's looks and manner.

She had expected her affections to be engaged by a worthy, preferably wealthy gentleman with whom she could settle down to raise a family in a union of pleasant companionship.

Dreams of love had played little part in her practical mind, even as a young girl. She had always known that her marriage would be arranged, would be a matter to be agreed by others, a question of money and property—though she had hoped that some regard would be given to her wishes, that she would not be forced into an uncongenial match.

Her father's bankruptcy and death had freed her from that prospect but faced her with other harsh choices. She had spent seven long years in servitude. Now, she was free to choose her own husband. She had had it all planned.

She had never imagined that her course would be strewn with traps and obstacles and offer temptations she would find it difficult to overcome.

Sitting beside him in the chariot, Leonora felt stifled. The close confines of a sedan chair would have been preferable—at least she would have had it to herself. Yet she could not truly be sorry that she had accepted his offer of escort. To arrive in a carriage with the Earl of Kelsey could do her no harm socially, despite her own lingering misgivings as to his worthiness, for everyone else seemed to accept him without question.

They spoke little as the coach threaded its way through the dark, narrow streets, each sunk in a reverie which apparently excluded the other, both acutely aware of the other's presence. A comment on the density of the traffic, a critical remark offered concerning the architecture of some building, represented the sum of their conversation.

Upon arrival at their destination Leonora realised the embarrassment she had been saved by Kelsey's offer of transport. No one, but absolutely no one of consequence, arrived at the Duchess of Broadshire's door in a sedan chair! She would have been utterly mortified had she done so, for the splendid carriages queuing up to discharge their passengers quite overshadowed the few chairs which, more easily manoeuvred through the throng, were conveying their passengers to the rear entrance of the mansion.

With the exception, that was, of an elaborately decorated chair surmounted by a coronet carried by two splendidly turned-out footmen and escorted by a magnificently attired attendant wielding a stick of office.

'Popinjay,' grunted Kelsey as a colourful figure, dressed in the first stare of fashion, stepped from its confines into the glare cast by a number of flambeaux and proceeded up the steps towards the light emanating through the open doors.

'Who is he?' demanded Leonora.

'Her grace's grandson, Viscount Grath. He is late if he is to help to receive her grace's guests. Took him an age to dress, no doubt. He considers himself a pink of the *ton*.'

'He does not lodge with his grandmother?'

'No. He has his own rooms elsewhere in Bath.'

'I imagine he belongs to the Vitus Club?' she suggested drily.

He smiled and his teeth gleamed in the dimness of the chariot. 'Naturally.'

No wonder the Duchess had defended Kelsey, thought

Leonora. But it must mean that he had not ruined the Viscount. Yet.

The coach moved forward slowly. There were four carriages ahead of them now.

'The Duchess must be entertaining a vast number of people,' murmured Leonora with growing apprehension.

'I believe we shall sit down some dozen couples,' responded Kelsey.

Were they to be regarded as a couple? Surely not. He was merely conveying her to the occasion, she reminded herself.

And so it proved. Leonora found Juliette in the room set aside for the ladies to discard their cloaks and tidy their hair. Afterwards she entered the brilliantly lit reception room to be greeted with generous warmth by her hostess and effusive gallantry by Lord Grath, who by this time had joined his grandmother at the door. Kelsey was already engaged in conversation with a group of gentlemen gathered by the fire.

The O'Briens were not present but the Earl and Countess of Chelstoke were, accompanied by their daughter Adelina with Lord Ransom hovering attentively by. The Countess beckoned and Leonora was constrained to approach her formidable aunt.

Her discomfort in being drawn into her aunt's circle did not last long, however. They were called to enter the dining room and sorted into pairs according to strict rules of precedence. Her partner, she found, was the ageing grandson of an earl she had never heard of, and, like herself, not in the direct line of succession.

They were at the back of the procession and sat as far away from the Duchess as the size of the table allowed,

although Lord Grath, acting as the host, sat at the far
end next to her. Kelsey was seated much nearer to the
Duchess. To Leonora's vast amusement, he had been
appointed to lead her aunt in.

Grath's collar points were so high he found it difficult
to turn his head to converse. A neckcloth, swathed up to
his chin, kept them in place. Beneath a violet silk brocaded coat with an upstanding collar, he wore an amazing
waistcoat in a large green and silver check with striped
lapels. Rings weighed down his soft hands and his
pleasant if slightly dissipated face wore a look of surprised pleasure as he turned his entire torso to speak
to her.

'Didn't expect to have the pleasure of so charmin' a
companion, m'dear,' he said as he helped himself to a
generous portion of stewed venison, ignoring the contents
of the soup tureen, which he pushed towards her.

'You are very kind, my lord,' said Leonora, helping
herself to a ladle of soup. 'As was the Duchess to
invite me.'

'Don't wonder at it m'self,' he returned, having swallowed hurriedly. 'Glad to have so splendid an article to
decorate her table.'

Leonora found she wanted to giggle. She had never
before been spoken of as though she were a branch of
candlesticks or a silver epergne!

As the meal progressed, with the soup replaced by fish
and all the other dishes in the first course being
sampled—veal, beef and turkey as well as the venison—
Leonora realised that Lord Grath was attempting to flirt
with her. He was, she decided, older than he at first
appeared—about her own age, she supposed—but
dressed in a fashion more appropriate to a young gentle-

man of adolescent years. She found that she quite liked him.

He was an open and shameless glutton.

'Had one dinner already, y'know, at the Club,' he informed her, chewing on a jugged pigeon from the second course. 'Sensible fellow, Kelsey. Sticks to the old time for dinner and serves up a substantial supper later. Means a fellow can eat there and still dine elsewhere if he must, and then eat again when he visits the tables later. Food is never so good anywhere else, mind—even Grandmama's cook can't equal André.'

With that Leonora had to agree. She had not partaken of dinner before coming out, satisfying a hunger pang with a cup of tea and a muffin. But Monsieur André's cooking was indeed superb. She would be spoiled for eating food cooked by anyone else for ever, she thought ruefully.

From time to time, despite the distance between them, she caught Kelsey's eyes on her and returned his regard. On one occasion he looked from her to Grath and lifted a brow. She glanced from him to the young lady seated beside him, new in Bath like herself, the daughter of a marquess and said to be possessed of a dowry of fifty thousand pounds. The pleats formed at the corners of her mouth and she, too, lifted a quizzical brow.

It was as though they were communicating in a secret language across the room. Leonora knew a moment of intense happiness.

And then he spoilt it all. The smile he returned smacked of smug satisfaction. He turned to the girl, a chit of seventeen who lacked all the finer attributes of address and grace, and she gazed back at him with large, pale, dazzled eyes.

Her features were somewhat indefinitely formed in a round face, but she had lovely golden hair and was not unattractive in an immature way, especially when she fluttered her eyelashes and smiled demurely at something that that reprobate Kelsey had said.

Leonora lost her appetite and was glad when the cloth was removed and the fruit and sweetmeats appeared. She could not have eaten another morsel of real food. She put a sugared almond in her mouth, finished up her wine and did not object when Grath refilled her glass for her. She smiled at him in the way the chit, Lady Flavia Collins, had smiled at Kelsey and watched interestedly as he blushed. Flirting, she discovered, was not so difficult after all.

It seemed an eternity before the Duchess stood and led the ladies into the withdrawing room, while the gentlemen gathered around the port and brandy decanters. Aeons of senseless chat passed before the gentlemen joined them to share the tea-tray.

Ransom made straight for Addie, with whom Leonora was sitting. She wondered why her cousin had been so set against the Earl, for he was not excessively old and quite presentable to look at. Her parents' opinion regarding his early demise appeared to Leonora to be founded mainly on wishful thinking. But it had persuaded Addie. She hoped the child would not be too unhappy.

Kelsey made straight for Lady Flavia while Lord Grath came to sit by her.

Leonora wanted to go home. Perhaps, after all, she was not really suited to life in the world of the *ton*.

Chapter Eight

Leonora's acute desire to go home lessened somewhat as the evening progressed and the card tables were brought out. She enjoyed a game of cards in congenial company and happily agreed to sit down to play a hand of whist.

Lord Grath, it seemed, was not eager enough for her company to refuse to join three other gentlemen who intended to play for higher stakes than the rest of the company. Kelsey was not numbered among these dedicated gamblers, for he was already seated at a table with the heiress and her mother. Unfortunately, the Duchess chose to lead her to join them.

'My grandson,' apologised the Duchess as she ushered Leonora to the table, 'finds it sadly tedious to play for mere shillings. But you know Lord Kelsey and so will not be entirely with strangers.'

Leonora would rather have sat down anywhere else in the room than opposite Kelsey, but could not object. Kelsey, she thought, must be extremely interested in Lady Flavia to forgo a more expert game to remain in her company.

'Thank you,' she murmured. She was not bad at whist and had played it almost every evening at Thornestone Park. But she guessed Kelsey to be a much more proficient and certainly a more devious player. His livelihood depended to some extent upon his expertise, for he was expected to sit at the tables from time to time to allow his members a chance to recoup some of their losses at faro or hazard. She knew she stood little chance of winning, but was defiantly determined to do her best.

Lady Flavia sat on one side of Kelsey and her mother on the other. Leonora, her eyes downcast, concentrated on her cards as far as possible, but every now and again her eyes met his across the green baize. She detected a gleam of irrepressible laughter in his and that feeling of intimate conspiracy assailed her again, for she knew he was sharing with her his amusement at the chit's behaviour.

Flavia had declared herself to be completely lacking in skill at the game and sought his advice at every turn, leaning towards him and showing him her hand. Kelsey, all sympathy, assisted her in the most charmingly patient manner imaginable.

'Do not be such a dimwit,' her mother chastised at last, shaking her plumed headdress in disapproval. 'Play your own cards, Flavia, and allow his lordship to concentrate on his. You cannot wish him to find you tedious.'

Flavia pouted and Kelsey laughed indulgently. 'Your daughter needs instruction, ma'am. I am not averse to supplying it,' he declared.

The Marchioness desisted from further comment, a thoughtful light in her rather staring eyes, which her daughter had inherited. If the Earl was prepared to endure her daughter's tiresome conduct, perhaps he had already

formed an attachment. . . Leonora, who could see the
thought taking root in the matron's mind, did not want
to believe it.

His lordship, however, was not playing well, distracted
as he was by his fair neighbour. The Marchioness, a
practised player, was not as skilful as herself, Leonora
believed. She set out to win as much of the modest stakes
as she could. The concentration kept her mind occupied
and saved her from dwelling in disgust on Kelsey's
behaviour.

By the end of the evening, to her immense satisfaction,
she had won several guineas, the only player at her table
to end the evening in profit.

A light supper followed, when Grath returned to her
side to fill her plate—and his own.

Midnight had struck before carriages were called and
Kelsey escorted her from the Duchess's residence.

The auspicious occasion was over. Her first entry into
the inner circles of the *ton* had, she knew, been a success.
To have the Duke of Broadshire's heir's heir paying court
to her must signify acceptance.

His grandmother had not attempted to dissuade him
from seeking her company. Perhaps, though, she knew
her grandson was merely indulging in a flirtation.
Leonora could not imagine that her grace would welcome
a mere earl's granddaughter as the wife of one destined
one day to succeed to the dukedom.

But Grath was, to date, the most acceptable of her
suitors. She would neither encourage nor discourage his
attentions, for the prospect of becoming a future duchess
had its attractions. It would put it beyond the power of
the gossips to do her harm. She would be free to chose

her own way, to enter fully into Society or to remain on the fringes, knowing that should she wish to claim it, her rightful place would be assured.

Kelsey sat sunk into his corner of the chaise. He had attempted no conversation, no intimacy. She was glad, she told herself severely, pressing herself into her own corner in a vain attempt to escape the almost tangible web he seemed to have cast about her.

Blaise was, in fact, afraid to move in case he should inadvertently touch his companion. The overwhelming attraction she held for him was something he should have recognised and conquered immediately after that first unexpected and unaccountable stirring when he had still thought her an unattractive and narrow-minded nuisance.

Now that he knew her for what she was, a beautiful, spirited, alluring young woman of character, and had been forced to sit so near to her for the chief part of the evening just past, he feared that the temptation to take her into his arms would prove irresistible.

He should never have offered his escort this evening. But the temptation to do so, to flaunt his assured place in Society and show his peers that he could walk in with the most sought-after female in Bath on his arm, had been too strong. However, he had no intention of becoming deeply involved with the person who was, unfortunately, his landlord.

If only Lady Flavia were as alluring! He could use the fifty thousand pounds she would bring him as her husband, were he prepared to give up his freedom. He could abandon the Club with that amount of money at his disposal. But he had no wish to do so at present. The price demanded would be too high.

He'd never actively contemplated such a course. He was no fortune hunter and had little wish to be branded as such. He had singled out the chit this evening because she had been useful in diverting attention from his growing obsession with Leonora Vincent. Also, the Duchess had seemed to expect it. Possibly she sought to prevent Grath from being snared by a chit she thought unsuitable.

He shifted slightly in his seat. She had placed Leonora next to Grath at table and Grath had shown signs of becoming besotted. Would the Duchess welcome that alliance?

Leonora would be worthy of the distinction.

But Grath was not worthy of her. Damned puppy!

Beside him, Leonora stirred as the coachman drew up in front of Morris House.

'This is the wrong place,' she said, drawing his apparently wandering attention to the fact.

'No,' he returned smoothly as the footman jumped down, lowered the step and opened the door. 'The Club closes at midnight of a Saturday, since few wish to remain longer without the ability to gamble. You may therefore mount the main stairs in perfect safety. Your maid will be waiting up for you and will open the door.'

Leonora did not seem grateful for this opportunity. Seething indignation made itself apparent in her every move. She snatched her hand away after he helped her down from the chariot and then stalked past him with her chin in the air.

'You overwhelm me with your consideration, sir,' she declared haughtily as she passed. 'Do not think that I have abandoned my intention to regain the use of these stairs at all times, as is my right. Goodbye, sir.'

He followed her in, amusement vying with wry regret

as she passed through the open front door, traversed the hall and began to mount the staircase, her bearing scarcely short of regal.

She was, he thought, magnificent. Still narrow-minded as the devil, but otherwise completely desirable.

He stood at the foot of the stairs, resisting the temptation to climb up after her. For he could scarcely attempt to seduce his landlord. Or. . .could he?

Leonora had feared that Kelsey might insist on seeing her to her own door and was relieved when he made no move to do so. She could not endure to engage in further converse with him that night. It was late and she felt quite out of sorts.

Nerves churned her stomach and her emotions were in such a state that she scarcely knew what she felt. She simply knew that she must escape his compelling presence or almost anything might happen. He was no puritan. He might attempt to kiss her.

She shuddered. To her dismay, the shudder was one of pleasure rather than disgust.

What was happening to her? She must not, could not, allow herself to fall in love with Lord Kelsey!

She managed to avoid him after church the following morning and Digby Sinclair attended the Assembly Room Ball on Monday, not his employer. Leonora was free to enjoy the attentions of several assorted gentlemen, including those of Sinclair and Lord Grath, without the distraction of Kelsey's presence. Grath twice asked her to stand up with him and took her in to supper. She could almost hear the eyebrows being raised all about her.

But she would have enjoyed herself more had Kelsey been there.

He wasn't present at the concert on Wednesday, either.

'He don't like concerts,' Sinclair, who was there, explained. 'Calls the sopranos' singing caterwauling!'

Lord Grath, though, who had attached himself to her side and ushered her to a seat in the front row, was entranced by the music and gazed raptly at the rather stout, middle-aged soprano as her voice soared to surprising heights.

'Delightful, ain't it,' he sighed as the audience clapped enthusiastically.

'You are fond of music, my lord?' enquired Leonora who had, herself, found the soprano's voice rather strained and tinny. She could almost sympathise with Lord Kelsey.

'Prodigiously, ma'am.'

She was grateful for Clarissa's company. Her background made her a pleasant, respectable companion and a lady could not attend most events alone, or walk about Bath sightseeing and shopping without someone to accompany her. Nor could she have received the increasing numbers of admirers who climbed up from the Vitus Club to call upon her. Lord Grath was becoming most particular in his attentions.

Leonora began to suspect him of entertaining serious intentions towards her. But although she liked him and found him an amusing companion, she could not, in the end, see herself as his wife. He needed to grow up, to eat and drink less and to dress more modestly.

So the days passed. Clarissa, in Leonora's opinion, had become surprisingly forward in her behaviour towards the gentlemen of their acquaintance. Perhaps that was her fault for relying so much on her friend to entertain them. She could scarcely reprimand her.

Kelsey, she deduced, was avoiding her. Whether he was attending Lady O'Brien or Lady Flavia she had no means of telling. She would not—could not ask the other gentlemen and they did not volunteer the information.

Shrove Tuesday was marked by the appearance of delicious confections Monsieur André called crêpes and everyone else spoke of as pancakes. His batter was paper-thin and the fillings divine.

Very shortly Leonora would have to decide whether to continue to enjoy the Frenchman's exquisite cooking or ask Dolly to prepare their food. Somehow she did not think that Dolly would be adequate to the task and, having become used to the best, she had no desire to suffer the worst in the way of food. So her mind was already made up. Unless the cost were indeed astronomical, she would pay Kelsey what he asked. Monsieur André's food was worth almost any price.

Ash Wednesday, of course, heralded the austerities of Lent. Not that most people let the fast make much difference to their lives. André served up less meat and more fish and his puddings tended to lack the richness of much cream. Sugary sweetmeats disappeared from the menu.

Leonora had finished with the book she had borrowed from the Reading Room and knew she should return it. She fancied delving into one of the intriguing accounts of travel in foreign countries she had seen there. So early one morning she let herself out of her apartment and descended the stairs to change her book.

The doors were all partly open and various sounds of cleaning and fire-laying came from beyond them, but as Leonora glided from the stairs to the Reading Room she met no one. She peered cautiously in, ready to excuse her presence to some servant, but there was no one there. The fire had already been lit and the place tidied. If someone did come back to finish off the cleaning it would not matter.

She replaced the volume where it belonged and then went along the shelves looking for a suitable travel book. She found one that looked interesting, an account of a journey through Egypt, liberally illustrated by sketches. Fascinated by representations of exotic animals like camels and of pyramids and the Sphinx, she decided to take it. As she turned to leave, the book in her hand, someone pushed the door wider open.

'I'm sorry to intrude—' she began, ready with her explanation—and then stopped.

Kelsey in dishabille proved more devastating to her senses than Kelsey in full evening dress. He wore slim dark trousers and a frilled, unbuttoned shirt. Surely he did not help with the cleaning! He should have been safely downstairs in his own apartment.

Leonora's heart began to knock. She stood where she was, unable to move.

'Miss Vincent!'

He appeared as shocked as she. Then a slow smile lifted the corners of his mouth in a way that turned Leonora's already trembling limbs to jelly.

'You were looking for something to read?' he asked, moving towards her. 'What have you found?'

'Eg-gypt,' stammered Leonora. Then, more strongly, 'A book about Egypt.'

'Ah!' He reached for it, took it from her nerveless fingers and riffled through the pages. 'Yes. An excellent account. I was there myself, once, on my rather curtailed Grand Tour during the Peace, in the year two. Luckily,

I was not caught in French-held territory when the war resumed, but my tutor thought it wise that we should return immediately to England. You have chosen well.'

Leonora swallowed. 'Thank you.' She managed a smile. 'I have given up fiction for Lent and I felt the need for something else to read.'

'Most worthy of you.' He handed the book back with a wry smile. 'I fear I am rather less virtuous. I give up nothing in Lent apart from the items André omits from the menu.'

She hoped he had not noticed her shaking hands. It was so difficult to breathe, let alone to talk, with him so close. She swallowed.

'The food is still excellent.' Unfortunately her voice was not quite steady, either. She cleared her throat. 'Perhaps I should remind you that you have not yet sent me your account for the first month. I should like to carry on with the arrangement if the cost is not too high.'

Something happened to his smile. To his entire expression. His hand reached out and a slender finger lodged under her chin.

Leonora shook. He must notice. She wanted to step back but her feet seemed glued to the floor.

'There will be no charge,' he murmured, his voice changed by some emotion he was visibly attempting to control.

'But. . .'

The words of refusal hovered on Leonora's lips but declined to emerge. Her breath stopped. His hands gripped her shoulders as he drew her closer. She saw his head dip and knew he was about to kiss her.

Her entire body yearned towards him, became putty in his hands. She longed for his lips to touch hers! For an instant, as his arms closed about her, she sagged against him. Then her inbred sense of propriety prevailed. She could not possibly allow such a liberty! She was no wanton that he should think to treat her so! Leonora allowed manufactured outrage its full play, dredged up all her resolution and pushed at his chest, the volume in her hand acting as a barrier between them.

'No!' she cried. 'No, Blaise, no!'

She was trembling, agonised, but not, he would swear, repulsed. He had felt that initial melting of her body, and how erotic it had been! But now he saw, surprised, that she was offended. Why? She was no chit straight out of the schoolroom to be frightened of a man's wish to kiss her. Her body had betrayed her. She had wanted him to. But. . .he drew a much-needed breath. . .offended?

'Why not?' he murmured, scarcely aware of what he was saying, so great was his need to control himself, his need to lighten the tension, taut as a violin string, vibrating between them. 'Is kissing something else you have given up for Lent?'

She choked and sparks flew from her beautiful, unusual eyes. 'Do not joke, sir! You are excessively impertinent! You cannot treat me as you would a lightskirt!' she protested.

'You think I was doing that?' So that was it! Amusement came to his rescue. The tension in his groin eased. Had she been aware of his desire? 'My dear Leonora. . .'

'I am neither dear to you nor have I given you permission to call me by my given name!' fired Leonora, unaware that she had just called him by his, so intent was she upon quelling the betraying reactions of her body while giving her genuine indignation free rein.

She could not allow him to think that she would willingly succumb to the demand, the passion she had glimpsed in his dark eyes and, alarmingly, felt pulse against her—yet her every instinct required her to do just that.

She must escape. If she did not. . .

His arms had loosened. Her fear of her own emotions at last unpinned her feet from the boards beneath them. She stepped back. He did not attempt to detain her. 'You. . .your behaviour is quite impossible in every way!' she flung at him as she made a hasty retreat to the door, the stairs and the security of her own apartment.

Blaise watched her go, frustrated beyond belief because she had denied him the opportunity to taste her lips. The woman set him on fire, did she not realise it? And he was damned certain she had wanted him to kiss her. Prudery and fear had stopped her.

Yet. . .she had called him Blaise. She had trembled at his touch like a young, untried girl—which, in everything except years, she was, he realised rather belatedly. Her expression had been anguished, torn, before she had turned to outrage to fend off his advance.

She had run away from him once before, after the Duchess's dinner, and he had decided to allow her time to miss him and perhaps seek him out. It had been a hard decision to keep to. . .and then, by chance, he had come face to face with her this morning.

He had, he knew, treated her as the woman of experience her age would suggest her to be, forgetting her history. And, God help him, forgetting the strict rules of propriety by which her life had always been ruled.

Outrage at impropriety had served her as an excuse. She had not shrunk from irregularity when determined to occupy the rooms above.

Yet. . .that irregularity had been different in kind. For a female of her sort to indulge in an amorous interlude with a gentleman neither her husband nor her fiancé would be to defy all the mores of her class. Nevertheless, he felt reasonably certain that it was not entirely decorum which had sent her scurrying upstairs to safety. Fear of her own emotions had played its part.

He would be forced to exercise some patience and not a little guile if he wished to seduce Leonora Vincent. Which he most emphatically did! For, now, simply to have the most alluring woman in Bath appear on his arm as a conquest was not enough. His eyes narrowed in anticipation. The seduction must be complete.

Leonora was still shaking when she reached the sanctuary of her parlour, the only room where, for the moment, she could be alone. She could hear Dolly in the dining room preparing for breakfast and Juliette would be in her bedroom tidying up and seeing to her mistress's clothes. Clarissa had not yet emerged from her room.

A glance at the clock told her it was not yet nine o'clock. But to her it seemed that a lifetime had passed since she had decided to venture down to change her book.

A lifetime *had* passed in one way, for she knew she would never be the quite the same person. How could she be when, propriety and common sense forgotten, she had longed so passionately for Blaise to hold her in his arms and kiss her until she lost the will to object when he took her to his bed?

Her cheeks burned at the immodesty of her thoughts yet she could not dismiss them. For she feared that she had been stupid enough to fall in love with the most unsuitable gentleman of her acquaintance. A man who ran a gambling club. Who made his living by exploiting other people's weaknesses. And who in any case was averse to the idea of marriage.

He'd surely never seriously consider marrying Lady Flavia for her fifty thousand pounds? Her stomach lurched and she felt sick. But she refused to think that badly of him. He didn't love the chit; she didn't even excite him. When he'd looked at Flavia, Leonora had seen no sign of real humour, only patient amusement, no hint of intimacy or of that darkly passionate expression he'd had in his eyes this morning.

Had he been seeing Flavia over the last couple of weeks? Not at the Assembly Rooms—she would have seen him there, or at private entertainments she herself had attended. But had he called on her? Had he escorted her about the town, as she had seen him squire Alicia? Because she had not seen him do so did not mean that he had not.

One thing she did know. He had not seen fit to mount the stairs to call upon her, with or without the excuse of some matter of business. All she had had was a glimpse of him once or twice, in the distance. He had been alone then.

She drew a breath. A degree of calm came to soothe her emotions. But she could certainly not contemplate accepting his charity over the matter of her food. She would demand an accounting. She would do it through Sinclair. For all he openly admired her he did not press his suit and would certainly never contemplate taking advantage of her as Blaise had done.

Why was she thinking of him as Blaise? And then she remembered. Hot blood flooded up her neck again.

Surely she had called him that to his face? Was that why he had presumed to use *her* name? Dear Lord, she must have been out of her wits to encourage him so!

She leaned forward, picked up the poker, thrust it vigorously into the coals, then held her trembling fingers to the resultant blaze. A shiver ran through her. Blaise. He had produced a blaze in her, she thought wryly. What was she to do?

'Why, Leonora!' came Clarissa's tones as the door behind her opened and her companion came in. 'You are up and about bright and early this morning!'

'I have some letters to write,' improvised Leonora quickly. 'But it is chilly and I wanted to warm my hands first.'

Clarissa nodded, not paying much attention. 'I wonder who will call this morning?' she remarked as she picked up the book Leonora had thrown down on a small table. 'This is new, is it not?'

'Yes. I've just been down to change the book I had. I thought we'd both enjoy it.'

'I'm sure we shall,' said Clarissa. Then, casually, 'Did you see Lord Kelsey?'

Leonora fumbled to open the desk. The leather-lined front fell down with a clatter, revealing compartments and drawers containing things which included pens, sealing wax, paper and a small knife. One day, she thought distractedly, she must clear out all her uncle's old papers.

'Why should I?' she said evasively.

'I just wondered.' Clarissa did not seem aware of her confusion. 'It is an age since he came up here and he has not attended the Assemblies recently. Do you think he is avoiding you?'

'Possibly,' said Leonora, her composure restored. 'He

likes us being up here as little as I like his activities below. We have nothing in common.'

'He was amiable enough when I met him in Milsom Street the other day.'

Leonora glanced sharply at her companion. 'You met him? You did not say.'

'It did not seem of much consequence,' said Clarissa with her usual placidity. Yet she looked conscious. As though, to her, it had been an incident of some consequence.

'There has been no reason for him to call on me recently,' Leonora pointed out reasonably, as much to convince herself as Clarissa. 'You must realise that whenever he has come up here it has been to find fault.'

'When we first arrived he sought us out at the Assembly Rooms, and he did come up in order to escort you to the dinner.'

Us, Leonora noted. Was that how Clarissa saw it? 'He was merely being polite, I daresay. He met Lady Flavia at the Duchess's, remember. He has an heiress to command his attention now.'

'Do you think so?' Clarissa sounded doubtful rather than dismayed. She glanced at Leonora from under her lashes. 'I've heard no mention of his interest in her.'

'Perhaps not. But he was making a fool of himself over her that evening.'

A small, secret smile caught the corner of Clarissa's mouth. 'Mayhap he did not wish people to think that his interest was fixed on you?'

Even to her own ears Leonora's laugh sounded forced. 'Because he had taken me up in his carriage?'

'It would have given rise to speculation, would it not,

had he also paid you attention during the evening? He would not wish for that.'

'Then why did he offer to convey me?'

Clarissa blushed. 'Perhaps because he sought an excuse to come up here?'

Leonora stared at her companion. 'To see you?' she gasped, appalled not only by the woman's effrontery but even more by her own reaction to the implication.

'Why not, Leonora? He has been exceedingly attentive whenever we meet.'

Leonora remembered the smiles they had exchanged, the evident sympathy he extended to her companion. But she could not interpret it as Clarissa did. Particularly since the episode downstairs earlier, with which she was trying so hard to come to terms and which she would die before mentioning.

'I should not depend too much upon that,' she said through a constricted throat. 'It appears to me that he is an accomplished flirt bent upon seducing every personable female in sight.'

Clarissa's eyes opened wide in shocked surprise, although Leonora doubted the sincerity of her horror.

'He has tried to seduce you?' she asked.

'Of course not!' Leonora hoped her denial did not sound too emphatic. 'But it is plain to see what kind of a man he is. A gambler. . .a flirt. . .a rake!' she finished dramatically.

Clarissa pursed her lips. Then their line broadened into a smile. 'You need not think I do not realise that I am beneath more than his passing interest, Leonora. No—' she waved a dismissive hand as Leonora opened her mouth to deny that any such thought had entered her head '—do not protest otherwise! But I find it pleasant to have such an agreeable gentleman treating me with kindness and respect.'

'Take care,' warned Leonora thickly. 'Do not allow yourself to be hurt—his honour would not extend—'

'Do not concern yourself, I shall do nothing rash,' returned Clarissa easily. 'My upbringing would not allow it. But I should not in the least object to receiving his particular attentions for a while. Unless, of course, it interfered with the more serious notice of some other gentleman.' She became suddenly fiercely earnest. 'I must wed, Leonora. I cannot bear the thought of returning to the Rectory.'

'No,' agreed Leonora. She had given little consideration to her friend's deeper desires and motives, merely noting that she seemed inclined to develop into a flirt. But, it seemed, the flirtatiousness was Clarissa's way of expressing her emancipation. 'Do you have a particular gentleman in mind?'

Clarissa shook her head. 'I shall not allow my interest to become fixed until I receive an offer.'

Leonora wished that she had been as wise as her companion.

'Do you have any expectations in that direction?'

'I am not entirely devoid of hope,' replied Clarissa guardedly. 'But do not look so mumchance, Leonora! You have Lord Grath on a leading-rein! He has title, expectations and, by all accounts, so great a fortune of his own that he has found it impossible to squander more than a tiny portion of it! You have only to bring him to the point and you become a future duchess!'

'But,' said Leonora, 'I doubt he will ever propose marriage to me. His grandmother would smother any such intention at birth. She would not count me a suitable match for a future duke.'

'He has spirit,' declared Clarissa. 'You could tempt him to defy his grandmother.'

Perhaps she could. But Leonora's ability to even consider an alliance with Lord Grath had deserted her. He was not Blaise Dancer.

Chapter Nine

Lent had little effect upon the social life of Bath, although the Duchess of Broadshire had chosen to hold her ball, the most glittering and prestigious event of the Bath Season, on the Tuesday after Easter, when feast rather than fast was in the ascendancy. The festival falling late that year, it was also shortly before she and many others departed Bath to prepare for their annual visit to London during its Season.

Leonora's best ball gown had been delivered as promised and so she had no hesitation in accepting the gilt-embossed invitation when it arrived.

That she was still upon her grace's list of guests despite her grandson's infatuation with a woman who continued to live in unconventional accommodation surprised Leonora a little. The Duchess, however, being the great lady that she truly was, had not hesitated to climb the service stairs to call upon her.

Unlike those of some of the few other matrons who had followed the Duchess's example, her visit had not been inspired by a prurient curiosity to see how she lived under such eccentric conditions, but rather by a genuine wish to mark her acceptance of the Earl of Chelstoke's niece into Society.

Leonora was forced to wonder whether, should Lord Grath propose marriage to her, his grandmother would actually approve. It seemed unlikely. More probably the Duchess was merely taking Leonora's measure in order to be more certain of killing off at birth any hint of such an engagement.

Kelsey would doubtless be invited to the ball. But despite her reluctance to be in the same company as his lordship, nothing short of complete indisposition could have caused her to decline her own invitation.

With the passing of the weeks the pile of invitations adorning her mantelpiece had grown, for in the face of the Duchess's approval, no one dared to snub her. She accepted most of them and, more often than not, Clarissa accompanied her to the receptions, concerts and routs she chose to attend. They seldom spent an evening at home.

A growing and uncomfortable sense of obligation made Leonora declare that she must hire a room in order to return all the hospitality they had enjoyed.

Clarissa looked up from her needlework, an alert expression on her face. 'When?'

Leonora allowed her embroidery to rest in her lap. 'When do you suggest? Before Easter, I think. I cannot leave it later. Everyone will be gone soon after the Duchess's ball.'

'I agree. The beginning of April, perhaps. That does not give us long—what form will it take?'

'A reception and supper.' She could not afford anything more elaborate. 'As you say, there is little time left. The invitations will arrive at short notice, I am afraid, and I must choose a day when few others are entertaining. We shall have to move quickly!'

She thrust her work aside and sprang to her feet, going to the open writing desk where her engagement diary lay. She perused it thoughtfully for some moments.

'Not in Holy Week,' she decided. 'I see we have a free Tuesday during the previous week. Can you think of any other event scheduled for the second day in April?'

'I cannot recollect hearing of any important event to which you have not received an invitation, Leonora,' said Clarissa, shaking her daintily capped head.

Clarissa's looks had improved almost beyond recognition during the weeks they had been in Bath, thought Leonora. New animation had given her face life. Her skin still inclined to sallow and she would never be beautiful, but on the other hand she was no antidote and had collected several admirers though, as yet, not a single proposal. But then, neither had she, so far, been the recipient of an offer.

'I will make a final check with the Master of Ceremonies,' Leonora said, dismissing her assessment of Clarissa's charms a little impatiently. Somehow, Clarissa seemed less ideal as a friend now than she had at Thornestone Park. She had developed a forward, rather self-centred streak which Leonora had not known she possessed.

'Where will you hold it? And what about the supper? Who will you ask to provide that?' demanded Clarissa, ever practical.

'If only I could persuade Monsieur André to provide the food. I wonder. . .if we serve a cold collation and he is given plenty of notice he may be willing to help.'

'He'd have to ask Lord Kelsey for permission but

otherwise I don't see why he should not. You will have to invite Lord Kelsey, won't you?'

'Kelsey?' A prickle of apprehension shuddered down Leonora's spine. She had not seen Kelsey since their encounter in the Reading Room a week ago. 'I do not see why. I do not owe him a return of hospitality.'

'But knowing him as you do—it will look too pointed—'

'Why? Everyone knows that we are at odds over his lease.'

'But, surely, not at such odds that you should choose to cut a peer of the realm in such an obvious manner? You cannot pick and choose, Leonora. You must invite all your acquaintances or none, unless you wish to become the object of speculation and censure.'

Leonora opened her mouth to say that she did not care and then shut it again. What Clarissa said made sense. But how would Blaise take her invitation? Would he consider it a signal that she was eager to end the stand-off that existed between them?

Was she? She did not know. All she did know was that she did not trust herself to repulse him again if he renewed his assault upon her senses. That keeping him at a distance was the only way to stop herself from casting aside her principles and begging him to make love to her.

If she were so weak as to do that, she could never hope to wed the likes of Lord Grath, or even of Captain Cunningham. But did it matter? Would not the world be well lost for love—if what she felt for Blaise was love and not simply carnal desire! How could she tell?

Certainly, were she honest with herself, she was not content at the moment and could see no future happiness without Blaise beside her. Yet convention held her in its grasp. So far, praise be, that grasp had proved stronger than the unwelcome tendrils of desire which held her in thrall whenever Kelsey came near her.

'Very well,' she conceded at last, 'but I shall hope that he will refuse the invitation. He has only to plead that he cannot afford to leave the Club. Meanwhile, I must arrange the venue and the supper before I can order the invitation cards. I will speak to Monsieur André immediately!'

She abandoned the desk and her list, swept from the room and almost ran down the stairs to see the cook.

Preparations for dinner were well under way when she entered the kitchen. Well-known and respected by now, her welcome into the steamy, aromatic, busy room where all the delicious dishes were prepared was as warm as the atmosphere.

'Mees Vincent! You honour us wiz a visit!'

'I have come to ask if you can help me, *monsieur*. I wish to entertain my friends and acquaintances, and intend to hire a room—one of the old assembly rooms, perhaps—in which to hold a reception. I wondered whether, despite your duties here, you could possibly consider providing a cold collation for the supper?'

The Frenchman's eyes opened wide. He shrugged expressive shoulders. 'But, *madame*, I regret—'ow can I? I am kep' ver' busy 'ere.'

It went against the grain but, 'Could you ask Lord Kelsey if he could spare you for a couple of evenings? You do have time off, do you not? The meals here are served sometimes without your presence in the kitchen?'

He nodded, rather doubtfully. 'It might be possible. Why you no ask heem yourself?'

A good question. Leonora smiled as winsomely as

she knew how. 'He will listen to you, *monsieur*. If you
persuade him that the service here will not suffer and
that you would like to do it, he may allow you to. To
produce a cold collation would be a challenge, would it
not? You could experiment with dishes you do not normally serve here.'

The chef's eyes had begun to glow with enthusiasm.
'I shall ask heem after dinner, *madame*. If he say *oui*,
then I shall make supper for you!'

Having thanked him most warmly, Leonora returned
to her apartments in a ferment of impatience. There was
nothing she could do, except make out a list of people
she must invite, until the cook had seen Kelsey. If he
refused to allow André to produce the extra dishes and
supervise their delivery and serving on the night, then
she would have to hire a large room in an hotel, where
the food was bound to be inferior.

For whatever reason, Kelsey had shown an inclination
to behave in a friendly fashion both before and during
the Duchess's dinner. Afterwards, he had chosen to avoid
her. Then had come that disastrous meeting in the Reading Room. Since then they had avoided each other.

Would the lingering remnants of his kinder feelings
prevail? Would he allow André to cook for her? Or would
he choose to make his continuing displeasure known by
his refusal?

Her uncertainty was soon resolved. Shortly after dinner
and before she had begun to change for an evening
engagement, Kelsey himself knocked on the door to her
rooms and asked to speak with her.

After returning from the Pump Room, which she had
visited not to take the waters but, as usual, to meet her

many acquaintances, she had changed into a becoming house gown. It was during this operation that the idea of holding a reception of her own had crystallised in her mind.

She wore it still. She fiddled with the blue skirts, arranging them about her to best advantage as she sat on the *chaise-longue* waiting to face Lord Kelsey's derision, maybe wrath. Since he had come himself rather than pass a message via his cook, she expected that he had come to express his disapproval of her suggestion.

'Oh, dear!' murmured Clarissa.

Her apprehension had communicated itself to her companion. But Clarissa's presence might take some of the sting from Kelsey's scorn.

When he entered the parlour he looked amiable enough, if rather aloof. As he bowed over her hand and greeted Clarissa with a formal nod he was every inch the accomplished man of fashion doing the pretty. Leonora murmured a word of greeting and braced herself for the worst.

'Monsieur André informs me that you intend to hold a reception early in April, Miss Vincent?'

He had come straight to the point. The query in his voice implied that he could scarcely believe André's word. She inclined her head in assent. 'Yes.'

'I see. Have you yet decided upon a venue?'

This mild, enquiring approach was unexpected. Leonora, conscious of him with every fibre of her being, clasped her hands in her lap, determined not to let him see the effect his presence had on her.

Meanwhile Clarissa, taking it upon herself to act as hostess, indicated that his lordship should seat himself, which he did.

Clarissa, it appeared, had controlled her tendency to blush when in his lordship's presence and could meet his eyes with perfect composure. Leonora had not noticed before, but since that earlier conversation Clarissa's infatuation must have died—while her own obsession with him had been growing.

Obsession it had become, for despite her avoidance of him he was never far from her thoughts. The sensations she'd experienced during those few moments in his arms had haunted her day and night.

And now here he was, in the same room, speaking to her in a casual drawl and playing languidly with his quizzing-glass the while. No wonder her pulse was beating hard and she had difficulty in speaking.

'It occurred to me, Miss Vincent, that despite the fact that my lease gives me exclusive right to the occupation of that part of this property, I should not entirely deny you the use of the formal rooms here. If it would please you to do so, you may use all but the Gaming Room for your reception.'

'What?' said Leonora faintly.

A mobile brow lifted and a slight smile curved his lips. Mischievous eyes laughed at her. 'I am offering you the use of the public rooms downstairs, Miss Vincent. All except the Gaming Room, which will remain closed.'

Leonora unclasped her hands. 'Why?' She still seemed unable to speak except in monosyllables.

'Because,' he said softly, 'I have come to admire your spirit, Leonora. You will not succeed in ousting me by legal means, but I am not so obdurate that I cannot sympathise with your point of view. It must be vastly inconvenient for you to be unable to receive properly. I therefore thought to save you the trouble and expense of being forced to hire suitable accommodation elsewhere.'

'Leonora!' cried Clarissa. 'How wonderful!'

Yes, it was. Leonora could not quite take in the enormity of what was being offered. Or why. His explanation left a great deal to be desired. Her insides had turned to jelly at the hidden implication—that he wished to please her. Even as the idea of refusing his offer on a point of principle crossed her mind, she knew she would not.

She managed to ask, 'You mean I may use them without charge?'

'Yes.'

'Will your members not object?'

'Some may, but they will have to accept my decision to close the Club for that evening. Those you choose to invite will, I believe, be excessively amused to escort their wives and perhaps their daughters to the place where they spend so much of their time. And the ladies will have their curiosity satisfied. I do not think you need fear having your invitations refused because of the venue.'

'No.' She could just imagine the sensation receipt of them would cause. Her composure returned all in a rush. A smile every bit as roguish as his lit her face. Her grey-blue-green eyes began to sparkle. What a fine jest it would be!

It occurred to her, suddenly, that she no longer thought of the Vitus Club as a gambling hell—she was quite ready to use the place for her own entertainment.

When had her opinion changed? Gradually, she supposed, over the weeks she had known Kelsey and heard his praises sung by the majority of her acquaintances. But she still could not admire him for the way he chose to make his living.

She lifted her eyes to the slate grey of his. Their expression was now somewhat sombre, but began to change when he saw the eager glow in hers. She realised that he had been wondering whether she would snub him, or accept his undoubtedly generous offer graciously. Her decision meant a great deal to him.

'Thank you, my lord,' she said. 'I am sensible of the sacrifice you are prepared to make, and gladly accept your offer.'

His tension had not been obvious, yet she could sense his relaxation by the way he shifted in his chair, crossing one elegantly trousered leg over the other and dropped his glass to hang by its ribbon.

'Capital! Then that is settled. Although you must realise that my hospitality cannot extend to offering additional cloakroom accommodation. The gentlemen normally leave their overcoats in the hall but that may not suit the ladies.'

'Since they may use the main stairs to reach it, they will not object to coming up here, I believe. I shall provide a room for them to leave their cloaks and Juliette and Dolly will look after their comfort and entertain their attendants.'

'Capital!' said Kelsey again. His eyes held warmth now. 'I shall inform André. He will consult you over the menu, of course, and every dish need not be cold, should you wish it otherwise. The kitchen will not be serving members with supper that evening and so will be entirely at your command.'

Leonora could scarcely believe it. Blaise, she thought, had changed. And he had called her Leonora in front of Clarissa. Did he realise it? She cleared her throat. 'How many people will the rooms comfortably hold?'

He grinned. 'You wish it to be a sad crush? Then invite everyone you know. I will engage to clear the rooms of clutter—we can remove some of the small tables from the Reading Room and introduce a few more chairs. The card tables seat between twenty and thirty, but there is room for others in there as spectators.'

Clarissa's eminently practical voice interposed itself. 'The Dining Room seats how many?'

He considered, brow puckered. 'With the food laid out on side-boards, as many as can squeeze round the tables. I could not exactly say. Do not worry, people enjoy a squash. As you must be aware, not everyone will stay the entire evening,' he added, directly addressing Leonora. 'They may move between all the functions being held on the same day.'

She pleated the skirt of her gown with fingers that had at last stopped trembling. 'I know. I have chosen the date to avoid any clash if possible. I want those who attend to be able to remain for as long as they are enjoying themselves.'

He rose with the lithe grace she so admired, which set her heart beating fast again. 'They will be. You are the sensation of Bath, Miss Vincent.' The graceless smile was back in his eyes. 'Why else do you think I offered you the use of my rooms, Leonora? I should have been damned for a confoundedly scurvy fellow had I not.'

She knew he had to be teasing her. Yet that did not stop icy tentacles of disillusion gaining a small hold on her heart. No doubt he believed there to be an element of truth in his words.

He bent over her hand. His eyes, roguish yet serious, were that possible, searched hers. 'Will you allow me to act as your host?' he asked softly.

Colour flooded her cheeks. She could not sustain his gaze. Only anger and resentment had ever allowed her to disregard his charm.

'How can I possibly refuse?' she said.

He pressed a kiss into the palm of her hand and closed her fingers over it. 'Thank you.'

He saluted Clarissa briefly and was gone.

Clarissa, no longer prey to a hopeless infatuation, watched his retreat with a thoughtful look in her prominent eyes.

'You could do worse than marry Lord Kelsey,' she observed at last, seeing that Leonora had no intention of commenting on his lordship's surprising offer. 'He will become a marquess one day. I believe you have managed to fix his interest.'

'Marry?' Leonora had difficulty in maintaining her composure. Where his lips had touched her palm still burned. 'Even were you right, and I scarcely think so, I could never wed a man with as few scruples as Kelsey. I shall choose a man of solid character and worth when I marry.'

'Such as?' murmured Clarissa with a wry smile.

'There is Mr Utley,' said Leonora defensively, mentioning a new arrival in Bath who had rapidly become one of her most ardent admirers.

'He is old enough to be your father and is a dreadful bore,' said Clarissa.

'But very worthy. Like the Duke of Wellington, he never gambles.' She allowed herself a small wry smile of her own. 'And he is very rich.'

'He also has two children from a former marriage. You do not mind that? You will accept him if he offers?'

'If he makes me an offer, I shall consider it carefully,'

said Leonora with precise accuracy.

For she would. It was just a pity that knowing Kelsey had spoilt her for every other gentleman under the sun and she could never contemplate marrying *him*, even were he to ask her.

Which in itself was extremely doubtful. Kelsey would only wed when he felt the need to set up his own nursery. He did not appear particularly interested in titles and estates, only in enjoying the life of a gentleman of considerable means and some leisure who could attract the favours of almost any woman he chose.

He had a cousin, she had heard, who was eager to inherit the marquessate. Who was hoping, no doubt, that Kelsey's reputedly shameless lifestyle would result in an early surrender of his lease on life.

The cousin would hope in vain, for Kelsey did little to damage his health. She merely wanted an early surrender of his lease on her property. Her hope held as little chance of being fulfilled as did the cousin's.

'Have you received an offer yet?' she asked abruptly, to change the direction of Clarissa's thoughts.

Clarissa grimaced. 'Not yet. Although I have hopes of Mr Bradshaw. He is in orders, as you know, and has no living at the moment, but he is a gentleman's son and the family does not seem to lack money. I do not regard his looks.'

Which were, regrettably, far from handsome since his face looked as though it had been squashed as a baby. Not that he could help that; he was otherwise unobjectionable.

'So you will accept if he comes to the point?'

'I think so. Subject to my father's approval, of course.'

'Of course.'

Leonora studied her companion. She found Clarissa

difficult to understand. She was almost thirty years old, but still considered it her duty to ask her father for permission to wed the man of her choice. She supposed he expected it.

As head of her family, Lord Chelstoke thought it only right that she, Leonora, should seek his blessing before she wed. In truth, he would like to dictate whom she should marry—he had made that clear enough before leaving Bath. But she had no intention of consulting her uncle or of asking his permission to wed. And had told him so.

'Well, then,' said Clarissa briskly, 'We have no excuse not to finalise our list and order the invitation cards, have we?.'

'No. And we shall need flowers. Kelsey does not require Mrs Parkes to decorate his rooms with flowers.'

Clarissa was writing on a sheet of paper. 'I should rather think not.' She made a note. 'Flowers. What else?'

'Leave the list out and we will jot down things as we think of them,' said Leonora, jumping to her feet. 'We must go and change, or we shall be late for her ladyship's soirée!'

The days flew past. Of necessity she saw more of Kelsey than ever before, for they had to meet to discuss and plan her reception.

Insidiously, and against her better judgment, their intimacy grew. If only he were not the proprietor of a gentlemen's club! If only he did not seem bent on squiring so many attractive females about Bath! For it seemed that, whenever she met him in the street or elsewhere these days, he had a different woman on his arm!

Sometimes, when it became necessary for them to visit

some merchant together, it was she who was so honoured. But she saw him with Alicia, with Flavia, even with the Duchess, although that gave Leonora no pain. There were others, too.

Suddenly, he appeared to be seeking more feminine company than he had before. He spent less time in the Club, more out and about in the town. He was often in the Pump Room when she and Clarissa went there to promenade.

'The numbers of visitors are thinning,' he explained one day at the tail end of March as, walking beside him, her gloved hand on his arm, she charged him with neglect of his business—rather acidly, she realised, after the words were out. 'Digby can manage quite well without me, he has plenty of assistants.'

'But he is entitled to time off,' Leonora pointed out.

They were in Milsom Street on a last-minute shopping errand. He stopped, looked down at her with rather intent eyes. 'And he gets it. Would you rather he escorted you tonight than I? It could always be arranged.'

He was hiring a chariot that evening to take her to a musical soirée arranged by the wife of one of his members. She knew he did not appreciate concerts and had been flattered by his offer to escort her. This was one of the occasions to which Clarissa had not been invited.

'Of course not!' said Leonora sharply.

Was he trying to escape what, to him, would seem a tedious evening? The thought of losing his company hurt so much that she turned and began to walk on, to keep moving, forcing him to do the same. Nevertheless, hard

as it would be, she must give him the chance to do as
he wished.

So she said, 'Unless you would rather not attend such
an event? I know how much you dislike listening
to music.'

'Not instrumental music,' he informed her. 'What I
cannot abide is the caterwauling of so-called sopranos.
Although,' he added, his tone light, 'in the right company
even that becomes bearable.'

Ignoring the implication behind his last words,
Leonora said, 'And I suppose there will be a card room
to which you may retire.'

'Doubtless Perry will have one set up. But why should
I wish to play cards, which I can do at almost any other
time, and so lose the pleasure of your company?'

As she flushed hotly, Leonora knew that, since she
had discovered her preference for Blaise Dancer, she had
been behaving more like a raw chit straight from the
schoolroom than a mature lady of five-and-twenty years.
'There is no need to bam me, my lord,' she said stiffly.
'We both know that beneath a surface civility we are
still at daggers drawn.'

'Are we?' he asked interestedly. 'I can assure you, my
dear, that I no longer cherish an ambition to have you
move out of your rooms. In truth, having a lady such as
yourself living above the Club gives it an added attraction
to certain members.'

'Those who wish to call upon me without being forced
to use the service stairs, you mean?' Leonora's tone was
withering. 'Naturally, you would appreciate a factor
which increased your profits.'

'Naturally.'

His voice had cooled, but she caught the echo of a

laugh beneath the surface. She looked up sharply. He was regarding her flushed and indignant face with something approaching fond, amused indulgence. She supposed she deserved such treatment, since she was behaving like an adolescent.

She drew a calming breath. 'I have no wish to quarrel with you, my lord, or to change the arrangements for tonight.'

'Leonora, why are you so prickly?' he asked softly, stopping again and turning her burning face to his by placing the silver knob of his cane beneath her chin.

'P-prickly, my lord?' stuttered Leonora.

'Prickly,' he repeated, his eyes now dancing with amusement. 'And, Leonora, will you not address me by my given name? Please call me Blaise, in private at least.'

'You have already decided to call me by mine, without permission, I collect.' If she sounded stiff now, it was because her heart was drumming so loudly she felt certain he must hear it and she had absolutely no wish to let him know how much she wanted to indulge in the intimacy.

She had lowered her lashes to screen her eyes from his gaze. 'Look at me, Leonora,' he ordered.

'My lord,' she answered, doing no such thing, 'we are in the middle of Milsom Street. People must be watching us.'

He chuckled. 'Do you fear for your reputation, Leonora? I thought you quite impervious to gossip?'

But he moved on, continuing to greet acquaintances as though nothing of moment was taking place between him and the woman whose hand rested on his arm.

'Of course I am not! If I wish to make a good marriage—'

'Ah!' he cut in. 'Of course. Like all females, you have marriage in mind.'

'What else is there for us?' Unconsciously, she had moved on from indignation to resigned acceptance of her lot. 'That is what we are bred and trained for, is it not? To bear children for our husbands and to run their households.'

She paused, expecting him to comment, but all he did was raise his brows. So she went on.

'The opportunities to earn one's own living are few for a female, particularly one born a lady. I chose to become a governess rather than be treated as a slave and married off at the first opportunity to a man of my aunt's choice. When he left me all he had, Charles Vincent saved me from a life of poverty and servitude. At least I am now free to choose my own husband.'

'And what do you look for in your future husband?' he enquired mildly. 'What sort of man will you choose?'

They had reached their destination. Leonora evaded the question by turning into the entrance. He was forced to open the door for her and the conversation died.

He did not attempt to renew it when, their mission accomplished, they walked back to Morris House.

He had taken to entering with her by the back entrance and parting from her at the ground-floor landing. If the servants found it curious that he should choose to use the service stairs, none had dared to remark on it. At least, not in his hearing, or in hers.

'So,' he said as they prepared to go their different ways, 'I shall call for you as agreed, Leonora. Perhaps, tonight, you will inform me of your requirements in a husband. I may be able to introduce you to just the right gentleman.'

His eyes danced, yet beneath the irreverent smile lay a thread of seriousness, to which Leonora responded.

'I believe you have already done your best in that direction, Blaise. Do not think I have not noticed your determination to introduce me to any and every eligible male who appears on the scene.'

'But no one, so far, has taken your fancy?'

'No one,' lied Leonora firmly.

Chapter Ten

The musical evening proved to be the usual sad crush and therefore a highly successful, enjoyable occasion. The ensemble played pieces by Mr Handel and Mr Mozart and in the intervals the guests strolled about exchanging the latest *on dits* or partook of light refreshments in the supper room.

Kelsey remained at Leonora's side for much of the evening, although from time to time they were parted by groups of friends who demanded one or the other's attention.

Leonora was not displeased by this, for they could not remain together for the entire evening without causing the tongues to wag faster than they already were.

Her own invitations had been issued and word had already circulated that Kelsey was to act as her host. Raised eyebrows and knowing looks had followed this piece of extraordinary news and Leonora knew that they were both already the subjects of speculation. This she chose to ignore. Gossip alone could not seriously harm her and her behaviour had been irreproachable.

She moved about amongst her acquaintances with an

187

easy conscience, amused rather than concerned by the furtive looks bestowed upon her by some of the dowagers. Her delight in the situation was marred somewhat, however, by the anguish of knowing that Blaise's attention was merely born of an impulse to flaunt his own success in engaging her interest.

For the bland manner in which he greeted her beaux and the assiduous attention paid to his own female admirers, while brushing aside any attempt to probe the nature of his involvement with Miss Vincent, told her much about his motives.

Was he, she wondered in astonishment, paying her attention in an effort to make them jealous?

During the second interval Lady Flavia Collins came bouncing up, having escaped the dampening presence of her watchful mother, who was engaged in consuming large quantities of the dishes on offer in the supper room.

'Why, Lady Flavia! How delightful to see you here!' greeted Kelsey fulsomely.

He bent in extravagant gallantry over the young girl's hand and made no objection when she clung to his sleeve, looking at Leonora, who already had her hand tucked under his other elbow, with daggers in her eyes. Were he desirous of making Flavia jealous he had succeeded to admiration, thought Leonora resentfully, unable for the moment to see the amusing side of the confrontation.

'You are neglecting me, Lord Kelsey,' Flavia accused petulantly.

'How can you think it? But—' a warning note crept into his voice '—you must be discreet, my dear. You would not wish to become the object of unkind gossip, I collect.'

'If we did, then you would have to offer for me,' retorted the shameless chit pertly, clinging the more fervently to his arm and gazing up at him with youthful adoration in her large prominent eyes, so like her mother's.

Leonora suddenly felt sorry for the girl. She knew instinctively that Kelsey had no feeling whatsoever for her. But that did not stop Flavia from pining after him. Any more than the knowledge of the shallowness of his attentions to her had prevented her from falling under the spell of his attraction.

'Do not depend upon it,' warned his lordship. He shook his head in admonition. 'You must not count on any such thing, my dear. As Miss Vincent will tell you,' he added lightly, his charming smile, intended to placate Flavia, causing Leonora to grind her teeth, 'I have no morals and no shame. In any case, to wed under such circumstances would scarcely secure a promise of future felicity, now would it?'

'You'd have my fortune,' sulked the child, glaring even more fiercely at Leonora. 'I won't marry anyone else.'

Kelsey studied her keenly, suddenly intent. 'Are your parents bringing pressure to bear on you, Lady Flavia?'

Colour flooded her round cheeks. For a moment she looked extremely young and vulnerable. 'They want me to accept Lord Dyke,' she said, naming a gentleman of mature years who had shown an interest in Leonora and her fortune before Lady Flavia's arrival on the scene. 'I hate him.'

'I do not blame you,' said Kelsey. 'He may be heir to a dukedom, but do your parents know that he is an acknowledged profligate and fortune hunter?'

'They say it doesn't matter because the gossip is probably exaggerated, they have plenty of money, and I should be a duchess one day,' said Flavia rebelliously. 'I would rather be your marchioness.

'I fear,' he responded quietly and, Leonora believed, for once absolutely sincerely, 'that that would be quite impossible.'

'Why?' demanded Flavia.

Kelsey sighed, liking the conversation no more than herself, thought Leonora.

'This is scarcely the time or the place to discuss such matters, Lady Flavia, but since you ask, it is because I am at present in no position to marry anyone,' said Kelsey austerely. 'And neither do I wish to, even if I were. My dear, you must simply keep on refusing your parents' suggestion.'

He removed Flavia's hand from his arm to hold it in his as he said, 'I will, if you like, inform them that Lord Dyke's reputation is not exaggerated. But do not attempt to trap me or any other gentleman into matrimony, Lady Flavia. It will not serve, at least it will not as far as I am concerned, and would only cause you and your parents great unhappiness.'

Leonora's anger had died under the assault of far more intense emotions. She wanted to move away, for she found being privy to such an embarrassing exchange, let alone being drawn into the argument without herself saying a word, acutely distressing. But when she made a move to remove her hand Kelsey pressed it against his side so that, without a struggle, she could not escape.

Why did he wish her to remain? she wondered unhappily. As a bastion against Flavia, who had now retreated, the tears already gathering in her eyes? And had he escorted her this evening because some of the other women with whom he had been flirting over the last few weeks were taking him too seriously and he knew he was safe with her?

He must believe that, for she had declared her aversion to the way he made his living and to his morals often enough. He had even quoted her on the subject, for his own purposes. It must be quite plain to him that she would never consider marrying him, however compromised. She would not, like Flavia, seek to force him into distasteful wedlock.

He felt safe with her. For some obscure reason this conclusion did not please her. None of the conclusions she had come to that evening did. But, maddeningly, she still revelled in being with him and would accept his escort again were he to offer it. And she remained tellingly elated at the prospect of his hosting with her her forthcoming reception.

She was an idiotic fool, for however safe he might feel with her, she felt far from safe with him! But if she had to pay later for her idiocy she would count the cost well spent. For on that evening, from that moment on, she was the exclusive focus of his attention. She basked in it and refused to contemplate the reason or the consequences.

Not until they were in the carriage returning to Morris House did he take up the matter of her marriage again.

'You were going to explain to me the attributes you desire in the man you will choose as your husband, Leonora.'

His voice, quiet, bland, almost imperceptibly slurred, came to her from the darkness of the other corner of the coach. There was about a foot of space between them on the seat and he had made no attempt to move nearer, although they had spent much of the evening in far closer contact. She had been dreading—dreading?—that he would take advantage of their isolation in such a confined space to attempt to kiss her.

Yes, dreading, because she must never let him know how much her body ached to be held securely in his arms, how her lips longed for the touch of his.

What kind of a man did she wish to marry? he asked. A man just like him except for the way he made his living. And flirted with other women. And, like tonight, sometimes drank rather too much. Not as much as his contemporaries, but enough to make her suspect that he was slightly foxed.

She had remained silent too long. He shifted slightly, impatiently. 'Leonora?'

'A mature gentleman,' she said at length, her voice tight because her throat felt constricted. 'One with whom I can converse easily and find companionship. A man of worthy character with a country estate of reasonable size.'

She fell silent. A short pause ensued.

Then, 'I am surprised at you, Leonora.' The light tone teased now. 'How dull that sounds! And no mention of love? A country estate is more important? Come, surely you are not too advanced in years as to have given up the hope of finding love?'

Not too old at all. But she had fallen in love with the wrong man. A man it would be impossible for her to wed.

'Love,' she replied austerely, 'is not necessary to a successful marriage. I am looking for companionship, security, and a father for my children. If love is present as well, then I should count it a blessing. But I am no longer so young as to be impractical. I do not expect it.'

The chariot drew up before the back entrance to Morris House. The Club was still open, men were still gambling on the first floor. Her resolution firmed. Blaise made no comment until they were descending the area steps to the back door.

'I trust,' he said then, a tightness in his voice that had not been there earlier, 'that you will find the man you are looking for, Leonora.'

No more was said until they parted as usual on the landing. Then Blaise, leaning a hand against the wall, Leonora suspected to steady himself, asked, 'Are you engaged tomorrow after breakfast?'

Leonora looked at him in the light of the candle she carried. He was smiling, though she could not see the expression in his shadowed eyes. She was close enough to smell the wine on his breath except that she, too, had drunk several glasses. Wine, she thought inconsequentially, was like onions. If you'd both partaken you could not detect the odour on the other's breath.

She said, 'No, but there is still much to do for the reception. Why?'

'It promises to be a fine day and you have been indoors working too hard. Some time off will refresh you. I therefore propose to take you out in my curricle. You have not yet explored the countryside around Bath, I collect?'

Leonora's breath caught. 'No.'

'And you must like the country, since you wish to live in it. So I shall oblige you by introducing you to the delights of the area. Will you come?'

'Thank you, Blaise.' His name came more readily to her lips now. Perhaps it was the wine speaking for both of them. Leonora clutched the candlestick with both hands to stop it trembling. The flame still wavered, but that could be accounted the fault of the draught. 'I should enjoy that above everything.'

'Capital. I shall call for you at noon. Unless the weather turns foul, of course. But I trust and believe it will remain fine.'

Leonora dressed warmly for the outing next day for March was, as was only to be expected, going out like a lion. Wind roared round the chimney pots and Juliette tied Leonora's bonnet on with a large veil that completely obscured her face. This suited Leonora, for she had no wish for Blaise to read her expression and perhaps recognise in it the consciousness his near proximity was bound to bring.

She had accepted the invitation whilst in her cups and had woken this morning inclined to regret it. But the weasely fear of what might happen had quickly given place to an anticipation of pleasure she could not deny. To escape the confines of the town for once!

He knocked on her door exactly on time. He too was warmly wrapped in a many-caped greatcoat, but had changed his tall beaver for a much shorter one with a curly brim.

She was ready. When he saw her veil, one corner of his mouth tipped up in a wry smile. 'A pity about the wind,' he said, patting his own hat, 'but it should keep the rain off. You are ready to risk a shower, I collect?'

'Oh, yes. The sun is brilliant, it is a gorgeous day. The trees are beginning to bud and I so long to see the countryside.'

Beneath the veil Leonora's cheeks were pink. But she

had herself well in hand, having firmly rehearsed in her mind all the rules as to the correct behaviour of a young lady about to be escorted out by a gentleman of her acquaintance, rules that she had been taught and had tried to instill into the minds of her charges.

A mature woman, she knew her own mind and was well able to deal with any advances Blaise Dancer might attempt to make. She had done so before. And she desired this outing into the country with a passion she could scarcely credit.

Life in a town could seem suffocating. Especially, she supposed, in a town where one could not escape the curious, critical eyes and gossiping tongues of the *ton*.

She felt restricted, not only in the air she breathed but in her movements, too. She had overcome the original scandal over her choice of abode, thanks largely to the gracious patronage of the Duchess, but should she dare to take one more step out of line the gossip would be cruel. She had concluded that an unescorted drive into the country with Lord Kelsey was a pleasure worth the risk.

His curricle waited, with a small groom in the livery stable's uniform holding the heads of the pair of matched bays drawing it. Kelsey was forced to keep his carriage and horses in livery, for there was nowhere to stable so much as a donkey at Morris House.

It was not, she noted, an extravagant outfit but the curricle was smart and well upholstered and the animals, if not prime cattle, were good-looking creatures. He handed her up into the swaying vehicle before going round to take his own seat.

He gathered the reins in his capable, gloved hands and took the whip from its slot.

'Let 'em go and jump aboard,' he instructed the boy,

and Leonora realised that the stable lad was to accompany
them. She was grateful. His presence would stifle gossip
and set her own mind at rest. She could forget everything
except enjoyment of the ride, for his lordship plainly had
no nefarious intentions.

Blaise allowed the boy time to mount the step behind
before giving his team the office to start. He did not
speak as he negotiated his way through the narrow streets
towards Pulteney Bridge.

Leonora had, of course, crossed Pulteney Bridge on
foot and walked as far as Laura Place, but had never
ventured beyond. The sheer cavernous length of Great
Pulteney Street, lined on each side by high, unbroken
terraces of new buildings, had disinclined her from
exploring further.

Sitting high in the curricle, however, the road did not
seem so long and she was surprised when, instead of
carrying straight on, Blaise turned off at Sidney Gardens,
leaving the chief of the traffic behind. He smartened up
the pace and the finely bred horses, straining at their bits,
enjoyed a brisk trot until they met a hill, when they
dropped back to a walk.

'When we get to a straight, level stretch of road on
the Downs I'll let them gallop,' Blaise said once the hill
had been safely negotiated. 'They need the exercise.'

'It's heavenly,' said Leonora, holding onto the swaying
carriage, her eyes sparkling behind the veil.

'I thought you might enjoy it,' remarked Blaise,
appearing thoroughly content himself.

He was no stranger to horses and he handled the ribbons with careless expertise. His team responded
instantly to his slightest command. Leonora had no fears

for her safety as the horses rose eagerly into an exhilarating canter.

Although the curricle was well sprung, she was bounced about on the seat and silently gave thanks that it was cushioned. But even had it not been she would not have complained. The speed, the fresh air, the sense of freedom and, she had to admit, Blaise's company, made any discomfort worth while.

Blaise had stuck his hat down firmly on his head and so far had kept it in place, though Leonora, glad of the veil swathing her bonnet, wondered how long that would last. The wind came in gusts and at one point she thought its strength might overturn the curricle, which was not the most stable kind of vehicle, but Blaise simply laughed, the reckless gleam in his eyes entirely matching her mood of wild delight. He drove so skilfully; how could she not trust his judgment?

This Blaise Dancer was a revelation to her. The languid air he so often adopted had quite deserted him. His concentration was sharp, his reactions fast. She supposed he was behaving as he might have done as a young man living on his father's estates, before penury had forced him to make his own living.

Like her, he had been country bred. Perhaps he secretly pined for the fresh air and open spaces as much as she did. Such a thought had never occurred to her before. He seemed so very much a part of Bath Society.

When they reached the straight Blaise had mentioned, he put his team into a gallop. The wind obligingly dropped for a few moments, the horses stretched their necks and the outfit fairly flew along. When the wind unexpectedly gusted again it rocked the carriage quite perilously and sent Blaise's hat hurtling away over the turf.

He said something Leonora could not quite catch as he brought the team under control and the curricle righted itself. By the expression on his face she judged it might be just as well. As soon as he could, he brought the outfit to a standstill.

'Go back and see if you can find my hat, Tom,' he instructed the lad. 'I can hold the horses.' Since they were blown he could do so quite easily, still sitting in his seat. 'I'm sorry if that frightened you,' he apologised, turning to Leonora. But she judged it was the loss of his hat that had made him swear, for his eyes fairly sparkled with with unholy joy.

'It was thrilling!' cried Leonora, the echo of excitement still in her voice. 'How excellently you drive, Blaise! I must congratulate you on keeping the rig upright—I half-expected to be thrown into the ditch!'

He laughed, a great outflow of released tension and triumph. 'Thank you, Miss Vincent! I shall treasure your approval, ma'am!'

Leonora laughed too. 'And so you should, my lord! But look at the view! Is it not magnificent? Thank you so much for bringing me up here, Blaise,' she added more soberly. 'I have not enjoyed myself so much for many a year!'

'You did not drive out at Thornestone Park?'

'Not far. There was no need to go far. I used to take my pupils round the estate and into the village in a pony trap.'

'So you can drive?'

'Only the pony. It was very fat and lazy.'

He chuckled. 'But you learned to ride?'

'I was taught as a child, and rode a great deal until

my father was forced to sell his cattle. I have not been on the back of a horse this ten years.'

'You will not have forgotten,' said Blaise, answering the wistful note which had unconsciously entered her voice. 'You could take it up again.'

Leonora could not admit that she could ill afford to keep a horse without revealing the slenderness of her fortune.

So, 'I shall consider it,' she prevaricated. 'Perhaps I could hire a mount occasionally.'

'There are plenty of bridle paths to explore. I hire a hack when I wish to ride on horseback. We must arrange to bring a couple of horses up here one day.'

'That would be delightful.' She would have to purchase a riding costume. 'When I decided to move to Bath I did not realise just how much I would miss the country.'

'Do you really miss it? I thought you were enjoying town life and society.'

'Up to a point,' conceded Leonora. 'I love Morris House, but I should hate to be obliged to live permanently in a town. Look at the smoke haze hanging over Bath even today, despite the wind.'

'So. . .' He hesitated. 'Whatever else happens, you will not always wish to live in Morris House?'

'Not all the time.' She turned her head sharply to look at him. 'But that does not mean that I will tolerate the Vitus Club operating on the premises for a moment longer than I can help.'

'The Club seems to be our main point of disagreement,' he said, somewhat ruefully, she thought. 'You really do object to gentlemen having a special place where they can meet together, socialise, relax or gamble as they choose, don't you?'

'It's the gambling mostly,' said Leonora. 'I know what suffering excessive gambling can cause. And the Club provides them with every opportunity to do it to excess.'

'A man must be allowed the freedom to go to hell if he chooses. No one can be coerced into prudence or rectitude, Leonora. Only the weak succumb.'

Leonora's throat had gone dry. 'We are taught to succour the weak,' she murmured.

Blaise's gloved hand covered both of hers, where they lay clasped in her lap. 'I am sorry, my dear, that we are so at odds over this. Let us forget it for this afternoon.'

Leonora nodded, smiled. She did not wish to quarrel with Blaise and spoil the outing. 'Where are we?' she asked.

'We are in the parish of Widcombe. The view of Bath is excellent from here. Look, there is the river and you can just see Pulteney Bridge.'

He leaned across her, one arm along the back of the seat, pointing with his whip. The horses, on a slack rein, were contentedly cropping the meagre grass of the verge.

Once again her breath seemed caught in her lungs. She could feel his, warm on her cheek. She was prodigiously glad of the concealing veil because she knew that her agitation showed on her face. Then he brought his face closer still, his eyes narrowed in his determination to penetrate the gauze of her veil.

'Leonora,' he murmured and, before she could take any evasive action, his lips found hers in a brief kiss.

The veil was between them, of course, but seemed hardly to interfere with the seductive warmth of his caress. His eyes sought hers behind the fine, protective material and what he saw there seemed to satisfy him. He smiled. 'There,' he said, that wicked, irresistible look in his eyes, the look which promised impossible delight. 'That was not so terrible, was it?'

'My lord,' said Leonora shakily, thoroughly ashamed of the quiver in her voice, 'you forget yourself. What must the groom be thinking? I shall be ruined if he chooses to report what he has seen!'

He withdrew his arm, looking behind as he did so. 'Tom saw nothing. He has recovered my hat, I see, but is still some distance off, dawdling along gazing all about him. He is not the slightest bit interested in us, only in enjoying his moments of freedom.'

Leonora glanced over her shoulder. He was right. The lad was strolling along, Blaise's hat under one arm, swinging a stick in the other and staring at something in the ditch which he poked at. Then he moved his gaze to the sky, where high clouds were scudding before the wind and a couple of large birds swooped. He was looking all about him and, as he drew nearer, Leonora heard his tuneful whistle. He was indeed enjoying himself and in no hurry to reach the curricle.

'I hope you are right,' she said stiffly. 'Though he should be attending more diligently to his duties.'

'I, for one, shall not tell him off,' grinned Blaise, not at all abashed.

Leonora relaxed. The kiss had been disturbing but had done no lasting harm. It had not been the first kiss she had ever received, but it had certainly been the most pleasing and exciting. Were she honest with herself, Blaise had only done what she had been longing for him to do. She thought he would probably try to kiss her again if he saw the opportunity.

She could guess his ultimate intention. He had no wish to wed. If he offered her anything it would be a *carte blanche*. Which she would, with appropriate indignation, refuse.

But she would not repulse him meanwhile. However upsetting to her emotions, she longed for him to kiss her again. To be held in his arms, for however short a period, would be bliss.

This decision she excused by telling herself that, since she would now be anticipating his amorous advances, she would be in a position to react with the proper degree of encouragement and restraint and to deflect his more immoral intentions. After all, she might never again be granted the opportunity to welcome the kisses of a man who so greatly attracted her.

Blaise had turned from her to accept the return of his hat, slightly dented and with a splodge of mud on its brim. He knocked out the dent and brushed the mud off as best he could, remarking that Lawrence, his man, would be obliged to clean it and would no doubt grumble at him for allowing it to be damaged.

Leonora laughed, glad to turn to a less fraught subject. 'Juliette has taken to telling me off if I damage a gown,' she remarked lightly. 'But you may blame the wind.'

'I shall,' he returned, placing the beaver firmly on his head once again. The boy was lifting the horses' heads, encouraging them to abandon the enticing grass. Blaise gathered the reins and let them feel their bits. 'Mount up, Tom.'

The remainder of the drive passed for Leonora in a daze of pleasure. He drove slowly along narrow, rutted lanes, taking her on a circular tour of the downs before joining a wider, more used road which led them back to Bath, via North Parade Road, at which point they were virtually home.

He deposited her at the back of Morris House, apologising for the need to abandon her there.

'I feel I must return the outfit to the stables myself,' he explained in a low voice, for Tom was holding the horses's heads while he escorted her to the gate at the top of the area steps and he did not wish the lad to hear. 'I do not quite trust Tom to take them back safely. But with your permission I shall call later, after dinner, perhaps, to make certain that you have taken no chill or suffered other unfortunate consequences from the outing.'

'Indeed, Blaise,' said Leonora giving him her hand to bow over, 'there can be no possible need, but I shall of course be pleased to receive you and to thank you again for a delightful afternoon.'

'It is I who should thank you, Leonora. I cannot remember when I have enjoyed a drive in more agreeable company.'

The blood heated her cheeks. Thank God her veil was still in place! 'Fustian, sir!' she chided. 'You, who may have the pick of all the most desirable females in Bath? You are bamming me, Blaise!'

'And you, my dear, have no idea how to gracefully accept a genuine compliment, I collect.' His eyes danced. 'That must be one lesson you entirely failed to teach your pupils.'

She replied in a light, bantering tone to match his. 'I was not,' she confessed, 'a very good governess, I fear.'

'When you arrived, I mistook you for a dragon,' he teased.

'As I took you for a rake.'

'And have you changed your mind, as I have mine?'

'Only partly,' she returned pertly. Then went on more

seriously, 'You possess all the qualifications, my lord.
Your conquests are legion, you gamble and drink, though
I must confess I have never seen you more than
slightly foxed.'

'Well, that's a mercy! But you must admit that my
reputation remains unsullied, my dear.'

His tone was still light but something in it made
Leonora sorry to have introduced a sour note at the end
of an otherwise amicable afternoon. She laughed.

'Much to my surprise, it does. I admit that I am somewhat prejudiced by your occupation of this house. Do
not mind me, Blaise. I admit to sometimes being a
grumpy old dragon. And I also admit to changing my
mind considerably about you. Now go and put your
horses away and then join us for dinner, why not? Tell
André what you wish to eat. Will you do that?'

'I accept your invitation with profound pleasure,
Leonora. Until later, my dear.'

Chapter Eleven

When, later, he joined them for dinner, Leonora feared that an awkward atmosphere might prevail. In fact, due largely to Lord Kelsey's easy manners, a pleasant intimacy developed between them, particularly when they retired to her parlour to drink tea and discuss their final plans for the reception.

It was, Leonora realised, the first time she had entertained anyone for longer than twenty or thirty minutes on her own territory, and the fact that it was Kelsey caused her a certain amount of inner confusion.

Clarissa was present, as was only correct, and during the next couple of days of frantic preparation she never once found herself alone with him. So Blaise had no easy opportunity to attempt the kiss she so desired and did not appear anxious to manufacture one. Yet, when their eyes met, she knew he was simply biding his time.

Her inner tension, already strung tight by the prospect of entertaining on such a grand scale, threatened to reach breaking point. But, somehow, she controlled her nerves and presented her normal calm front to the world.

The tension was still there, however, and she prayed

that something would happen soon to relieve it. Otherwise the fine thread of her control might snap and she'd do something stupid—like throw herself into Kelsey's arms regardless of who was looking!

Blaise was an excellent organiser. She should have realised his ability before, given the the way his Club was run. She herself was no mean operator and Clarissa had been used to running many of her father's parish events. Digby Sinclair possessed talents in that line too, or he would not have lasted as Blaise's manager. And, although they had arguments over minor matters, the four of them did not seriously fall out once during the harassing business of planning, directing servants and dealing with tradesmen.

Everything down to the very last detail was arranged so that, when the day of the reception arrived, she had nothing left to do but to go down, once the Club had closed its doors, to oversee the arrangement of the masses of flowers imported for the occasion, before dressing herself.

After a light meal at noon she therefore shed her gown, dismissed Juliette, took a deep breath, lay on her bed and tried to relax.

Exhaustion swept over her. The reviving trip into the country seemed an age past. Yet it was only three days since she had laughed in exhilaration in the face of the wind, and been kissed.

Reliving that excursion in every delightful detail, she dropped into a deep sleep that allowed no room for dreams. Except that, on the brink of stirring, Blaise's face appeared in her mind, so that he was the subject of her first waking thought.

His irreverent smile and questing eyes had a habit of haunting her. How could she ever have thought him disagreeable? Yet other memories, of his disparaging expression when first they met, of his distaste of her ownership of the property and, more particularly, her presence on the premises, beset her too.

He *had* been disagreeable at first. He had seemed ruthless, an awkward, impossible tenant with whom she must deal. She, she supposed, had appeared prudish and power-crazed, threatening him with eviction and, from his point of view, possible financial ruin.

Yet even then the underlying nature of the man, his fairmindedness, the humour with which he normally met life's challenges, had been evident. She had come to like him despite herself and, what was even more surprising, to rely on his judgment. Then to desire him. And, she feared, to love him.

But despite all his endearing and efficient traits, Blaise was still responsible, however much he denied it, for encouraging his members to squander their fortunes at his gaming tables. She could not forgive him that. She must never forget it, either.

Juliette came in to wake her and she sat up sharply. She felt eager, refreshed, ready to meet the demands of the evening.

On this special day the Club would close its doors at five o'clock so that the rooms could be cleaned, the furniture rearranged and the place made fit to receive the guests.

André had prepared a mouthwatering array of cold dishes, to be stored in the cellar, the coolest place in the house, until wanted. The food, which Leonora was convinced would surpass any offered by other hostesses in Bath that Season, would be brought up at nine. André and his assistants meanwhile would be busy heating up the soup, baking hot pies, pasties and biscuits, and preparing the steaming bowls of punch.

She donned a simple house gown and shot downstairs to play her part in the last-minute preparations and returned an hour later, happy that everything had been arranged to her satisfaction.

As Juliette put the finishing touches to her toilette, Leonora surveyed her bedroom, which was to be used as the ladies' retiring room. An array of mirrors, scent bottles, combs, even needles, thread and scissors, had been set out ready. There was water in the pitcher and soap and towels on the washstand. Bowls of potpourri stood about the room, filling the air with their delicate perfume.

Juliette stood back to scrutinise her handiwork and, satisfied, held a mirror so that Leonora could inspect the back of her head.

'You look wonderful, Miss Vincent,' she said admiringly. 'Madame Fleur was positively inspired when she designed that gown.'

'Yes,' agreed Leonora, quailing inwardly, for she had not yet received the modiste's account and feared it would be sky high. It was surprising how fast her modest inheritance was dwindling.

But the summer would see a lessening of the social life of Bath. She could drop into obscurity and rally her resources ready for the autumn—for she was determined to carry out her original plan, to live in style for a full Season, which meant remaining in Bath Society until the following March at least. She had, as a new and accepted mover in first circles, so far only experienced the latter part of the Bath Season.

However much Madame Fleur charged, she could not begrudge the money spent on this gown. Low-necked, showing the swell of her breasts whilst preserving her modesty, with small puffed sleeves and the newly fashionable lower waistline, it flowed from the ribbon-defined waist in shimmering turquoise folds of a different, slightly darker shade than that of her sumptuous ball dress, which she intended to wear for the first time to the Duchess's ball.

She stood, and the material of her gown shimmered because the silk weave was shot with silver threads, which changed the colour as she moved. Madame Fleur had shunned lace and frills as decoration and instead had worked exquisite embroidery and appliqué to finish the neckline, using a multi-coloured flower design of great intricacy and beauty. A narrow panel of the same work ran down from the waistline, broadening out before it split to show an ivory underskirt and trailed back to decorate the hem of the not-insignificant train.

Madame's friend the milliner had fashioned a small headdress to match. She twirled in front of the mirror and gave a happy, excited laugh. She appeared to be wreathed in flowers.

Juliette buttoned up Leonora's long silk gloves, then she picked up her fan and a small reticule and waited for Juliette to drape a fringed scarf of fine silver and ivory gauze across her back and round her elbows so that the ends fell in shimmering wisps. The finishing touch.

She turned from the mirror. 'Thank you, Juliette. As ever, you have worked a miracle. Remember, refreshments will be served to the maids at supper time,' she went on, still not believing that she had no cause to fuss. 'If they need anything before then—'

'I shall send Dolly to fetch it,' put in Juliette quickly. 'Do not concern yourself, ma'am. I shall see that both the ladies and their servants are happy, and manage quite well with Dolly's help.'

'I know you will,' Leonora admitted with a grimace. 'I am sorry, Juliette, I know how capable you are.' She drew a breath. 'I suppose Miss Clarissa must be ready by now. Go and see, will you? If she is not, I shall go down without her.'

Juliette returned almost immediately.

'Miss Worth is experiencing some difficulty with her hair, madam. She asks if I may be allowed to assist her?'

'Of course, if you would not mind, Juliette. I shall expect her to follow shortly.'

So it was alone that Leonora descended the stairs, some fifteen minutes before the first guests were expected to arrive.

She reached the landing below and experienced a renewed shock of pleasure. The normally opulent but masculine surroundings of the Club had been transformed, had become a floral bower. Blaise had engaged to supply the flowers, saying that several of his members had flourishing hot houses full of pot plants and blooms which he could plunder at minimum cost.

The pot plants could all be returned. Leonora had arranged the cut flowers herself only an hour or so ago, having a gift in that direction. They would last in her rooms upstairs for several days, afterwards.

Both Dining and Reading Rooms were similarly decked with plants and flowers, though the Card Room was less lavishly adorned. She inspected them all in turn,

acknowledging the servants still swarming about execut-
ing last-minute tasks. Digby Sinclair was in the Reading
Room, directing matters there, but Blaise had yet to
come up.

The entrance hall had also benefited from her talent
for flower arranging. No one would be able to accuse
her of parsimony in the matter of floral decoration, she
thought with satisfaction. The first impression was all
important, and she had decorated the entrance hall lavishly. Ivy and other climbers trailed from pots and urns
to wreath the banisters of the stairs, leading her guests
on and up.

Every candle in every chandelier was alight throughout
the place, the cut glass scintillating. The silver wall
sconces flickered and gleamed in their candles' flames.

She sighed her satisfaction. She would not be ashamed
for the Duchess of Broadshire to enter here.

His sitting-room door was ajar. She trod across and,
for the first time in days, found Blaise alone. Everyone
else was upstairs, apart from a youthful footman already
stationed at the front door ready to open it to the first
arrivals.

Blaise was immaculately dressed and stood, one foot
on the fender, looking pensively into the fire, a glass of
what she supposed was brandy in his hand. As she entered
he looked up, straightened, and tipped the contents of
his glass down his throat.

There was scarcely need for greeting; they had parted
only an hour or so since.

'So,' said Leonora brightly, 'everything seems to
be ready.'

He moved across and pushed the door to without quite
closing it. 'You look exquisite,' he said.

She made a deep curtsy in acknowledgement of the compliment. 'Thank you, my lord!'

'So damned exquisite that I cannot help myself,' he said, stepping near and taking her chin in his strong, cool fingers.

So this was the moment. Leonora met his eyes shyly but boldly. What he read in them she could not tell, but in his burned a flame she had not expected and knew could not be assuaged under the present circumstances.

'Blaise,' she murmured.

'My dear.'

His breath was warm, perfumed by the brandy. Her lips parted of their own accord as his mouth came down.

Its touch was light, persuasive, tormenting, plucking at her lips but not lingering. She returned the kisses, delighting in the short, sensual contacts, the sudden withdrawals.

His fingers still held her chin. His other hand rested lightly on her waist, where it would not harm her gown. He had not taken her in his arms and her hands were encumbered by the things she carried. The most she could do was to lightly hold his upper arms.

This was not the moment for deep passion, passion which would disarrange costume and coiffure. She had known it, and perhaps that was why she had ventured into his room. Despite her yearning, the unpredictable responses of her body, for her the wooing must be slow. She had not been made or brought up in a way that enabled her instincts to overcome her reason all in a moment. Otherwise she would not have run from him in the Reading Room.

She had come a long way since then, but not quite far enough to abandon herself to the full enjoyment of physical love without taking some lessons first. With the footman outside the door and guests expected at any moment, nothing too demanding could happen.

His hand shifted to cup her cheek. For a moment, both breathing deeply, they gazed into each other's eyes. His shone black as pitch in the shadowy light but a small smile curved his mouth.

Those finely chiselled lips, she thought, her gaze wavering down from the intensity of his, were the source of her enervating weakness, of the delightful languor inhabiting her body. Those lips and the touch of his long fingers stroking her cheek. A strange pain had started somewhere in her abdomen. A pleasurable pain. How could a pain be pleasurable?

The hand at her waist shifted, rose to cup the other side of her face. She noticed with some astonishment that his fingers trembled slightly. He bent his head and kissed her again, a longer caress which she returned. Their lips clung, but he did not attempt to deepen the embrace.

'You are no longer outraged?' he murmured, the intensity of his dark gaze turned to wicked teasing.

Commanding all her self-control, she tapped his arm with the fan still in her hand, and extricated herself from his hold.

'Familiarity,' she responded, equally teasing, 'breeds contempt. Or so I am informed.'

'Ah. So that was contempt.' He trailed his fingers down from her chin to the cleft between her breasts. 'Then I look forward to sampling your adoration, my love.'

Leonora's knees needed stays. The pain in her stomach had turned into a quivering pulse of ecstatic feeling and she knew that her body had opened to receive him. It was not shame that swept over her in a wave of heat but something much more primitive. She was quite incapable of speech.

He, damn him, seemed unmoved. Yet now that she could see his grey eyes properly they shone with that sultry flame she had glimpsed once before. He could not quite control his responses, for his fingers still trembled.

He said, 'I hear carriage wheels. Our guests are arriving.'

His voice had thickened. What she did not know was that his last caress and the evident response it had incited had brought Blaise near to losing his control. She had not looked down, thank God, and their bodies had not been close. He'd been a damned idiot to fool around at such a moment.

'We should go up,' he said. 'Will you go first?'

He dared not offer her his arm. The bulge in his small-clothes was rapidly diminishing and, if he did not touch her again, would be gone by the time they reached the upper landing.

But he had to quell his body's reactions when, for one unguarded moment, he allowed his imagination to dwell on the pleasures inherent in the imminent conquest of Leonora Vincent.

They stood to receive their guests, at first each very conscious of the other's nearness. Quite soon, though, the concentration needed to efficiently host the reception took all their attention.

Blaise proved himself the consummate host and Leonora, while inexperienced, had been born and bred to the duty.

From the start, the evening was a success, but the success was confirmed when, half an hour before supper was due to be served, the Duchess of Broadshire, escorted by her grandson, was announced.

Leonora, who had abandoned her station at the door long since—as had Kelsey—rushed to greet them. Kelsey quickly joined her, emerging from the Card Room, where he had gone to make certain that those guests amusing themselves there were happy.

Leonora made a deep curtsy and Blaise an elaborate leg.

'My dears!' said the Duchess graciously, her small form glittering with sequins and jewels, a rather old-fashioned, high-plumed headdress upon her greying head, 'How nice to be here!' She glanced about her with sharp-eyed appreciation. 'So this is where the gentlemen gather! What a splendid occasion this is! Grath, go and find me a lemonade, for I declare I am quite dying of thirst!'

'Allow me—' began Kelsey, only to be waved to silence.

'Grath will go.'

As the colourful, plump figure of her grandson disappeared into the throng, the Duchess made a gesture of helpless regret.

'My apologies, my dears, but I could not avoid it,' she said brusquely.

Both Leonora and Blaise gazed at her enquiringly.

'Could not avoid what, ma'am?' asked Blaise.

'The Regent. Just arrived in Bath. Called on me, and when I told him I had engaged to come here this evenin' he insisted on comin' too. He'll be here in a matter of minutes. I rushed ahead to warn you.'

'His—His Royal Highness?' gasped Leonora.

'Thank you for your warning, your grace,' said Kelsey, quite self-possessed. 'It is some years since I had the pleasure of being presented at St James's, but the Regent visits Bath occasionally and when here he uses the Club, as a guest. He will not be on strange ground.'

'No, he said he'd been to the Club, knew you well. Was intrigued by the idea of Miss Vincent's holding a reception here, though. Ah, this'll be him. I'll leave you to cope,' said the Duchess with an impish grin Leonora could scarcely believe.

'Blaise—' she began, her voice unaccountably hoarse.

'Do not concern yourself, my dear,' said Blaise soothingly. 'He will not remain long. I'll look after him.'

'But I've never. . .'

'Been presented? Now is your chance, my dear Miss Vincent! And so much less expensive and worrying than having to attend St James's!'

'I'm not. . .' She looked down at herself deprecatingly.

'Dressed for it? Of course you are,' said Blaise bracingly. 'You look superb, and you know it! Pretend you've known him for years, as you would have done had you not been deprived of your London Season.'

A commotion down in the hall made him cock his head, listening. 'Here he is. Bear up, my love!'

That was the second time he'd called her his love that evening. Leonora only wished it were true, and not just a figure of speech. All the same, the easy way he treated her and took this terrifying visit in his stride certainly eased her own nerves.

The heavy tread of many feet on the stairs made Leonora realise that the Regent had not arrived alone. A bunch of some half-dozen splendidly attired gentlemen

approached across the landing, most dressed in the first
stare of fashion, one or two in sober black, the mode of
dress Beau Brummell had made fashionable.

The massive figure leading them, with its alarmingly
protuberant belly, could be mistaken for no other than
the Prince. He was, she thought, almost as grotesque as
the cartoons in the broadsheets suggested. Yet when he
came near and she curtsied deeply before him, his smile
was quite engaging.

Blaise made his bow. Then, as though from a distance
because her mind was in such a whirl, she heard him
say, 'Sir, may I present your hostess, Miss Vincent? She
is niece to the present Earl of Chelstoke. The previous
earl was, of course, her grandfather.'

The Royal hand was graciously extended. Leonora,
still sunk in her curtsy, kissed the ring of state. Still
graciously, the Regent lifted her to her feet.

'Pleasure, m'dear,' he said, and Leonora looked into
a multi-chinned, dissipated face which nevertheless held
considerable charm. But she shuddered to think of his
poor wife and mistresses, who had to sleep with him.

Her mind in focus again, she realised the trend of her
thoughts and colour stained her cheeks. A new awareness
of the lithe, powerful body of Kelsey, who was naming
the Prince's companions, all of whom bowed to their
hostess and bent over her hand, overwhelmed her.

'Generous of Kelsey to let you use his rooms,'
observed the Prince conversationally, 'demned if it ain't.
What made you offer?' he demanded of Kelsey.

Blaise gave his easy, languid smile. 'Miss Vincent is
my landlord, sir. By holding the lease of these rooms I
have prevented her from using them herself and so she

could not easily offer return hospitality. I thought it only fair.'

'Decent of you, Kelsey, 'deed it is. Pity the Club is closed, though. Was lookin' forward to some gamin' meself.'

'There is whist in the Card Room, sir, should you wish—'

'Pah! Females playin' in there, I'll wager?' At Blaise's nod, 'Thought so. Low stakes.' He flapped a bejewelled hand dismissively. 'Is supper served yet?'

'At any moment, sir. André has prepared it.'

'Capital. Wish I could tempt him from you, m'boy. He's an artist with food.'

Blaise merely smiled. André had his own reasons for remaining with Lord Kelsey, reasons which neither man would wish to bruit abroad. Kelsey had literally fallen over André, at that time a despairing foreigner in a strange country. André had followed his aristocratic master to England, a master who had been thoughtless enough to abandon him there by dying. Blaise had picked him up from a London gutter, cured him of his addiction to drink, employed him in his own kitchen at Longvale Park, the Kelsey estate, and brought him to Bath with him.

Grath, having seen his grandmother comfortably settled with her lemonade, came up as they moved from the door and was immediately absorbed into the Regent's set. They all went through to the Dining Room, where supper was just being served.

Blaise, his hand in the small of her back, guided Leonora along with them.

The Regent knew most of the other guests, who all bowed or curtsied as he passed, acknowledging them with a wave of the hand or a brief greeting. His object was to reach the tables where the food was spread. His purpose achieved, one of his entourage filled a plate at his direction and acquired a brimming glass of port wine.

A seat was, of course, instantly forthcoming. Clarissa saw to that, for she was overseeing the serving of supper. No one presented her to the Royal visitor, nor did she expect it. Her lack of standing in Society precluded such a distinction.

The Regent ate voraciously for some minutes, finished his wine and called for more, which he quaffed like water.

Leonora, hovering with Blaise, had, by an effort of will, conquered her earlier confusion. But, watching the Regent and tapping her fan in a different kind of agitation, she whispered, 'He has spoiled the evening.'

'On the contrary—' Blaise had his mouth disturbingly near to her ear; she could feel his warm breath on it 'you have been fortunate. His presence will establish you in the highest ranks of the *ton*.'

'You think so?' The question was rhetorical and he knew it. She spread the fan and waved it to shield her mouth. 'But the atmosphere has changed.'

'Naturally. You cannot have the person who is virtually your Sovereign attend your reception without it causing some slight constraint. But your guests are honoured, not upset, by his presence. Behave naturally, Leonora. Do not neglect the others. Circulate. I will attend His Royal Highness until he leaves.'

She nodded, reluctant to leave his side but aware of her duty. 'I pray it may be soon!'

It was. Prince George took his leave amidst bows and curtsies and the atmosphere in the rooms returned more or less to what it had been before his arrival. Except that people looked at her with new respect and, for the first time, she felt truly accepted as one of them.

This was the end towards which she had worked and planned. She must not feel discouraged because it was the presence of the gross and despised Regent that had secured it for her.

Grath it was who brought her a plate of food, which she found it impossible to eat. Cunningham brought a more welcome glass of the heady wine of Burgundy. She drank it quickly and felt herself relax.

Kelsey moved amongst the guests, talking to Alicia, Flavia, the Duchess, Flavia's mother and father. He disappeared into the Card Room but did not remain long. Digby Sinclair had been stationed in there to see that those who sat down to a hand of whist were not neglected. Servants carried supper in to players reluctant to leave their game.

By the time the last guest had departed, more or less on the stroke of midnight, Leonora was in a euphoric, if exhausted, mood. The success of the evening had indeed been assured by the unexpected arrival of the Regent.

Blaise held her arm to lead her down to his room. 'Come and relax with a nightcap,' he suggested.

'Clarissa—' murmured Leonora.

'May find her own way upstairs, I believe,' said Blaise firmly.

Leonora followed happily enough, for she wanted to talk over the evening's events with him. There were too many servants still about clearing up for her to fear being quite alone with Blaise—if, indeed, she did still fear such an eventuality. In all honesty she had to admit that she desired it. However, she was too tired tonight to expect to enjoy whatever awaited her alone with Blaise Dancer.

'The Regent will be king soon, I suppose,' she remarked. 'He is not popular, and he has no male heir.'

'Times are hard,' said Blaise. 'People resent his extravagance. The labouring classes are angry—look at all the trouble there's been over the new machines.'

'And the price of bread.'

'Quite. But even with the Corn Laws the landowners are unhappy; they have lost almost half their income because of bad harvests, and money is tight.'

'Yet they still gamble.'

'Yes. Gambling is endemic in human nature, my dear. They hope to recoup their fortunes.'

'And you are the one to profit.'

They had reached his door. Once inside, he closed it firmly behind him and remained silent until he had poured her a glass of wine and himself one of brandy.

She had seated herself by the glowing coals. As he handed her her glass, he lifted his own in salute.

'Here,' he said, 'is to profit,' and drank. 'Do you not admire my business acumen?'

She twirled her glass in her hand, gazing into its tawny depths. When she looked up she wore a serious expression.

'Yes,' she admitted. 'I do. But I deplore your moral attitude, Blaise.'

'Ah. My moral attitude.' He tipped the remainder of his drink down his throat and poured another, his back turned. 'Lawrence has the night off,' he announced to the room at large. Then he spun round. His eyes glinted with an emotion she could not define but felt certain contained anger. 'In what state are your morals, Miss Vincent? Will you spend the remainder of this auspicious night with me?'

Chapter Twelve

Leonora gazed up at him, her eyes strained wide.

How could she have been so foolish as to mention morality when she longed to be led by slow, delicious stages into the immoral consummation he had just so baldly suggested? Now he had made it quite impossible for her to do anything but protest.

'Are you offering me a *carte blanche*? she demanded aggressively. Aggression stopped her from bursting into mortifying tears.

Blaise, his temper roused by her stubborn refusal to acknowledge that the method he had chosen to recoup his fortunes was both legally and morally defensible, returned her look with a lofty glance down his aristocratic nose.

'If that is what you wish to call it.'

Curse it! Everything had gone wrong. He had planned this seduction with some care, believing her ready to be tempted into his bed. Earlier this evening he had been certain of success.

Now his plans lay in ruins. She had chosen to accuse him of unprincipled dealings and, piqued, he had thrown the question of morals back in her face. Of course she would refuse him now. The disappointment, the frustration, ripped through him like a knife.

Leonora would have risen to stalk in dignified outrage from the room if she had felt capable, but she doubted whether her knees would support her. So she sat where she was, her heart yearning after this impossible man, but knowing now that she was not ready to fling herself headlong into a dangerous and possibly ruinous affair.

'What else should I call it?' she demanded. 'I do not imagine your proposition included making me an honourable offer of marriage?'

'No, certainly not. Neither, my dear, do you wish for one.' His voice was brutally curt. 'You have made it abundantly clear that you despise me and would consider me out of the question as a husband but—' he paused only a moment before going on in a softer but infinitely challenging tone '—but I believe you want me. As I want you.'

Her eyes darkened as colour rushed into her already hot cheeks. Want. How crudely he put it. She hungered for him, ached to be part of him. She said, 'You flatter yourself, Blaise.'

'Do I?'

That conscious rush of blood had confirmed what he already believed. He had been a fool to allow his temper to deprive him of an undoubted pleasure—the first of many, he had expected.

Normally, he cared little for the opinions of others. No one else had the power to provoke him as she had. The reason, he realised with a flash of dismay, was because it mattered very much what Leonora Vincent thought of him.

Not only did he value her good opinion, she enchanted him. He wanted her so badly he was prepared to swallow his pride and anger to get her. To make the first move towards reconciliation. He reached for her hands and drew her to her feet. Before she had time to protest he had her fast in his arms.

His kiss, though not demanding, was as seductive as he could make it. He felt her instinctive resistance melt, her lips soften under his, her body sag against him and the quality of the satisfaction he experienced at her surrender came as yet another surprise. He had taken his pleasure with many women, but to feel Leonora yield against him filled him with new, untried emotions.

'You see,' he murmured on stopping to draw breath. 'My lovely Leonora, you must see what pleasure we could share.'

She had seemed lost in his embrace, but he had failed to fully overcome her resistance. Resolution returned to her eyes and her body stiffened.

'It is easy for you, Blaise,' she said, her voice not quite steady. 'You would suffer no damaging consequences from a casual liaison. But I—I have to be certain that I want you enough to make any sacrifice of reputation—any chance of pregnancy—worthwhile. You have to convince me, Blaise.'

'My dear.' Her coiffure did not matter now. He threaded his fingers through her abundant hair, spilling pins and releasing ribbons, and drew her mouth back to his. She responded, he thought, despite herself.

'I want you very much,' he murmured. 'But, my dear, you have already made it abundantly clear that you do not consider me suitable as a husband, even were I presently in a position to offer you or any other female marriage. I am not, as you well know. So there can be no question of matrimony between us—but were I free to wed, you are the woman I would choose to share my life.'

Surprisingly, he knew his words to be true. He kissed her again and Leonora was helpless to resist the lure of him. Recklessly, she kissed him back and felt her senses swim. Yet somewhere, beneath all the racking emotions tearing her apart and the exquisite pain he evoked in her body, her mind remained on guard.

'And were you not engaged in an enterprise of which I so heartily disapprove, I should probably choose you above all others to share mine,' she confessed in a voice choked with suppressed emotion.

His pulse quickened and he knew that she must be able to feel the pounding of his heart in his chest. Simply as a man, then, she would consider him as her husband. Knowing this somehow heightened his excitement, made his victory complete and the whole prospect of marriage, when it became both possible and necessary, more acceptable, were it with a woman as agreeable as Leonora.

Yet, thank God, a marriage between them was quite impossible, she had admitted as much. That left him able to pursue, with a clear conscience, the affair he had already planned. She would come to him without the tiresome commitments wedlock imposed.

He gazed steadily into her gorgeous eyes, filled now with incipient passion for him. He suppressed a groan of desire and said, 'You do me great honour, my love.'

He kissed her again, lightly this time, though it cost him a great exercise of will not to crush her to him and devour her lips. 'But if you come to me, you need not fear that I should abandon you were you in trouble. And conception can be deterred if not absolutely prevented.'

She knew it, of course. It was one of the things she had planned to arrange when at length she felt ready to abandon herself to his arms—when she had been persuaded over the hurdles of reticence, respectability—yes, of fear, too—which she knew were strewn in her path.

She wished, though, that he had not said it. That he had not reminded her of his experience in these matters. That they could have gone ahead without precautions and fear, able to accept the birth of a child, if it came, with joy and love.

That they could lie together legitimately. That marriage between them was not so impossible.

His hands slid over her body, careless now of damaging her gown. She breathed in his essence, felt his desire hard against her belly. And, again, her body opened like a flower to receive him.

Almost swooning, she moaned; she couldn't help herself. Her arms tightened about his neck and she pressed herself closer.

'Blaise,' she gasped.

'Leonora!' His urgency, suppressed, made his voice gruff. His arms tightened. 'Say you'll stay here with me tonight!'

Leonora, surfacing suddenly from the perfumed realms of unreality in which she had been floating, stiffened and pushed away him.

'No!' she cried. 'No, Blaise! I cannot! Everyone would know...and I'm not ready...not prepared...'

His hands dropped away. She saw them trembling. He was breathing heavily, grim, angry again, his colour high, his desire obvious. For a moment she feared he might try to force her, but of course he did not. Even in an extremity of thwarted passion, Blaise Dancer was first and foremost a gentleman.

He turned away, gripping the mantel, his forehead on his knuckles.

'Then you had better go,' he said thickly.

'Yes.' She swallowed. 'But, Blaise, I haven't said no absolutely.' Her voice quivered. It took resolution to go on. 'I-I do want you to. . .to make love to me. B-b-but not here.'

He turned, almost wearily, the expression on his face bleak.

'Where, then?'

'I don't know,' she admitted miserably.

They stared at each other. He took a deep breath and the intense, angry, passion-filled man confronting her disappeared, changed in an instant into the elegant, languid Lord Kelsey of Society's drawing rooms, who bestowed on her a rueful smile that turned her heart and drawled, 'Then I must think for us.'

She could only imagine the power of the will that had wrought the transformation. He reached out for her hand and she did not deny it to him. Abstractedly, he kissed the tips of her fingers, one by one.

'I go to Longvale Park, the Kelsey residence, after Easter,' he mused. 'You could join me there. I employ only servants I trust implicitly. You need not fear gossip.'

'I could rely on Juliette not to talk if I brought her,' said Leonora faintly. 'How long would it be for?'

'I planned on going on to my parents after a few days.' He grinned, teasing her. 'But I need not go so soon, or for long. I intend to be away from Bath for about a month.'

'A month?' repeated Leonora. 'You mean we could spend a month together?'

Her whole body glowed. She had never for one moment contemplated being invited to his home, to live with him there.

But—not as his wife, mistress of his household. She quelled the small, chill voice in her mind, pushing it aside as of no consequence. After all, even were he to offer her marriage she would not accept.

'Exactly so, my love, apart from the few days I must spare for Huntsford Towers.' He looked deeply into eyes which at that moment were the most entrancing mixture of blue, green and grey that he had ever seen. His voice deepened. 'Will you come?'

'And...afterwards?' wondered Leonora, part of her brain retaining some common sense.

'Afterwards?' He repeated the word as though he had never thought of any afterwards. A quizzical smile appeared in his eyes and his fingers tightened round hers. 'We shall have to wait and see, shall we not? We may well be tired of each other long before the month is up.'

'But suppose we are not,' said Leonora huskily, knowing full well that she would never tire of living with him. 'We could not continue the liaison here.'

'No?' He looked interested. 'Why not?'

'Because we could never keep it a secret.'

He sobered, took her fully into his arms again. 'And that would matter so much to you?'

'Yes,' said Leonora tightly. Her palms rested against the brocade of his waistcoat. 'I should be ostracised, should never be able to make a decent marriage.' Suddenly, her nerve deserted her. 'Blaise, I do not believe that I can come with you at all!'

Still holding her to him, he lifted her chin so that he could search her eyes. 'Yes, you can,' he told her. 'We want each other. It is the most natural thing in the world for us to come together. Only convention can keep us apart.'

'I am stupidly conventional,' she whispered.

He kissed her lips tenderly. 'No, you are not,' he denied persuasively. 'You chose to live in your uncle's apartment despite the peculiarity of its situation and the gossip your decision would cause.'

The tingle from that kiss travelled through her body. Her hands clenched into fists as she fought off the inclination to surrender without further protest. 'That was different. Gossip without substance can be distressful but cannot in the end cause irredeemable harm.'

'There will be no gossip,' he assured her. 'Do you think me unpractised in the art of avoiding it?'

'No,' said Leonora somewhat grimly. No one could prove that Alicia was—had been—his mistress. The O'Briens had returned to Ireland last week. 'I imagine you have found plenty of opportunity to engage in deception of that kind.'

'Then trust me. All will be well.'

For her, things could never be well unless she wed him. She digested that truth, feeling as though she were being torn in two. She might never be granted the chance of such happiness again. If she had to sacrifice her future for it, did it matter? Her future would be bleak without him, whether she indulged her desire now or not.

Which was the most important? Accommodating her puerile fear of stepping further outside the boundaries of convention and facing the painful consequences, or experiencing, enjoying, for however short a period, the bliss Blaise was offering and for which she yearned?

And, if she had his child, she would still have it to love when he had passed out of her life.

He saw her hesitation. 'Well?' he asked, 'Will you come?'

The serious, anxious tone of his voice convinced her.

'Yes,' said Leonora softly.

Clarissa had already expressed her desire for leave of absence to see her parents after Easter. Leonora would, they decided, take her companion into her confidence and leave Bath with her and Juliette as though she were going to visit Thornestone Park. At a convenient point Blaise would meet her with a coach and take her to Longvale Park with Juliette, while Clarissa carried on to her home. This would be a couple of days after Blaise had returned to his estate.

Their plan devised, he escorted her up to her door and kissed her again before parting. Leonora knew, as she entered her apartments, that she probably looked well-kissed, but could not help that.

She did not intend to say anything to Clarissa that night. Everything was far too close, she needed time to digest the happenings and decisions of the last hour. She would find convenient moments to tell both her and Juliette in the course of the next day or so.

As she had feared, Clarissa was waiting for her in the parlour. 'You were a long time,' she accused Leonora.

Sharp eyes were scrutinising her in an uncomfortable way. Leonora hoped her air was one of innocent fatigue. 'You should have gone to bed,' she said. 'We had things to discuss over a nightcap.' In an attempt to deflect Clarissa's attention she remarked, 'Fancy the Regent honouring me by coming to my reception!'

'Yes.' Clarissa did not sound particularly impressed. 'I did not speak to him, of course. He really is gross, don't you think?'

Leonora smiled reminiscently. 'But quite charming.'

'I did not find him so.' Clarissa closed that subject with an offhand shrug. 'I am quite exhausted,' she went on, sounding anything but. 'I waited up because I wanted to know if you were pleased with the way things went. With the way supper was served.'

'Very pleased,' said Leonora, yawning. 'I am most grateful to you, Clarissa. But we can discuss it in the morning. I am tired, too. We shall all feel better after a good night's sleep, I collect!'

'I declare,' said Clarissa with a small laugh, 'I feel too excited to sleep! You must, too.'

'Perhaps, but I shall retire immediately and hope to relax enough to rest. Our cose will keep until tomorrow.'

Whether Clarissa guessed at the thorough kissing she had received Leonora did not know, but Juliette, seeing the state of her mistress's gown and hair, must have done so.

She was far too well-trained to remark on it, however.

Breakfast was barely over the next morning when Dolly announced Mr Utley, who requested the privilege of a private interview with Miss Vincent.

'Oh, dear!' said Leonora, replacing her cup in its saucer with a slight clatter. 'Show him into the parlour, Dolly.'

When Dolly had gone, she grimaced. 'He has come to make his declaration, I collect.'

Clarissa's eyes had narrowed. 'At last. Will you accept it?'

'No.' Not after her arrangement with Blaise last night. Utley was a nice enough gentleman, too nice to be cheated, although she now knew with absolute certainty that she could never wed him, not unless forced into it. 'I have tried not to be too encouraging. I trust he will accept my refusal without rancour. Excuse me, Clarissa.'

Mr Utley, greying and plump, had indeed come to ask for her hand. He went down on one knee to do it.

Leonora, embarrassed, refused, expressing her regret and gratitude in the most courteous and gentle manner at her command.

He struggled to his feet and bowed. 'I cannot pretend that I am not disappointed, ma'am. You would, I am assured, make me a perfect wife and my poor children a loving mother. Will you not reconsider?'

'I regret, sir—'

'I place all my not-inconsiderable wealth at your feet,' he interrupted earnestly. 'You would never want for a well-furnished place to live and could entertain on a lavish scale. I should not be ashamed to have the Prince Regent as my guest, you know. I could afford it. You are acquainted with him. He might be persuaded to accept an invitation were it to be issued by you. . .'

Seeing the determined way in which Leonora was shaking her head, he abandoned his effort to persuade her. His leavetaking was both dignified and cordial.

He really was a nice man, even if, like so many others, he wished to use her position in Society to raise his own consequence. The Prince Regent's visit must have finally decided him to declare himself. She might have disappointed him by her refusal, but she knew that she had neither hurt his pride nor broken his heart.

Her companion's show of interest in her lively account of the proposal did not deceive Leonora. Clarissa cared that she had received an offer while she, so far, had not. But there was nothing Leonora could do about that, and so she ignored Clarissa's faint air of resentment.

But it did not seem an appropriate time to confide her future plans.

When, half an hour later, Lord Cunningham was announced, also requesting a private interview, Leonora raised her eyes to the heavens.

'It seems that the Regent's patronage has concentrated a number of minds.' She sighed. 'You had better leave me, Clarissa. I cannot deny him his interview.'

Cunningham took his stance before her, large and confident. He did not kneel. 'Well, my dear Miss Vincent,' he boomed, as though he were issuing orders on his quarterdeck. 'Can see ye'd make an admirable admiral's wife.'

He laughed, pleased with his play on words. 'Admirable admiral's wife! Clever, eh?' and carried on without waiting for Leonora to respond. 'So I've come to make you an offer, ma'am. Just say the word and I'll make you Lady Cunningham quicker than hell would scorch a feather!'

He was, in his own eyes, doing her an immense favour. Leonora was too amused to be upset by his condescension. She stifled an inclination to giggle—so childish!— smiled serenely and, with suitable expressions of sensibility and regret, declined his offer.

'How many more, I wonder?' she said ruefully afterwards. 'I must tell you, Clarissa, that I shall not be in a position to accept any of the offers I may receive.'

Clarissa stared. 'Why not?'

Embarrassed colour rose in Leonora's face and she hesitated. But she had to tell Clarissa of her plans at some time and it was of no use putting off the moment any longer.

'Because I have already accepted a *carte blanche*,' she declared quietly.

'You have *what*? You will be ruined!' cried Clarissa, scandalised. She stared in disbelief at Leonora and then observed dourly, 'Lord Kelsey, I collect?'

Leonora nodded. 'Yes. It was arranged last night.'

'I could see he'd made some kind of advance, Leonora, but I never for one moment expected you to succumb to such a scandalous proposal. You cannot do it! It would be against every teaching—'

Leonora's voice was low but she kept it even. 'I know. And I'm afraid that I do not care.'

'You must seek advice from my father, Leonora! He will guide you into the correct paths. Come to Thornestone with me!'

Leonora had not expected Clarissa to be pleased, but had not thought to meet such fierce opposition. She cleared her throat. 'I am truly sorry if my decision distresses you, Clarissa, but my mind is quite made up. I intended to ask you to help me.'

'Help you to fornicate?' grated Clarissa, appalled.

'Help me to find perhaps the only true happiness I ever shall, Clarissa,' Leonora contradicted. 'I could never marry him while he runs the Vitus Club, even if he asked me to, which he will not. So if I wish to find out what it is like to be bedded by the man I love, I must go to him unwed.'

Clarissa was finding it all too much to take in. 'You

love him? I thought you disliked him intensely!' she observed harshly.

'At first I did. Or thought I did. But I cannot help myself, Clarissa. I find I love him. Although I trust you will not breathe a word of this to anyone!'

'You will not condone his running of a gaming club, yet you will give yourself to him outside the bonds of matrimony?'

'I fear so. To me, the two things appear quite different. Our making love together concerns no one else but ourselves. But when he encourages gentlemen to squander fortunes at his tables the result is likely to affect entire families, perhaps for generations to come.'

'I shall not say a word to anyone, of course, but, Leonora—'

'Thank you. I pray you will help us, Clarissa, for whether you do or not I intend to join him at his estate immediately after Easter.'

Clarissa, still disapproving, asked doubtfully, 'How do you wish me to help?'

Leonora's relief showed itself in a brilliant smile. 'By departing in a post chaise to visit your parents as you planned, and sharing it for part of the way with me and, I trust, Juliette. As far as people here will know, I am visiting Thornestone Park. Kelsey will meet us that evening at a suitable inn, having brought with him a coach and a woman to accompany you on the remainder of your journey the following day. Kelsey will escort Juliette and myself to Longvale Park.'

There was a moment's silence while Clarissa considered her words. Then, 'While I cannot approve of your scheme,' she said in her most righteous voice, 'I cannot deny our friendship, and the kindness you have shown to me, by refusing your request. But I fear that I shall not be able to bring myself to return to Bath as your companion. My father would not allow it.'

'You have promised to tell no one, Clarissa. I pray you will not confide in even your father.' She could not bear the idea of that kindly man's distress were his uncompromising daughter the one to inform him of her fall from grace.

'No. I will find some other excuse for not returning to Bath.'

'Thank you,' said Leonora, a little less inclined to be grateful for Clarissa's help than she had been a few moments earlier. 'So it is settled, then. We will leave Bath on the Monday following the Duchess's ball. No doubt you will wish to write to warn your parents of your expected arrival on the Tuesday.'

'Of course. I shall do so without delay.'

'Meanwhile,' said Leonora cheerfully, 'we carry on as usual. I am quite looking forward to hearing Mr Handel's *Messiah* this evening.'

'And the singing in the Abbey over Easter,' agreed Clarissa a little stiffly.

Juliette readily agreed to accompany her mistress to Lord Kelsey's estate. Dolly, appraised of her supposed plan to visit Thornestone, seemed happy enough to remain at Morris House to look after Leonora's apartment while she was away. Dolly did not seem to suffer from home-sickness and had made friends of the kitchen and household staff employed by Blaise, so would not lack for company. Mrs Parkes would keep an eye on the girl.

Digby Sinclair returned to his home a week before Easter to celebrate the festival there. He would be back in time to take over the running of the Club before Blaise himself departed. Blaise had other competent staff and the Club continued to operate smoothly. Its doors were closed on Good Friday and Easter Sunday.

Blaise and Leonora maintained, in public, the same relationship as they had before—coolly friendly, Blaise mildly attentive, with an edge of suppressed animosity hovering between them over their forced sharing of Morris House.

Private moments were few, but when they could be arranged, Leonora slipped into the crook of his arm on her *chaise-longue* or, on the days when the Club was closed, went down to share his large armchair while they kissed and talked.

She was grateful for these interludes, short as they were, for they helped her to overcome the mental hurdles still strewing her path. She'd agreed to go to Longvale Park and she would, but Clarissa's now-silent disapproval was hard to bear, the necessary secrecy a sharp reminder that what she proposed to do was, in the sight of God and Society, a sin.

Outwardly, a Society butterfly had emerged from her chrysalis state of governess, but the inhibitions of her upbringing, though buried, still remained in her mind. Ladies did not engage in secret rendezvous, did not allow themselves to be alone with a gentleman, let alone allow him the freedom to kiss and cuddle her in such a way as to render her eager to experience, and quite powerless to refuse, the ultimate intimacy which would surely be demanded at Longvale.

She was, she knew, hopelessly, helplessly in love.

*   *   *   *

Blaise escorted her to the Duchess's ball, since to do so would not be setting a precedent and in any case, on this occasion, Clarissa had been invited too. Speculation as to their precise relationship had been rife after the Duchess's dinner but, lacking stimulation, had withered away until Blaise had co-hosted her reception. However, the fact that his Club's rooms were used for the occasion caused surprise rather than additional conjecture.

In order to dampen new gossip, he largely ignored her during the ball, standing up with her only once. Knowing why he was being frugal with his attention, Leonora was able to enjoy the grand occasion almost to the full. The aquamarine ball gown suited her to perfection and she did not lack for presentable and congenial partners.

Grath was especially attentive. He stood up with her twice and insisted on taking her in to supper.

Leonora readily accepted his attentions, hoping that they would deflect any suspicion of intimacy between Blaise and herself, but she took care not to appear too encouraging. She did not wish to disturb the Duchess or to lead Grath to anticipate acceptance of whatever offer he felt disposed to make.

When the Duchess sought her out for a private word, Leonora immediately feared the worst. But her grace did not appear unduly concerned.

She came straight to the point. 'Grath is rather taken with you, m'dear. You realise, of course, that I should have to oppose any union between you?'

It was said kindly. The Duchess's shrewd eyes did not waver from hers. Leonora found herself smiling.

'I have no designs on Lord Grath,' she assured her hostess. 'I like him and find him agreeable company, but have formed no kind of attachment to him. I have always known myself to be an unsuitable match.'

'A pity,' said the Duchess bluntly, 'you'd've been good for him. But there you are, his marriage is already arranged. Duke's granddaughter.'

'Does he know?' demanded Leonora.

'Yes. Don't like it above half, but he'll do as he's told. At least, I trust he will. Don't want an elopement or anythin' of that kind. He's an impulsive sprig.'

Poor Grath. But it probably meant that his interest in her was not serious, and more than likely dishonourable. She tried to reassure her hostess. 'You need not fear that I shall tempt him into any stupid action, your grace.'

'No, didn't think you would. I like you, m'dear. Why not come to London while I'm in residence there? Stay with us in Grosvenor Square for a few weeks. The Duke'd enjoy meeting you, I collect. Come and spend part of the Season with us.'

Overwhelmed, 'You do me a great honour, ma'am,' Leonora said, dipping a curtsy. 'I had not planned on entering into London Society at all. I'm not certain when—'

'No need to make up your mind now. Let me know when you're coming, if you decide to come at all. Now—' briskly '—I am neglecting my other guests. Enjoy the remainder of the evening.'

'I shall.' Leonora curtsied deeply. 'Thank you again, your grace.'

'Might find a more suitable husband than Grath in London,' was her grace's parting shot.

Blaise's footman rode on the box with the hired driver and Juliette had been carried to and fro by sedan chair. Inside the chariot, with Clarissa perched, silent and disapproving, on the pull-out seat between them, they had no opportunity for privacy.

'I'll be waiting at the King's Head in Gloucester on Monday evening,' Blaise reminded them. 'Miss Vincent, you will not mind sharing a room with Miss Worth and your maid, I collect?'

'No, I shall not mind.' What else could she say, with Clarissa there?

'We will leave the inn in separate parties on Tuesday and change passengers between coaches near the bridge over the River Severn. You can then travel east, Miss Worth, while we cross the river to go north and west. We should all reach our final destinations that day.'

'The post boys will be curious,' observed Leonora.

'They will be well rewarded to stay mum and in any case no one is likely to question them. Don't worry. Our secret will be safe.' He chuckled. 'Do you not find the intrigue exciting?'

'Up to a point,' admitted Leonora, although in truth anxiety rather outweighed excitement. She was, she supposed, too old for this kind of thing. One should be eighteen and oblivious to the possibility of calamity ahead to enjoy to the full the thrill of a clandestine assignation. 'What I do find exciting,' she added softly, despite Clarissa's presence, 'is the prospect of spending the next weeks at Longvale Park.'

'I am glad you find it so.' said Blaise. 'I cannot wait to introduce you to my estate.'

'I do not find your plans at all exciting,' put in Clarissa austerely.

'I am sorry,' said Blaise mildly. 'But we are both grateful to you for overcoming your scruples and helping us. If I can ever be of service to you, you have only to ask.'

'Thank you, my lord,' said Clarissa primly. 'I do not, however, imagine I shall need assistance in the future. I have just accepted Mr Utley's hand in marriage, subject to my father's approval, of course.'

'Mr Utley?' gasped Leonora. 'But—'

'While courting you, Leonora, he had noticed me. When you refused him, he decided to ask me to honour him by becoming his wife.'

'I see,' said Leonora weakly.

'I wish you every happiness,' said Blaise. 'Utley seems a decent enough fellow. Your stay in Bath with Leonora has reaped you a great reward. As you say, you will require no favours from me.'

They drew up at the front of the building, for the ball had gone on into the small hours. He handed both ladies down, leaving his footman to dismiss the chariot, and led them indoors. All was quiet, even the servants had retired.

'You go on up,' Leonora instructed Clarissa once they were inside. 'I will follow in a few moments.'

Blaise bowed formally over Clarissa's hand and then followed Leonora into his sitting room.

'Well, I declare!' exclaimed Leonora. 'Of all the cunning creatures I have known, Clarissa Worth beats everything!'

'But Utley did ask you first, my love. Clarissa was only his second choice.'

He was laughing at her, but Leonora could not help that.

'She raised all kinds of objections to my accepting him! And then she goes and takes him herself!'

'And do you wish, now, that you had received his offer more favourably?'

The amusement was still in Blaise's voice as he handed her a nightcap of spiced wine, then sipped his own brandy.

Leonora realised that she was reacting rather stupidly. She made her tone light as she said, 'He is very rich. No doubt that weighed with Clarissa.'

'But not with you.'

The laughter had left his voice. His eyes rested steadily on her over the rim of his goblet.

'My dear,' said Leonora, 'I have enough money for my needs. Had he been young, handsome and dashing I should probably have said yes.' She met his eyes, blinked rapidly and lowered her gaze quickly to stare at the glass in her hand. 'But not, I think, just at this moment.'

Blaise had been forced to exercise more restraint than he liked over the last couple of weeks. But the look she gave him when she raised her eyes again promised that his moment was near. He made no move to persuade her to advance their union. He could afford to wait a few more days.

He lifted his goblet in salute. 'Until next week, my love.'

'Next week,' echoed Leonora softly.

After she had drunk her wine he removed the glass from her hand and took her in his arms.

'I shall leave here as early as possible tomorrow, so we shall not meet again until Monday. Your arrangements are all in hand, are they not?'

'Yes, Blaise. I shall not change my mind.'

'And neither shall I,' he assured her before he sealed their bargain with a kiss.

Chapter Thirteen

A week—well, not quite a week, but the best part of one—seemed a very long time to wait see Blaise again.

By Friday her things were packed, ready to leave, and a whole weekend stretched barren before her. To fill a dull Saturday afternoon alone, for Clarissa was out with Mr Utley, Leonora decided to undertake a task she had been putting off for weeks.

Her great-uncle's writing desk was still in a dreadful mess. She had sorted the important papers and thrown obvious rubbish away to make room for her own things. But over half the drawers and cubbyholes still required attention.

Stifling a sigh of boredom, she reluctantly began on the unwelcome task. She did not want to delve deeply into her great-uncle's private affairs. She wished to discover no dark secrets of which she would rather remain ignorant.

When, after an hour of diligent sifting, she had come across nothing more revealing than old bills long ago settled, ancient Navy Lists, and a few letters from her grandfather to his brother and from the present Lord

Chelstoke to his uncle, mostly concerning the family estates and an allowance that she had not known Uncle Vincent had received from them.

With much of the desk empty, curiosity made her search for and find what she had guessed would be there—most of this design of desk had at least one—a secret drawer.

She found the right knob to push, hidden amongst the carving on a decorative panel. The drawer sprang open and inside she discovered the remainder of her inheritance, her source of future independence.

In a damaged, padded box marked with a French maker's name lay an exquisite set—a necklace, brooch and earrings—wrought in gold and set with rubies and diamonds. She fingered the pieces reverently.

Behind the box lay a salt-stained, oiled-leather pouch. She took it out and untied the drawstring at its neck with trembling fingers.

Inside she found more pieces of jewellery, just as fine, although the items did not match. They were simply a jumble of gold, silver and enamel set with multi-coloured precious gems, which, on closer inspection, she judged might have been worn by a wealthy gentleman of fashion in a previous age: brooches, heavy rings, snuff boxes, chains and fobs, a locket containing a lock of fair hair—all skilfully wrought of the finest materials.

Crumpled in the bottom of the pouch lay a stained piece of paper. She extracted it, smoothed it out and tried to decipher the faded writing. The words were still readable: *My share of items found aboard captured French man-of-war off Jamaica, 1782.*

She sat back, the paper in her hands, the precious gems strewn across the writing surface of the desk. She could scarcely believe what she had discovered.

Treasure her great-uncle and others had found and kept for themselves four-and-thirty years ago, presumably after the Battle of the Saintes—and who could blame them? She felt no qualms over appropriating the pieces, for they had been lost in the confusion of a famous action at sea.

She knew instinctively that the jewels were valuable. French noblemen had captained warships in those days before the Revolution and perhaps one such had commanded the surrendered vessel. . .been killed. . .and her great-uncle had been one of the prize crew. . .

She allowed her imagination to run wild for a few moments before she pulled herself together. Her hands were still shaking with excitement. Her great-uncle had not sold the jewellery, but left it to her with the contents of his home. He had indeed left her a fortune, one no one had known he possessed.

Her heart beat fast as she contemplated what the discovery meant. Realising their value might prove arduous, involving a visit to London to find a reputable jeweller but—

She no longer need feel obliged to take measures to prevent conception! For the cache she had found must surely be of sufficient value to provide her with the means to retire to the country to pose as a young widow while she raised Blaise's child, were she lucky enough to have one. If she were not—

Then she would have to make fresh plans when the time came. If she could bring herself to it, a husband might still be the best answer, if she could attach an agreeable gentleman.

She replaced the gems in the secret drawer. They

would be safe there until her return. By then she would
know more clearly what her future held.

Gloucester, discovered Leonora, was a fine city and the
King's Head a respectable hostelry, in addition to being
a posting inn.

The journey had been fast, uncomfortable but unevent-
ful, apart from the need to change coaches and horses
twice on the way. Hired post chaises, the teams of horses
which drew them and the post boy postilions who rode
them, plied backwards and forwards between post houses
situated at approximately ten-mile intervals.

Clarissa would have to proceed in the same way the
next day, changing every ten miles, but Leonora was
grateful to presume that she would ride in greater comfort
in a carriage belonging to Blaise, though it would be
drawn by post horses, which would have to be changed.
He did not, he had explained, keep enough carriage
horses to form a team strong enough to pull a
heavy coach.

In Bath he lived as though in command of modest
wealth, but not of riches. Had he been wealthy enough
to keep a stable full of horses he would not have felt the
need to found the Vitus Club, she supposed. She would,
then, have had no reason to refuse to wed him—had he
asked!—but would probably not have met him.

Oh! Why did things have to work out in such a difficult
and complicated way?

Why had he been thrown in her path? If he had not,
she could not have fallen in love with him. Or why, since
she had met him, did he have to lack the funds to live
decently without involving himself in an activity of
which she could not approve?

The questions seemed unanswerable. But when she entered the inn and asked for Lord Kelsey, she was shown into a private parlour. To see him sitting at a table with a flagon of wine before him made her heart turn over—she knew now that nothing mattered except being with him.

How could it, when he jumped to his feet and smiled at her like that?

'Serve the supper in fifteen minutes,' he ordered the burly, friendly landlord.

'Very well, my lord.'

He was known here, there could be little doubt of that. She supposed he made the King's Head a normal stop on his way between Bath and Longvale Park or Huntsford Towers.

Perhaps they were used to his having assignations with ladies here.

She thrust that doubt aside as unworthy. She knew that unmarried gentlemen kept mistresses, that Kelsey was no different. She was about to become one of them. She would not dwell on that.

Kelsey indicated a door through which, across a passage, they would find a room where they might tidy themselves after the journey. Meanwhile their bedroom was being prepared for them.

Feeling decidedly better after washing the dust from her hands and face and having Juliette tidy her hair, Leonora returned eagerly to the parlour, where the steaming dishes were just being set out upon the snowy cloth.

Lawrence was in attendance on his master, and a middle-aged woman dressed in plain, decent clothes sat quietly in a corner.

The six of them made the small room seem rather crowded but it was cosy and comfortable. The inn had done well, providing a tureen of thick pea soup, large bread rolls, a pot of glistening brown beef stew, a chicken roasted on a spit, a piece of cold ham, a large wedge of crumbly cheese, carrots braised in sugar and butter, and baked parsnips. A rich feast.

'I did not realise I was so hungry!' said Leonora as they took their seats at a table set for three. Places and food had been set for their attendants at another table. They had been provided with the soup and the stew—but not the chicken or ham—plain boiled vegetables and a loaf of bread.

'Capital,' she sighed, her first hunger assuaged. 'Not quite up to André's standard, but still excellent!'

'Why else do you think I patronise the place?' demanded Blaise, taking up his wine glass. 'They employ an experienced cook, and their business prospers.'

'Like yours,' remarked Clarissa, who, now she was almost wearing an engagement ring, regarded herself as anyone's equal.

'Yes. I am lucky to employ André.' Blaise drank. 'When is Mr Utley to speak to your father?' he asked, filling his glass again from the replenished flagon.

Clarissa glanced down, looking conscious. 'He is to visit Thornestone at the weekend. That gives me time to explain, so that my father knows what to expect.'

'A wise arrangement,' said Blaise with a nod.

They retired to bed soon after the meal.

The next morning all three ate an early breakfast before starting on their way again.

Blaise had made the arrangements, speaking to the

post boys before the two carriages set off. And so it was within sight of the gently flowing Severn that Leonora took final leave of her companion.

Clarissa's face wore a sombre expression. 'I cannot condone what you are doing, Leonora,' she said painfully, 'and I fear for you. But I hope you will find happiness and will think your flouting of convention worth while.'

'That is generous of you, Clarissa. And I pray that you will be happy with Mr Utley and not find his children too much of a trial.'

'At least,' said Clarissa with her intrinsic honesty, 'it will not matter if I prove to be too old to bear him children myself. Mr Utley will suit me very well, I think.'

And one day you will be a very rich widow, thought Leonora, but did not say it aloud.

She looked across and caught Blaise's eye as he stood waiting for her.

No, she would not change places with Clarissa for all the tea in China.

Leonora held out her hand. 'Goodbye, then, Clarissa.'

To her surprise, tears suddenly gathered in Clarissa's eyes. Impulsively, she put her arms about Leonora and gave her a hug.

'I'm sorry, Leonora,' she whispered.

'Sorry? Whatever for?' demanded Leonora, returning the embrace. After all, they had been close friends at Thornestone.

'For flirting with Lord Kelsey—although at the time I did not know that you were interested in him—and, God forgive me, for pursuing Mr Utley after you refused him. He would still have taken you, you know, had you changed your mind. I assured him that you would not

do so.' Blinking back tears, she met Leonora's astonished
eyes. 'But I needed to wed, and to wed well, Leonora.
Can you forgive me?'

'Mr Utley is not the only chance I have thrown away
because of my feelings for Lord Kelsey,' said Leonora
truthfully. 'Of course I forgive you. You have nothing
with which to reproach yourself, Clarissa, and I sincerely
wish you happiness.'

'Thank you,' gulped Clarissa.

They kissed, and parted. Leonora doubted whether she
would ever see her former companion again. She was
a strange creature, she decided, torn between her deep
religious convictions and the call of her basic instincts,
something she had failed to understand in the past.

In Blaise's coach, with Juliette and Lawrence sitting
opposite them, they could not say much or indulge in
any kind of touching or kissing, which Leonora found
wretchedly frustrating.

However, Blaise kept her entertained with a commen-
tary on the villages and verdant countryside through
which they passed, until at last, tired despite the greater
comfort of the journey, they reached the Kelsey estates,
noted several tenant farmhouses and eventually passed
through the gates of Longvale Park, opened by a woman
from the lodge who dropped Blaise a respectful curtsy,
to drive through the grounds to the house.

The manor house, sprawling, elegant, came into view
round a bend in the drive. Brilliant April sunshine was
reflected back at them from mullioned windows set in
the stone façade and dormers peeking from the roof.

'It is not large,' said Blaise deprecatingly but with that
in his voice which told Leonora that he was proud of

his residence. 'It has only five guest bedrooms and no ballroom. In my parents' time here the hall was used for dancing. But it does have a fine drawing room and the morning room, at the back of the house, overlooks the terrace and the shrubbery.'

'Longvale is about the size of the house my father owned until he lost it at the card table,' said Leonora, but her voice sounded sad rather than angry.

'It is not as grand as Huntsford Towers, which will also be mine one day. That is a fortified medieval building, more of a castle than a manor house, but my forebears have managed to modernise it and make the fifteen bedrooms and the rooms in everyday use reasonably comfortable.'

'Will you enjoy living there?' asked Leonora. He had not made any mention of taking her to see either it or his parents. She was not a prospective bride, she reminded herself, but merely a mistress. Probably a short-term mistress.

'It is the Whittonby seat,' he was explaining. 'I spent my first years there. I love it. But Longvale goes to the eldest son together with the courtesy title of Kelsey. It provides me with my own establishment and, nominally, an income until I inherit Whittonby.'

'It is beautiful, yet you are scarcely ever here,' murmured Leonora.

'At the moment it is impossible,' said Blaise in a tone that told her he did not wish to discuss the matter further.

Inside, the dust sheets had been removed and fires lit, but the place still retained a faint odour of disuse and damp. Yet although old, the furnishings were in excellent condition—the woodwork gleamed with polish and the mirrors shone brightly in the lingering rays of the sun entering through sparkling windows. Nor she could detect any trace of tarnish to mar the perfection of the silver salvers and candlesticks in either the large hall or the small room, furnished with a number of chairs and a side table, into which Blaise took her.

Juliette had been led off by Mrs Wilson, the housekeeper, a buxom woman who treated Blaise with the respectful familiarity of an old family retainer, while Lawrence directed the transportation of their luggage up to the bedrooms and Wilson, the butler, poured them a drink.

'Thank you, Wilson. I'll ring when Miss Vincent is ready to go to her room to change.'

'Very good, my lord.'

Neither Wilson or his wife had blinked an eye at her advent, although she fancied Mrs Wilson had subjected her to a close scrutiny. Only time would tell what conclusion the woman, who obviously adored her employer, had arrived at.

'I do not keep many servants here,' Blaise apologised when the tall, spare man had gone. 'The Wilsons manage the house well enough with a small staff. One day—' he paused to smile mischievously at her and raised his glass in salute of the promise '—one day, when I have made my fortune I shall retire here, keep a full household staff and entertain occasionally as I should.'

She supposed that would be the day when he wed, too, for he would need a wife to help him, and a family to bring the place to life and provide heirs. But when she did learn of his marriage, although she would suffer agonies of frustration and jealousy, she would know that she had once been lucky enough to attract Blaise Dancer's attentions herself.

To voice her opinion that he would need a wife would hardly be diplomatic under the circumstances, so she merely raised her own glass and said, 'Then I drink to that day.'

He pulled her to her feet and, for the first time since they had parted in Bath, took her in his arms and kissed her.

Leonora, as always, became helpless when that happened. She knew that tonight he would demand more than kisses. She wondered how she would feel then, whether she would suffer the embarrassment she feared? But he was experienced, he knew exactly how to coax her body into joyous surrender. She knew that, so why was she suffering from last-minute nerves?

It was, she suspected, because the last and final hurdle was so near. Once she had jumped it she could not turn and go back.

She would never again be a virgin.

Tension mounted in her through supper, a tension quite different from the waves of awareness that seemed to fill the small dining room where it had been served.

She had been allocated a room near to, but not adjoining, the master bedroom where Blaise slept. The Pink Room, it was called, the reason obvious. Warming pans were already airing the large, canopied, silk-hung bed when she went up to change. Her clothes had fitted easily into a large cupboard and triple mirrors topped the silken-skirted dressing-table.

That the silk was falling apart in places did not matter. What did matter was that Blaise should later join her in the comfortable-looking bed and make her indissolubly his.

The time came for her to retire. Blaise rang for someone to escort her to her room, took her hand and kissed
her palm, curling her fingers to keep the the caress in.

'An hour,' he murmured. 'Come, let me light you a
candle.'

A number of unlit candles stood on a table in the hall
beneath a flaring branch fixed to the wall. Blaise chose
one, touched its wick to a flame and handed her the
holder as a small maidservant arrived in answer to his
summons.

'Take Miss Vincent up to her room, Maisie,' he
instructed. 'Sleep well, Leonora.'

There could be no pretence of true formality here. Her
being a lone guest in a gentleman's house was strictly
against the rules, but they would preserve a decent front
before the servants as far as possible. Not to do so might
incite reluctant service, even veiled impudence from the
servants who did not know her.

So she dutifully followed the diminutive figure of
young Maisie up the sweeping staircase and to the door
of her room, where Juliette was waiting with a tub of
steaming water.

'I thought that, after the journey, you would wish to
cleanse yourself thoroughly,' Juliette explained the presence of the bath as she added some drops of perfume.

'Most thoughtful of you,' said Leonora gratefully. It
had been in her mind to take a scented bath tonight, but
she'd forgotten to order it. Her problem, she had thought,
would be the time it must take to heat the water and have
it brought up. Trust Juliette to anticipate her needs and
wishes!

Leonora finished her ablutions, the tub was removed
and her preparations for bed completed. Juliette extracted

the bedpans, helped her under the covers, doused all the candles but the one she carried and left to go to her own room, which was some distance away. She would not be within call.

The bed was deliciously warm, soft and so comfortable that, despite her nervousness, tiredness quickly overcame Leonora and she was drowsing when she heard the scratch on her door.

Was it him? Whoever it was had not waited for an invitation to enter and carried no candle.

'Blaise?' she murmured nervously.

'Who else were you expecting, my love?' came his amused retort as he crossed the room quickly to stand by her bed.

The curtain at that side had been left open. He loomed over her, a darker shadow with a faint luminosity where his face might be. But it was Blaise, she would have known that by the scent of him, that distinctive mixture of sandalwood, brandy and clean male sweat—faint now, but still there beneath the effects of the recent cleansing he, too, had undergone—which was essentially Blaise Dancer.

And in that moment, slightly befuddled with sleep as she was, all her inhibitions, all her fears disappeared. She whispered 'Blaise!' in a strangled voice and reached up to wind her arms about his neck.

He gave a short, rather breathless laugh as he released himself from her clasp in order to discard his dressing robe. Then the covers lifted, the mattress sank under his weight and she was gathered in his arms.

He wore no nightshirt. Her shy yet eager, exploring hands felt only bone and muscle under smooth flesh. He kissed her, gently at first, while he removed her frilly nightcap and asked softly, 'You are ready for me, my love?'

Leonora had never felt more ready for anything or anyone in her life. She read no more into his query than her willingness to have him love her.

'Oh, yes!' she whispered.

He immediately abandoned restraint and plundered her mouth with demanding lips and seeking tongue.

Their teeth clashed. Leonora, taken by surprise, let them part as she struggled for breath, then gave herself up to the delicious tangling of tongues as he probed the recesses of her mouth and she tasted the nightcap whose perfume still lingered on his breath.

At first his hands held her head still, his fingers buried in her hair. Soon, his mouth still possessing hers, he reached down to ruck up her night shift until he could reach the hem and gather the unwanted garment under her arms.

He traced the smooth lines of her body, murmuring sounds of pleasure and encouragement because her muscles tensed at this first invasion of her modesty. Only after she had relaxed again did he lift his head and move so that both hands could touch her exposed breasts.

Leonora gasped as the sensations, the spears of exquisite pain, ripped through her body making her hips shift of their own accord. She had already opened to him, as she had so many times before. But now he replaced one of his hands with his mouth, teasing her stiff nipple with his lips and tongue while his fingers probed the secret places between her thighs.

He gave a grunt of satisfaction and moved again to put her under him. She could feel his throbbing hardness against her and instinctively spread her legs to accommodate him. So fierce was her response that she thought her body might split apart—she felt damp, moisture seemed to be seeping from her and she could not understand that.

Blaise rose above her, supporting himself on his elbows. 'I'll try not to hurt you more than I must,' he murmured and next moment plunged himself into her depths.

It did hurt, just a little, but only enough to make her catch her breath. She could feel him pulsing inside her and for Leonora that was enough to compensate for almost anything. For this long moment, as he lay there, quite immobile, breathing deeply, he was hers and no other's. This was her moment of triumph, fulfilment, joy. There was no thought in her mind for the future. Now was everything.

Then he began to move. His lips found hers again as he thrust. Sensations flowed from both his actions to make her mind whirl, her hips shift, her arms tighten about him, her insides to wobble in delicious anticipation of something stupendous.

He had buried his face in the pillow beside her head. She tightened her arms still further and whispered, 'Oh, my love!'

He shuddered convulsively and collapsed on top of her, his breathing suspended until he let it out on another long tremor. His heart gradually stopped hammering in his breast and only then did he stir, not to leave her but to kiss her again, this time on the throbbing pulse in her neck.

Eventually he rolled aside, drew her close and tangled his legs with hers so that their bodies were entwined.

His fingers combed her long, silky hair as he kissed her again, but still did not speak.

'Was it all right?' whispered Leonora, beginning to wonder at his silence.

'All right?' He was on the edge of rueful laughter. 'My dear girl, you have left me bereft of words to tell you how wonderful you are.'

'You were not disappointed?'

'No, my love. It was you who should be disappointed. I wanted you so desperately that my desire overcame my good intentions. I finished too quickly. But next time, I promise, you will find fulfilment too.'

'I was not disappointed, Blaise. I cannot imagine more pleasure to be possible. You have made me so very happy.'

'You are an uncommonly passionate lady,' he murmured into her hair. His hand stroked her shoulder, touched on her breast, traced the curve of her waist, the swell of her hips, before he restored her shift to a more decorous position and smoothed it down. 'Sleep now, my love. We have four weeks to explore the full depths of our passion. You are the most perfect companion and lover I have ever known.'

And that must be some compliment, thought Leonora dreamily as she dropped into blissful sleep. Her emotions had been so restricted, first by her upbringing, then by her duties as a governess that, apart from her devastation at the death of her parents, she had experienced few deep feelings for anyone, let alone the vivid kind that were sweeping her now.

Dawn came early at that time of the year. It was just breaking when Leonora woke to find Blaise leaning over her. It must have been his featherlight kiss on her eyelids that disturbed her.

She smiled. 'Blaise.'

He was still there beside her in the bed.

'I have to return to my own room soon,' he whispered. 'The servants will be about before long. But first. . .'

She turned into his arms without hesitation. This time, however, he insisted on removing her shift before he began. Their loving was slow, infinitely pleasurable, his assured, hers still tentative but becoming more bold by the minute. She discovered where he liked to be touched. They laughed when they found each other ticklish, Leonora batting his hand away from her waist with a confident gurgle. 'Don't!'

'Then I shall have to touch you here,' he responded, with a wicked smile she could just see in the light filtering through the thin curtains. 'Do you prefer that?'

She did, oh, she did! His stroking thumb racked her body, sent her soaring into realms of delight, but there was something missing. . . Before she could decide what it was, she had climaxed and lay shuddering in his arms.

When she descended to earth again she knew what had been missing. 'You didn't. . .you weren't. . .'

She trailed off, unable to say it in words. He had not been inside her.

'I know, my love. I wanted to be certain that you knew pleasure this time. But now I'll take mine, too. Then you'll know just how wonderful our union can be.'

He began to make love to her all over again. When he entered her she knew what to expect and was not surprised when the wobbles inside became a climax. Only this time they both shouted together and momentarily died together and that sharing brought the ultimate joy.

They recovered and lay quiet for a while, savouring the aftermath of a perfect union.

Then Blaise stirred. 'I must leave you, my love.' He kissed her mouth. 'Breakfast is served at nine.'

'I'll be there,' promised Leonora, nevertheless clinging to his fingers for as long as she could.

In the strengthening light, with the bed curtains drawn back, she could see his strong body so clearly, the broad shoulders, slim waist, taut stomach, lean yet muscular thighs. The dark hair on his chest in which her fingers had tangled and against which her cheek, at some time, had rested.

He caught her gaze on him as he tied the belt of the gown, and smiled. 'I'll show you the stables after breakfast. You can choose a mount to suit you and we'll ride out to take a look at the estate.'

Leonora, jerked into full awareness, sat up in the bed, holding the sheet to cover her bare breasts. This brought a delighted smile to his lips.

'Your modesty overwhelms me,' he murmured. 'You have seen me. Am I not allowed to see even your most delectable breasts?'

Colour sprang to Leonora's cheeks. She had not thought it possible to be embarrassed by Blaise again, but she had been mistaken. 'I am saving the treat,' she assured him, blinking up at him as flirtatiously as she knew how.

'You wicked tease,' was his parting shot as he ruffled her already tousled hair and disappeared from her sight.

She heard the door close quietly behind him and only then began to wonder what she should wear. She still had no riding costume. Still wondering, she slipped back into languorous sleep.

The days that followed were more enchanting than she had ever imagined possible. They behaved like all lovers, laughing, touching, taking every opportunity to fall into each other's arms.

The staff must have guessed at their relationship—it was obvious whenever they were together, which was most of the time—but the Wilsons' reaction was one of benign tolerance and this set the attitude of everyone else in the household.

The master could do no wrong and no one would dream of criticising the woman chosen as his mistress, especially as she seemed to make him happy and they could not otherwise fault her. As time went by they even evinced a certain affection towards her.

She quickly regained her riding skills and, mounted on one of his hacks, accompanied Blaise about his estate and all the tenant farms attached to it. In showing her his domain, he displayed a degree of pride she had not expected.

His bailiff, or agent, or whatever he chose to call the tall, weatherbeaten man charged with the running of the estate and the Home Farm, talked to him easily, discussing matters of organisation and farming, quite aware that his lordship understood and was interested in every aspect of the business.

Kelsey did not, she discovered, neglect his estate; what's more, he oversaw the running of that of his father the Marquess. This she found out when a stranger appeared a few days after her arrival and was introduced as the agent in charge of the Whittonby estates based at

Huntsford Towers. He was younger than Falconer, the Longvale bailiff, but had a natural authority and spoke to Blaise as easily as did the other man.

Blaise spent the whole morning with the two men, who were invited to take a light repast with Blaise at noon, before setting out on horseback for an inspection of the Home Farm. There were, it seemed, some innovations they wished to show Wainwright, as the man from Huntsford Towers was named.

She was introduced merely as his landlord and friend on a visit to Longvale Park. At first she had felt embarrassed and awkward in the new man's presence but, like the rest of Blaise's staff, he showed no surprise to find her there.

'You know Bath?' she asked in some surprise as she waited with both men for Blaise to join them for the nuncheon.

'Why, yes, ma'am,' said Wainwright. 'I go there once a month to report and consult with his lordship.'

'You do?'

'We both do,' put in Falconer. 'Being upstairs you wouldn't see us, Miss Vincent. Between us, we report on all the Whittonby holdings, scattered as some of them are. Without his son's acumen and guidance Lord Whittonby must have lost most of his lands by now.'

'My father's health deteriorated after his investments failed,' said Blaise, who had entered as Falconer spoke. 'If I wished to have an inheritance at all, I had to do something about it. Will you have another drink?'

He addressed Wainwright and Falconer, who both accepted refills of the excellent ale being offered.

'Thank you, my lord,' said Wainwright, 'And here's to the continued success of your schemes. They've taken a deal of money in the past, but without them the poor harvest last year would have sunk us, I fear.'

'I consider the money well spent,' said Blaise briefly. 'Ah, the meal is served.'

Later that day Leonora questioned him about his schemes, and the money required to execute them. 'It comes from the profits of the Vitus Club?' she asked.

'Yes. I had to do something. The property was mortgaged and the estates yielding virtually nothing. The Vitus Club, my dear, has been our salvation.'

'I see,' was all Leonora said. But her appreciation of Blaise Dancer had changed drastically. She had never imagined that she could come to love him more than she already did, but she had.

Chapter Fourteen

Expecting it, whilst half-hoping that it would not show up, Leonora was faced with telling Blaise when, nearly, at the end of their second week together, her monthly bleeding began.

She put off the telling until he came to her in the darkness of the bedroom that night. There was nothing for it but to be blunt.

'I'm sorry,' she whispered as he slipped out of his gown, 'but I am indisposed at the moment.'

'Your bleed?' At her murmur of consent he appeared to hesitate, but only fleetingly. 'That is no reason for us to sleep apart, my love,' he declared with a pleasing demonstration of affection. 'At least you are not breeding.'

'No,' agreed Leonora without much enthusiasm.

By this time he had given up creeping back to his own room before the servants were up. They knew, they understood, and it was so much more pleasant to remain in the warm bed together until it was time to rise.

As they discovered each other's bodies their love-making grew more deeply passionate, more fulfilling, more joyous. Leonora, at least, clung to those shared moments of complete union with the fervour of desperation. She knew that, before long, the idyllic interlude must end. Back in Bath, secretive and rushed, their times together could never be the same.

April had turned into May and spring arrived in a burst of green foliage, with white blossom to smother the hedgerows. Never had Leonora appreciated a spring more. To her senses, heightened by love, the sky looked brighter, the birds sang more melodiously, the colours— greens, yellows, pinks and whites—intensified. Everything, including herself, sparkled with vibrant life.

The weather was not perfect all the time but this did not deter them from riding out whatever it was like, even in rain. Leonora had pressed a warm travelling gown into use for riding, which she covered with a thick, felted cape belonging to Blaise when necessary. Even dull, damp days possessed a definite charm that spring.

She grew to love the old house, the estate, the local village and the rolling countryside, while the almost daily exercise of riding, once the initial aches and pains in unused muscles subsided, brought a rosy flush of health to her face, a new and welcome strength to her muscles. The general sense of wellbeing came from being so extraordinarily happy.

But, inexorably, the time drew near when she must return to Bath. Blaise was committed to visiting his parents and the Whittonby estates before his return. He had already delayed his visit for too long, he said.

Her sense of occupying some high place where nothing but joy could touch her began to fade. She was forced back to earth.

Blaise's ardour, during those last days, seemed to dim. He even took to returning to his room at night after a brief visit to her bed. Leonora did not protest or attempt to cling. She knew what it meant. He had grown tired of her and this was his way of telling her so.

She could not fault his manners and he made love to her with undiminished fervour, but he had withdrawn part of himself, an important part, the part that ensured that they shared the delightful, day-long intimacy to which she had become accustomed over those first enchanted weeks.

When the day of departure came he escorted her back to Gloucester. They travelled largely in silence. Juliette was present, of course, though Lawrence, busy preparing for the visit to Huntsford Towers, had not accompanied his master. But their silence was not due to the presence of a third person. They seemed to have nothing left to say to one another.

Leonora had almost forgotten Clarissa, so wrapped up had she been in her own happiness, but now, as the carriage clattered over the bridge and through the cobbled streets of Gloucester, the memory of her erstwhile friend came back. She knew that Clarissa had reached the Rectory safely, for the woman who had accompanied her there had returned to Longvale within a couple of days.

'I wonder how Clarissa does,' she remarked.

'Excellently well, I imagine,' said Blaise. 'Utley was a good catch for her.'

Yes, Clarissa would soon become Mrs Utley. The respectable Mrs Utley. She did not need to be reminded of that.

'I once thought you interested in her,' she remarked,

punishing herself as much as testing him.

He chuckled, and for a moment Blaise her lover returned. 'She wished to flirt and I was not averse. Besides, you were so antagonistic I decided to tease you.'

'How ungallant of you,' said Leonora, her pleasure in this demonstration of his early notice swallowed up in her present misery over their imminent parting.

She, Leonora, had turned down Mr Utley's and several other tempting offers in favour of Kelsey, who would seek to end the liaison when he returned to Bath in a week or so—that had become painfully obvious over the last days. He was, delicately, dispensing with a mistress of whom he had tired and would soon find himself another one. She should, without delay, set about finding a husband as she had intended.

If only her heart did not ache so.

They went to bed separately in the inn that night, of course.

Next morning Leonora wondered whether Blaise had slept any better than she had. His dark eyes had little sparkle and he seemed to experience some difficulty in dredging up his usual engaging smile. Other than that, he was his usual attentive self and took leave of her with all the courtesy she could wish.

'I shall return to Bath by the end of the month,' he told her as they parted. 'I cannot leave the affairs of the Club unattended for longer. We shall meet again then. Goodbye, Leonora. And thank you, my dear.'

She nodded. 'Thank you, Blaise. I have enjoyed myself immensely.' She wanted to cry but refused to let him to see how much this parting upset her. She smiled bravely. 'Goodbye.'

She turned quickly and got into the post chaise.

Blaise stood, an elegant, beloved figure, his beaver tipped back on his dark hair, watching the chaise out of the yard. Looking back, Leonora knew that it would be a long time before she could bear to see him again.

Her mind had been made up in the dark hours of a sleepless night. She would accept the Duchess of Broadshire's invitation, go to London for the remainder of the Season and then perhaps travel on to stay somewhere by the sea.

She had no wish to return to Bath in the immediate future, if ever.

She wrote to the Duchess to say she was taking advantage of her grace's kind invitation, and set about her preparations for the visit in a whirl of nervous energy, determined to be away within a day or two.

She decided to take Dolly with her, as well as Juliette. The Duchess was bound to have plenty of accommodation for her guests' servants in her mansion in Grosvenor Square and she had no idea when she would be returning to Bath.

The travelling was tedious but accomplished in a couple of days. The valuable jewellery lay hidden in the bottom of her trunk under all her finest gowns. Knowing it was there, Leonora felt that she could afford to travel by post chaise rather than by the Stage or Mail.

In the rush and excitement of planning, travelling, arriving and being made to feel warmly welcome, Leonora did not realise, until she had been installed in Broadshire House for several days, that her bleed had not appeared on time.

Could she be pregnant? A combination of excitement and worry gripped her for the next week, until she could be quite certain that her show was not simply late. Meanwhile she joined in all the glittering routs, visits to exhibitions, musical evenings and soirées to which the Duchess insisted she accompany her, and danced at Almack's. The Duchess, of course, had no difficulty in obtaining the necessary voucher.

It was all exciting, London was splendid if a little noisy and odorous, the eligible gentlemen were particularly attentive.

The problem was, she wanted no one but Blaise Dancer, Earl of Kelsey. And he was not in London.

Lord Grath was, although he did not stay at Broadshire House but had rooms in St James's. However, he often visited his grandmother and attended many of the same functions. His attentions to her continued to be marked and nothing Leonora could do, short of snubbing him, which would show lack of conduct, could make him desist.

The Season was drawing to its close. Everyone, soon, would be departing for their estates or to the sea. It was in this atmosphere of change that Grath sought her out one morning in the small parlour where she had been sitting, reading.

He bowed before her with such a speaking look that she guessed his purpose before he began.

'Prinny has commanded me to Brighton,' he announced.

'Really, my lord? How delightful for you.'

'Yes, but it means I have to bring myself to the point, ma'am, for we shall be parted.' He dropped impressively to one knee and flung out his hand. 'Miss Vincent, you must realise the high regard, the respect and affection in which I hold you. In short, Miss Vincent, I love you. You know my prospects and I pray that you will do me the honour of accepting my hand in marriage.'

He reached the end of his declaration and looked at her expectantly. Leonora drew a breath.

'Do, please get up and take a seat, my lord,' she said prosaically. 'I am, of course, honoured and gratified that you should hold me in such high regard——'

'Do not refuse me!' cried his lordship, jumping impetuously to his feet to grasp her hands.

She released them and waved him to a nearby chair, which he took reluctantly, sitting on the very edge.

'But I must, my lord,' she continued, avoiding the dawning disbelief in his gaze, 'for you are already promised to another, I collect.'

'Grandmama has been talkin' to you,' he accused. 'But I don't regard that. Emmy ain't much more enthusiastic than I am for the match. I can persuade my parents——'

'I pray you will not even try, for even could I consider you free, I regret that I could not accept your gracious proposal.'

He looked stunned. Then he began to recover.

'I collect that your interest is fixed elsewhere,' he said in an offended tone.

Leonora found it impossible to restrain the colour which flooded her cheeks. 'That, my lord, can be of no concern to you.'

'But it is! If you love someone else then I am undone!' he cried dramatically. For all his histrionics, he regarded her shrewdly and concluded, 'That rogue Kelsey, I collect. He'll not wed you, y'know.'

Leonora tightened her lips as a shaft of pain shot through her and suppressed an impulse to hit Lord Grath, with angry words if not her fist. If she did that, she'd upset his grandmother.

'My lord,' she uttered, 'you may suppose what you like, but it can make no difference to my answer. I much regret that I cannot agree to marry you.'

At that moment the Duchess walked in, on some errand of her own. She stopped short. Grath's expression and attitude told her what was happening.

'Am I intrudin'?' she asked mildly.

'Not at all, ma'am,' said Leonora quickly, before Grath could find his voice. 'We had finished. Lord Grath has just done me the great honour of offering me his hand in marriage, but I was forced, regretfully, to reject it.'

'So I should think,' said the Duchess briskly. 'What possessed you, Grath? You've been promised to Lady Emily since you was twenty. You are not free to propose marriage to anyone else.'

'I like Emmy well enough,' said Grath sulkily, 'but she's little more than a child, I don't love her, any more than she loves me.'

'And you fancy yourself in love with Miss Vincent, eh? Well, let me tell you it won't do. You'll wed Lady Emily for the sake of the duchy. She is seventeen now, quite old enough for marriage. The match was fixed on years ago by both families and cannot be set aside.'

'I could elope,' said Grath mutinously.

'But not with me,' put in Leonora briskly. 'I would advise you to look again at Lady Emily.' The young girl was in town and Leonora had met her. 'She is a delightful creature and you really are very well suited, you know.'

'I would suggest that you take your leave, Grath,' said

the Duchess forbiddingly; despite her diminutive size, she could be extremely forbidding.

Her grandson departed in a dignified huff. The Duchess sighed and Leonora breathed deeply.

'I am sorry, your grace,' she apologised. 'I really did not see the proposal coming.'

The Duchess darted her a sharp glance. 'No, too wrapped up in your own predicament, I dare say. Will Kelsey wed you?'

'What?' gasped Leonora.

'You're breeding, child. You've been in Kelsey's pocket since February. Recently spent a month at Longvale, so I have heard.'

The walls seemed to be closing in on her. 'How?' she managed to ask.

'Servant's gossip. Your maid, Dolly. She don't suspect anything wrong, she's too naïve, but she's proud of being left in charge at Bath while you were away.'

'But she did not know I went to Longvale! Except. . .I suppose I or my maid might have said something after our return. . .it is possible she overheard,' groaned Léonora. 'Dear madam, I had hoped no one would notice my condition as yet.'

The Duchess sat down beside her on the sofa. 'Doesn't Kelsey know, my dear?'

'No! And he must not! Please, your grace, do not tell him!'

'Why? Do you not wish to wed him?'

'Oh, yes. More than anything. I did think once that I could not, because of his involvement with gambling. My father, you see—'

The Duchess knew all about that. Leonora gathered her thoughts so that she could speak coherently. 'But I see now that I was being prejudiced and blind. No man is obliged to gamble away his home. My father succumbed to weakness; certainly he was entrapped in a gambling hell, but no one forced him to enter its doors.'

'Ah.' The Duchess reached out and placed her small, brown-spotted hand over Leonora's. 'You have come to see that Kelsey is no callous predator intent on cheating others out of their fortunes?'

Leonora nodded, adding, 'But I never thought him quite as bad as that.'

'He is, my dear, a rather arrogant young man who set himself the task of restoring his family's fortunes. The Marquess is in no state to help. Kelsey runs all the estates as well as the Vitus Club, and has already paid off a large part of his father's debts from the profits, but I believe the property is still at risk and it will take him a few more years to accumulate enough funds to undertake all the necessary repairs.'

Leonora looked down at their clasped hands and then up to meet the Duchess's bright, penetrating gaze.

'I realised much of that while I was at Longvale. I came to appreciate his real worth, and I no longer judge him by the narrow-minded conclusions I jumped to on first acquaintance,' she admitted.

The Duchess smiled. 'Well, that's a mercy!'

Leonora smiled back, rather wryly. 'You see, I was much put out to find him in possession of the greater part of the house I had inherited and was ready to think the worst of him without any real evidence.'

'So, you would like to marry him.' The Duchess sat back, releasing Leonora's hand. 'D'you love him?'

There was little point in denying it. 'Yes.'

'But you do not wish him to know that you are increasing. Why not?'

'Because he does not love me, ma'am. He thought I was taking measures. . .and I will not blackmail him into a marriage he does not want. You see, he is not in a position to set up his nursery yet, quite apart from feeling disinclined to forfeit his freedom.'

'You can't know that for certain,' interrupted the Duchess.

'I can. He told Lady Flavia Collins as much when she attempted to persuade him into an alliance. She had a dowry of fifty thousand pounds, so his reluctance is not only due to lack of funds.'

'Most young men are disinclined to enter parson's mousetrap until they are forced—either by circumstances or because they fall in love. Kelsey has been no different but—'

'I know,' cut in Leonora quickly. 'But although he. . . desired me, he does not love me and has already tired of our affair. So I cannot marry him.'

The Duchess pursed her wrinkled lips. 'I wonder. Will you travel to Brighton with me next week, Leonora?'

'Dear madam! I should be delighted. Although—I had thought my pregnancy would not show for at least another month, and that I could wait until then to disappear. But you have already recognised my condition and I do not wish any rumours to reach Blaise.'

'Others will not inspect you so closely as I. But— Kelsey may notice in a few more weeks. You are bound to see him when you return for your things, and he knows you well.'

'Then I shall send Juliette. She can be trusted to clear out the apartments and leave with my belongings without indulging in gossip or giving in to pressure to reveal my whereabouts. Kelsey will achieve his aim of gaining use of the entire building. The rent he pays to my agent will increase my income.'

'And you intend to retire from Society, to disappear?'

'Yes. I shall call myself Mrs Vale, recently widowed and left with an unborn child to bring up.'

'You have it all planned, I collect. You have sufficient funds?'

'Yes, ma'am. Sufficient to bring up Lord Kelsey's child as it should be. My chief regret is that he or she will not be entitled to claim their proper title or position in Society.'

'Well, my dear, you must do as you think best. I think it quite safe for you to accompany me to Brighton for a while and I shall value your company. Were it not for certain rather important considerations, I could have welcomed you as a granddaughter.'

'Poor Lord Grath! I pray he will quickly recover his spirits.'

When the Duchess left her, Leonora sank into deep thought. She had had the jewellery valued and been pleasantly surprised by the total amount quoted. She had not sold it yet. She would try other jewellers before finally making up her mind how much to sell and to whom. She wanted the best possible price for each piece.

She still had no idea where she wished to settle and, once moved, she would have to let Juliette go. A personal maid was a luxury she would not be able to afford. Dolly, though, she would like to keep with her, despite her indiscretion. She must have a word with her about indulging in such heedless gossip. However innocently poor

Dolly had repeated what she had heard, she must learn to hold her tongue.

Next morning she woke feeling sick and so remained behind at Broadshire House while the Duchess made her morning call. Her pregnancy had not so far troubled her and she prayed that it might continue so, that her present indisposition was due to an upset stomach—otherwise she would be unable to properly enjoy her time in Brighton or provide the companionship the Duchess desired.

By noon she had recovered sufficiently to sit in the small parlour and read, her favourite place and occupation when alone.

She had not been settled there for long when a footman knocked and opened the door to announce, 'Lord Kelsey has called, madam. Since her grace is out he has asked to see you. May I tell him that you are at home?'

'No!' Leonora's response was automatic. Panic rose in her throat in a renewed attack of nausea. She could not possibly face Blaise now! 'Tell him I am not receiving visitors.'

'But you are,' came a harsh voice from the door as Kelsey shouldered aside the footman and strode into the room.

'My lord!' remonstrated the poor man, hurrying in behind him and attempting to cut him off. 'Miss Vincent,' he appealed to Leonora in distress, 'shall I call for assistance?'

'To remove his lordship?' Leonora, still agitated, had nevertheless recovered much of her poise. The nausea had subsided again. She felt in control of herself and tried to make her tone scathing. 'I hardly think that will be necessary. No, it is all right, Jones,' she told the footman quietly. 'I will speak with Lord Kelsey, since he is so insistent.'

Why was he here? The Duchess had had no time to contact him and in any case had promised not to do so.

She did not offer her hand. She could not bear for him to touch her. She must get rid of him as soon as possible or she might fall to pieces.

'My lord,' she said stiffly as the servant disappeared, 'you wished to see the Duchess. How can I be of help?'

Blaise stopped a short distance from her. He inclined his head in a bow, as courtesy demanded. His taut features did not relax into smile.

'Why so formal? Why are you here, Leonora? Why did you leave Bath?'

Had he truly expected her to wait for him, after his behaviour towards her at the last? But then, men were notoriously arrogant when it came to their relationships with females: do this, do that, go away, wait for me, come to bed, don't trouble me. Expecting to receive devotion however badly they treated the object of their attentions.

She lifted her stubborn chin. 'The Duchess had asked me to join her here, on the evening of her ball. I did not promise to wait for you, Blaise. I did not think you would wish it. So I decided to take advantage of her invitation to London.'

'You did not think I would wish you to wait for me?' He picked up on her excuse, his voice incredulous. 'After what we shared at Longvale?'

Misery flooded through Leonora as she remembered all the delight they had known. She stiffened her resolve, forcing herself to dwell upon those last days when he had withdrawn in mind and spirit, leaving a rather impersonal passion as his only expression of lingering regard.

'You had grown tired of me,' she asserted. 'I could tell. And I could not face a loveless intrigue, all the secrecy and shame, even for you, Blaise. So I decided to leave.'

'Tired of you? A loveless intrigue?' Again he responded to only part of what she had said. 'Would it have been loveless for you, Leonora?'

She drew a breath. This was proving even more difficult than she had feared. Pain took the remaining colour from her cheeks, revealed the lines of strain and brought the mortifying tears to prick her lids. She fixed her eyes on her clasped hands and blinked rapidly.

All in a moment he was kneeling beside her, his large hand covering both hers. She jumped at the shock of his touch and his grip tightened.

'Leonora,' he said huskily, 'it would not be loveless for me. It was because I had discovered how much I loved you that I may have seemed distracted during those last days at Longvale. I did not know what to do.'

'You. . .love me?'

She had scarcely managed to find her voice at all and it came out as a choked whisper. She looked up, her eyes glazed with unshed tears, to study the intent face so near her own.

Lines of strain were evident on his face, too. His initial aggression had gone, replaced by what she could only interpret as desperation. He looked as devastated as she felt.

Could she believe what her ears and her eyes told her?

That Blaise really did love her?

He was repeating that he did. 'I did not fully realise how much until you had gone,' he said. 'I missed you

quite painfully. I felt incomplete, my life seemed pointless without you. I returned to Bath all eagerness to see
you again, to declare my love. Imagine my dismay to
find that you had fled!'

'Oh, Blaise!' She leaned towards him, pulled him up
and he sat beside her, their hands locked together. 'And I
thought you had tired of me! Oh, my love, I am so sorry!'

'Does this mean,' he asked gruffly, his face alight
with hesitant surprise, 'that, as I'd hoped, you return my
regard?'

'I have loved you for an age,' she confessed softly.

Some minutes passed before he reluctantly stopped
kissing her and spoke again.

'But, financially, I knew I was still in no position to
marry, my dearest love. I wanted to rush after you to
declare my love, and in the end I did, but I have nothing
to offer but a mortgaged family estate, a pile of debts,
and the prospect of several more years when I must
receive the profits from the Vitus Club to keep the
estates' affairs above water.'

His voice dropped to a tone of fierce disgust. 'I cannot
give up the very thing which will prevent you from even
considering me as a suitable husband, my dear.'

She stroked his face, traced the lines about his eyes.
'You wish to marry me?' she asked in wonder.

'Desperately.' He took her chin in his fingers and
forced her to look at him, as he had done once before.
'I know you do not approve of my occupation, but could
you. . .would you consider making me deliriously happy
by agreeing to accept my hand in marriage? I cannot
guarantee to bring my finances about quickly enough to
ask you to wait but. . .could you force yourself to marry
a gambling pauper, my sweet love?'

His eyes probed hers. Serene now, because he loved her, she met his gaze candidly.

'I am not without a dowry, Blaise. I have Morris House, some bonds and jewellery. I had planned to live on it, but if it would help you out of your difficulties—'

'No. My dear girl, I am no fortune hunter. I could have wed a fortune years ago. It is you I want, not your money—'

'But as my husband you would have command of it.'

'No,' he repeated. 'I must extricate myself from my own difficulties. I cannot, at the moment, give up the Vitus Club even to please you, Leonora.'

'I do not ask you to.' She paused, wondering how best to explain. 'Blaise, I have come to know and love you for what you are, not the rogue my imagination painted you. My only excuse for my behaviour is that my father was ruined by a swindling gamester. My experiences since that disaster did rather colour my attitude to the very notion of anything other than social gambling, and to those who make a living by it.'

He grinned wryly. 'I cannot blame you. I admit that my view of certain speculative business enterprises has been jaundiced by my father's crippling losses. So I can understand. But you have not yet promised to marry me!'

She smiled, her eyes seeking his. 'I promise.'

There followed another rather prolonged interlude during which Blaise was heard to regret that they were not back at Longvale, where he could have taken her straight to bed.

'We must marry quickly,' he proclaimed. 'I could not endure to suffer a long engagement. If you are willing, I will move in with you upstairs in Morris House. With

Clarissa gone, Juliette could have her room. That should give us ample privacy.'

'Until we need to set up a nursery,' murmured Leonora, suddenly nervous again. Blaise had suggested she take steps to avoid conception. Suppose he wished, for financial reasons, to avoid starting his family yet?

'When that happens,' he said, untroubled, 'we shall rent a house in Bath and move into that. I could not bear to have you living far away at Longvale Park without me.'

'I could not bear to leave you!'

He laughed a little. 'I am reassured to hear it! The Club can take over the top floor of the house for bedrooms. When the day comes that I can abandon the Club—or perhaps keep it going under management as an investment, for I must confess that to have it amuses me—and spend all or most of my time in the country, I shall be the happiest of men.'

'You are like one of those creatures that changes its colour to match its background,' Leonora told him fondly. 'In town you are the perfect Society gentleman. At Longvale you become a typical country squire. And I believe that, like me, you prefer the country.'

'I do. We suit each other to perfection, my dearest. While I was at Huntsford Towers I told my parents of my intention to ask for your hand. They have no power to prevent our marriage, of course, but I should like you to meet them as soon as it becomes convenient. I know they will approve of you.'

'After the wedding,' said Leonora firmly. Now came the most difficult moment of a difficult morning. 'I believe we could be wed in three weeks, by Special Licence?'

He laughed. 'In such a hurry, love? People will suspect us of anticipating the official union!'

'It is because we did that it would be wise for us to wed quickly, Blaise. My dearest, I am already increasing.'

He was so still, so silent, that she though him displeased, angry. But when she dared to look she saw a great grin of sheer happiness irradiating his face.

'So your precautions did not work,' he observed happily.

'I did not take any,' confessed Leonora softly. 'I wanted your child whether you wed me or not, my dearest, dearest, Blaise. I intended to retire to the country and bring it up as a gentleman or lady, just as you might have wished.'

'Without telling me? he demanded, outraged.

'Yes,' she admitted. 'I had no wish to compel you into parson's mousetrap, and you might have felt obliged, whatever you told Lady Flavia. But,' she teased him, 'having its father on hand will be so much more agreeable. And its place in Society will be assured.'

'Hmm,' he muttered, mollified. 'You should not have taken what I said to an impertinent young lady to be my final word on the subject!'

She smiled, bringing the entrancing pleats to bracket her mouth. 'You sounded most convincing!'

'I intended to!' Then he smiled again. 'I did wonder about those precautions of yours, my love, but I said nothing because deep down I did not mind if you began breeding. I wanted to be forced to marry you.'

Leonora gasped. 'Blaise!'

He kissed her again before he went on, 'If we have a boy, the Whittonby succession will be assured— Leonora, I cannot tell you how overjoyed I am. A quiet wedding, I think, at Longvale. And I suppose I shall have to do without you in Bath for several months, although Digby can probably take over for much of the time. No one will then know exactly when the child is born. That should avoid any harmful speculation.'

'Somehow, things seem to have worked out well,' murmured Leonora contentedly.

'Our love,' murmured her future husband, 'was bound to win in the end. It is so much more important than any obstacle we imagined was impeding its path.'

Lord John Blaise Dancer was born at Longvale Park the following February. Leonora, tired but content, watched her husband cradle the tiny scrap who one day, God willing, would become Earl of Kelsey and much, much later Marquess of Whittonby. Tears ran down her cheeks, perhaps as the result of weakness but much more likely of sheer happiness.

Kelsey, returning his son to his nurse's arms, kissed Leonora tenderly. 'You have wrought a miracle, my wife,' he murmured.

The credit chiefly belonged to nature and the accoucheur, but it was nice to have him think so.

'You did have a little to do with it, my love,' she murmured drowsily, and heard his joyous laugh ring out as she drifted off into sleep.

ARE YOU A FAN
OF MILLS & BOON®
HISTORICAL ROMANCES™?

If YOU are a regular United Kingdom buyer of Mills & Boon Historical Romances we would welcome your opinion on the books we publish.

Harlequin Mills & Boon have a Reader Panel for Historical Romances. Each person on the panel receives a questionnaire every third month asking for their opinion of the books they have read in the past three months. Everyone who sends in their replies will have a chance of winning ONE YEAR'S FREE Historicals, sent by post—48 books in all.

If you would like to be considered for inclusion on the Panel please give us details about yourself below. All postage will be free. Younger readers are particularly welcome.

Year of birth..............................Month..........................

Age at completion of full-time education......................

Single ❑   Married ❑   Widowed ❑   Divorced ❑

Your name (print please)..

Address...

....Postcode ....

Thank you! Please put in envelope and post to:
HARLEQUIN MILLS & BOON READER PANEL,
FREEPOST SF195, PO BOX 152, SHEFFIELD S11 8TE

MILLS & BOON®

Historical Romance™

Coming next month

THE LOVE CHILD
by Meg Alexander

Regency
The first part of an exciting new trilogy

Sebastian, Lord Wentworth, was not fooled by
Prudence's disguise—she may have been dressed
as a boy so that she could search for her family
—but to him Pru was *distinctly* feminine.

AN UNPREDICTABLE BRIDE
by Helen Dickson

1645
How could Jane possibly marry a Parliamentarian
and a man she hadn't seen for three years? It was
only when she finally met Edward again that she
realised it might be easier than she thought.

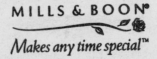

MILLS & BOON®

Makes any time special™

HEATHER GRAHAM POZZESSERE

If Looks Could Kill

Madison wasn't there when her mother was murdered, but she *saw* it happen. Years later, a killer is stalking women in Miami and Madison's nightmare visions have returned. Can FBI agent Kyle Montgomery catch the serial killer before Madison becomes his next victim?

"...an incredible storyteller!" —LA Daily News

1-55166-285-X
AVAILABLE FROM FEBRUARY 1998

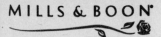

MILLS & BOON

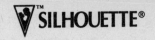

SILHOUETTE®

SPECIAL OFFER £5 OFF

FLYING FLOWERS

Beautiful fresh flowers, sent by 1st class post to any UK and Eire address.

We have teamed up with Flying Flowers, the UK's premier 'flowers by post' company, to offer you £5 off a choice of their two most popular bouquets the 18 mix (CAS) of 10 multihead and 8 luxury bloom Carnations and the 25 mix (CFG) of 15 luxury bloom Carnations, 10 Freesias and Gypsophila. All bouquets contain fresh flowers 'in bud', added greenery, bouquet wrap, flower food, care instructions, and personal message card. They are boxed, gift wrapped and sent by 1st class post.

To redeem £5 off a Flying Flowers bouquet, simply complete the application form below and send it with your cheque or postal order to; **HMB Flying Flowers Offer, The Jersey Flower Centre, Jersey JE1 5FF.**

ORDER FORM (Block capitals please) Valid for delivery anytime until 30th November 1998 MAB/0198/A

Title ....Initials ....Surname ....

Address..

....

....Postcode ....

Signature..Are you a Reader Service Subscriber **YES/NO**

Bouquet(s) **18 CAS** (Usual Price £14.99) **£9.99** ☐   **25 CFG** (Usual Price £19.99) **£14.99** ☐

I enclose a cheque/postal order payable to Flying Flowers for £................................or payment by

VISA/MASTERCARD ☐☐☐☐☐☐☐☐☐☐☐☐☐☐☐☐ Expiry Date............/............/............

PLEASE SEND MY BOUQUET TO ARRIVE BY ..../........./........

TO Title ....Initials ....Surname ....

Address..

....

....Postcode ....

Message (Max 10 Words) ....

....

allow a minimum of four working days between receipt of order and 'required by date' for delivery

e mailed with offers from other reputable companies as a result of this application.

x if you would prefer not to receive such offers. ☐

tions Although dispatched by 1st class post to arrive by the required date the exact day of delivery cannot be guaranteed. e until 30th November 1998. Maximum of 5 redemptions per household, photocopies of the voucher will be accepted.